THE POWER OF LOVE

Minutes later, after a quick shower, Riva walked to the bedroom with plans to behave herself. She squeezed lotion into her palm and began massaging her body with it.

"Let me do that," Lance offered, squeezing the sweet-smelling lotion into his palm and sliding the straps of her nightgown off her shoulders. Riva closed her eyes, enjoying his soft touch.

"No." She turned to take the lotion from Lance, stopping him from touching her. She couldn't help but notice the heated desire smoldering in his eyes. "I think I can . . ." Riva started, then was interrupted as Lance gathered her in his arms, his hands stroking her hips, igniting a fiery passion that she knew would force her to break all her rules. She didn't care anymore. She tingled and shivered with excitement, not wanting to stop. She felt feverish as Lance's mouth covered hers again. Riva's thoughts began to spin, her common sense warning her to stop, but she wouldn't listen. Lance lifted her into his arms and gently laid her on the bed, exploring and sampling every inch of her body, until Riva felt as if she were spinning on an axis, reeling somewhere between space and time. She accepted him, allowing scorching flames to flow until they were satisfied.

THE
POWER
OF LOVE

Marcella Sanders

BET Publications, LLC
http://www.bet.com
http://www.arabesquebooks.com

ARABESQUE BOOKS are published by

BET Publications, LLC
c/o BET BOOKS
One BET Plaza
1900 W Place NE
Washington, D.C. 20018-1211

All Kensington Titles, Imprints, and Distributed Lines are available at special quantity discounts for bulk purchases for sales promotions, premiums, fund-raising, and educational or institutional use. Special book excerpts or customized printings can also be created to fit specific needs. For details, write or phone the office of the Kensington special sales manager: Kensington Publishing Corp., 850 Third Avenue, New York, NY 10022, attn: Special Sales Department, Phone: 1-800-221-2647.

First Printing: December 2001
10 9 8 7 6 5 4 3 2 1

Printed in the United States of America

I dedicate this book to those who were my inspiration: Wayman and Josie Jackson, Juel Jones, and Charles Smith.

Special dedication to Mrs. Marion Jones, Mrs. Annie D. Jackson, Mrs. Alma Robinson, and my aunt and fourth grade teacher, Mrs. Pleasant Coleman.

Thanks for being the light in my life.

ACKNOWLEDGMENTS

Many thanks to all the people who contributed their support: my editors—Karen Thomas, who is so patient, and Chandra Taylor, for keeping me on the straight and narrow; to my husband, Tommy, for answering questions on automobiles; to Ava Garner for her input on crime, warrants, and surveillance; to Courtney, Z.J., Patricia Jackson, Melvin Jackson, Velma Davis, Williar, Jackie, Valerie, Ralph, DeWitt Hall, Francis Perkins, Hilda Kelly, Louise Gordon, Renee Gordon, and Jason Prudent, for their wonderful support.

Dear Readers:

Let Riva and Lance sweep you into their world of attempted murder, prime suspects, and lots of love.

I hope you enjoy the POWER OF LOVE.

Best wishes,

Marcella Sanders

P.O. Box 640084
Miami, FL 33164-0084

One

Riva Dae Cain twisted the crimson straw, stirring the piña colada while nibbling the tart pineapple she'd unhooked from the edge of the goblet, and listened to jazz as she waited for account manager Jasper Wade to join her inside of the café.

As always, Jasper was on time. Through the tinted window, Riva watched Jasper cross the street. Jasper's black suit was a perfect fit for his short, portly body. Although Jasper was dressed nicely, Riva didn't understand how he survived the ninety-degree south Florida heat wearing a black suit.

She crunched down on the last thin slice of pineapple and watched Jasper maneuver his way to the sidewalk as he removed the black straw hat, displaying a sparse amount of black thin waves on his balding head.

For a moment Jasper stood underneath a gangly palm, as if he needed to rest after the short walk across the street.

Riva looked away from the window, reflecting on her and Jasper's last meeting. Jasper never agreed with her about anything except that she, like all the other employees, should address him by his first name.

Riva turned her attention back to Jasper, who

was still standing underneath the palm. Its wide leaves were like outstretched hands waving against the gentle breeze stirring the sizzling late afternoon. Jasper Wade could stand under the tree as long as he pleased, Riva mused, but he was meeting with her today. Riva turned away and took another sip from her drink, reminding herself that she would not yield to Jasper's attempt to wreck the advertising project. However, Riva needed one more chance to talk to Jasper before she met with Isaiah Fuller. Riva hated telling Fuller that Jasper was refusing him the lipstick ad he wanted because of problems Dae Advertising had experienced with him several years ago.

"Riva." Jasper pulled out a chair and sat across from her, drawing her out of her thoughts. His light brown skin was damp with perspiration, and he appeared to be almost out of breath.

"Jasper," Riva acknowledged him, raising her voice over the round of applause from the small crowd acknowledging the local jazz player, who'd finished entertaining the late-afternoon diners. Riva eyed Jasper closely, observing how he carefully placed his black straw hat in the chair next to where he was sitting.

"Riva, I have made up my mind. I will not authorize the advertisement for Isaiah Fuller until he has paid in full for the lipstick advertisement, and I mean it."

Riva felt the skin between her smoothly arched brows knitting into pleats. One would think Jasper was the owner of Dae Advertising, instead of her father, Mason Dae. "Jasper, Mr. Fuller is one of our oldest clients. You can give the man a break," Riva remarked. Earlier that week, when she and Jasper had met in his office, she had been so loud that everyone on the creative team walked past or stood in the corridor near Jasper's office. Riva was sure the employees had been listening to the argument.

To make matters worse, Riva had marched out of his office, pushing her way through the nosy bystanders, and yelling that Jasper was uncompromising, stingy, and too old for his job.

"I have told you once and I'm telling you again: I am not giving Fuller a break."

"Okay." Riva collected her composure. "Dae Advertising had a problem with Fuller years ago before I began working for the company." Riva studied Jasper's round, chubby face, looking for signs assuring her that Jasper would relent and give in to her suggestions. Instead of seeing any signs of hope, Riva noticed that Jasper's light brown cheeks appeared feverish from the heat he'd walked in from. "Most people fall on hard times," Riva continued.

"I understand that, and so does Mason," Jasper assured Riva. "The problem is, when Fuller gets back on his financial feet, he talks a whole lot of nonsense about how he's going to take his time paying the company." Riva noticed Jasper's serious expression. "The last time we almost had to take him to court."

"Would you like to order now, sir?" A young male waiter dressed in black pants, a white shirt, and a black vest had hurried over to their table and now addressed Jasper.

"I'll have a glass of ice water, and I'll order dinner later," Jasper replied, not taking his eyes off Riva.

"Yes, sir," the waiter said to Jasper, then turned to Riva. "May I refresh your drink?"

"No, thanks," Riva answered.

"Will you be ordering dinner later?" the waiter asked Riva.

"I'll let you know," Riva said, imagining that the waiter was counting his tips. If she ordered nothing more than a piña colada, he would probably come up short on his expected gratuities for the day.

"Of course," the waiter replied, and moved to another table across from her and Jasper.

"But Mr. Fuller has had several projects since then," Riva said, continuing her discussion with Jasper, understanding that when Isaiah Fuller had spouted "nonsense" to Jasper and her father, she wasn't even out of college. Riva had no knowledge of the adversities her father and Jasper had encountered with Isaiah Fuller, and she could care less as long as Isaiah was paying his bills now.

"Tell you what I'll do," Jasper said. The smile crossing his lips drew his cheeks upward in apple-dumpling fashion.

"And what would that be?" Riva countered with trepidation about what Jasper had in mind.

"I'll authorize a regular white car instead of the limousine."

"What?" Riva didn't even know why she was shocked at Jasper's suggestion.

"Riva, I don't have a problem with Fuller wanting a limo and a professional model for his lipstick ad, but I do have a problem with him wanting Dae Advertising to pay for the cost of his ad, and his promise to pay later. I know Fuller. He does not pay his bills on time." Jasper looked at Riva, as if to study her reaction. When she didn't say anything, he continued, "But I will authorize a regular white car to be used in the ad instead of a limousine."

The waiter slowed down at their table, set a glass of ice water in front of Jasper, and moved swiftly to the back of the café. "Thanks." Jasper had twisted around in his chair to respond to the young waiter, but Riva was sure he hadn't heard Jasper.

"Jasper, that's ridiculous. A regular white car . . . it's not like we're *buying* a limousine for the project. We're renting, remember?" Riva turned her attention away from Jasper and looked around the room, which was now more crowded than when she had arrived.

"I know that. But Fuller has found himself on hard times again, and I don't want any trouble out of him." Jasper took a long swig of his water. "As far as the model goes, one of those young clerk-typists will be perfect."

Riva's idea to hire a professional model for the ad for frosty pink lipstick went up in smoke right before her eyes. Nevertheless, she stayed as calm as she could. "Jasper, I agree with you that there are some attractive typists. But that's not what I had in mind," she remarked with forced composure.

"I disagree," Jasper countered, taking another drink from his glass. "The silk dress can be a nice thin sleeveless cotton dress," Jasper said, holding the glass in midair.

"That's it!" Riva shouted, almost knocking over her drink as she banged her fist against the table-top. "You will not ruin this project just because you and Daddy almost had to sue Mr. Fuller." Riva was fed up with Jasper's cheap ideas and his old memories. She was sure Jasper was the oldest man in the business and probably remembered things that had happened before the Civil War."

"Calm down, Riva." Jasper waved a meaty hand in her direction.

"Calm down? I don't think so," Riva shot back at him.

"This way we can save money. Now, I just had an another idea about that white car. I saw a nice Lexus in the parking lot. I think the car belonged to one of the new employees. Maybe, if we're lucky, we can borrow the car and save on a rental."

"Don't even think about it." Riva dared Jasper to continue.

"Now, Riva." Jasper patted the table.

"Don't you 'now, Riva,' me!" Riva was so absorbed in her conversation with Jasper that she hadn't noticed the music had softened. "You let me tell you one thing: not only are you old—you're cheap!"

Jasper didn't seem to have heard a word Riva said, or at least he didn't seem to have paid attention to her statement regarding his age and his ability to save money. Instead Jasper continued: "I was also thinking that instead of placing the ad in the magazine you requested, we could go ahead and place the ad in the magazine I suggested in our first meeting."

Riva rose from her seat and grabbed her purse. "I have had it with you." She placed one hand on her slender waist, her short red manicured nails extended out over the side of her round hip. "You know as well as I do that magazine is for women in their thirties, forties, and beyond."

"Yes, but the circulation is high," Jasper replied.

"And you know good and well that I want the ad to run in a well-circulated magazine for the teenage and young-adult market."

"When Mason retires, and you're running this company, you'll understand." Jasper pushed away from the table and stood to his full height, nearly a head shorter than Riva's five feet, ten inches.

"You listen to me, little man. . . ." Riva stopped. She wanted to tell Jasper to go play in traffic in the middle of I-95. Instead she whirled around, leaving Jasper. She stopped at the register and paid for her drink, noticing that everyone in the café was looking in her direction. On her way out, she almost bumped into inquisitive Phillip Davis from the creative team, as he walked into the café with his buddy Johnny.

"Hello, Riva," Phillip said to her, and stared as if he were giving her the once-over.

"Hi, Phillip." Riva noticed his wry grin. "Excuse me," she said, heading out to the sidewalk. Her spa appointment was in three hours, and she already had a headache from arguing with Jasper.

The heels of Riva's yellow shoes clicked against the sidewalk as she moved swiftly down the street to the office to pick up her laptop and get her truck. She waited for the traffic light to change, and pushed away a palmetto leaf that grazed her bare arm. Riva squinted against the sun, then took her sunglasses from her purse and put them on. She realized that her headache was no match for the afternoon heat, and crossed the street.

Three blocks down the street, Riva walked into the drugstore. Welcoming the crisp air, she headed down the aisle to the headache remedies and selected and paid for a bottle of aspirin. As soon as she returned to her office for her laptop, she took a pill and headed home. With any luck her headache would be gone by the time she arrived at her apartment.

However, the drive home wasn't much better, and promised to be as horrid as the verbal fight she'd had with Jasper. Two crunched automobiles in the middle of I-95 turned the highway into a parking lot. Riva groaned and turned on the radio.

A news report stated that two undercover officers had been missing since last week. Riva let out a murmur and pressed her palm against her forehead. That was her exact reason for filing for divorce, Riva thought as she listened to the broadcast. She'd had nightmares that her husband, Lance Cain, would go missing and months later his remains would be found in a deserted wooded area.

Riva inched closer behind the car in front of her, as a police officer directed traffic to move to the next lane. Lance had made her crazy, Riva realized, thinking about her soon-to-be ex-husband. He had promised her before they were married that he would work inside the precinct. Lance kept his promise until one year into their marriage; then he took a promotion, working undercover, and didn't bother to tell her until he had signed on and was driving an unmarked patrol car. He told her he'd taken the job so they could save money and upgrade from the apartment they'd bought to their dream home. That way they could start a family.

The problem was, Riva didn't understand having a family when he or both of them could end up dead and wouldn't be around to raise their children. She recalled the incident that led to her filing for a divorce almost eight months ago, and tried to dismiss the ugly memories of her and Lance's car accident, which had been caused by a person who was trying to kill him. After she filed for divorce, Lance left the police force and took a job with a private-detective agency owned by a retired police officer who had once been his supervisor. Riva didn't know if Lance's new job was safer. It didn't matter now. Soon she and Lance would sign the papers that would ultimately end their marriage.

But Riva had a serious problem: she still loved Lance Cain. It seemed strange to her that their separation hadn't dissolved her feelings for him. Riva forced the thoughts of her and Lance's separation, and the final meeting in two months that would cut all their legal bindings to each other, from her mind.

She changed lanes and finally start moving at a faster speed.

Ten minutes later, Riva pulled into her parking space, cut the engine, and got out, taking her purse and the bag of over-the-counter medicine from the car seat.

It appeared to Riva that more than half the people living on the sixth floor were gathered around the mailboxes in the lobby. She unlocked her box and took out her mail, which consisted of supermarket sales papers and a clothing catalog. She closed the mailbox and followed the crowd to the elevator, waiting with the other tenants until one of the neighbors got off, pushing her way through the crowd.

"Hold the door," Riva heard Lance call. "Sixth floor," he said.

Riva noticed Lance turn to the side and squeeze into the packed elevator, inching his way toward her until their bodies were pressed together. He was handsome as ever, dressed in a blue suit.

"Hi," he said.

"What are you doing here this time of day?" Riva asked. It wasn't unusual for him to visit her once a month when they had attended counseling for their separation. Seeing Lance at this time of the day surprised her, especially since their sessions were over.

"I wanted to see you," Lance said, flashing her a grin that seemed to light up his light brown eyes.

"Did something good happen?" Riva asked, noticing that he was still grinning and that his light brown complexion seemed to glow.

"Yeah, I got some free time. Can't I want to see you?" Lance asked.

Riva smiled. She would enjoy his company while she had a chance to be with him. At least she and Lance hadn't stopped being nice to each other.

The elevator stopped on the third floor, and several people got off. Riva moved away from Lance, unpinning herself from his muscular body and his heady cologne, which had the power to make her forget her worries and unearthed fiery desires and lingering passion. Those times were over now. She and Lance would no longer give each other the power to ignite passion.

Riva looked up at him. Lance Cain was six feet, three inches tall and had an athletic physique and a set of light brown eyes that still held her captive. "I'm surprised to see you," Riva said, noticing that Lance's curly black hair was cut shorter than usual.

"What, you think because our sessions are over, I wouldn't stop by to see you?" Lance flashed Riva another pearly-white smile.

Riva's smile faded. Their counseling sessions were designed to help them work out their differences, with the hope that they could reconcile their marriage. "I can't visit for long; I have an appointment at the spa tonight," she whispered, to keep the others on the elevator, who were deathly quiet, from hearing what she was saying to him. Her headache hadn't subsided much, so she couldn't afford to miss her appointment. The warmth of the water always relaxed the tension that coiled around her muscles like tight bands, stretching her nerves to the limit. Then, of course, the fight she'd had with Jasper hadn't helped.

"I won't stay long." Lance moved close to her. His gaze held hers as he lowered his head so close she could smell his fresh, minty breath.

Riva was so busy looking into Lance's eyes, sharing his gaze, she didn't even know the elevator had stopped on her floor.

"Will the lovebirds please vacate the elevator? I have dinner to make," a woman Riva had once met at the condo-association meeting said.

Excusing herself, Riva pushed her way through the remaining crowd, feeling Lance behind her. Lance had the ability to put a brake on her thoughts of the project that Jasper was threatening to botch by any means necessary.

"How have you been?" Riva asked Lance as she turned the key in the lock and walked inside her bright apartment.

"I'm fine, and you?" Lance walked into the living room and pushed his hands into his pockets, pulling his suit jacket back, and exposing the black revolver strapped to his shoulder.

Maybe if she had bought new furniture and changed the pictures on the walls, her memories and her love for Lance would have faded by now. Instead everything in the apartment was the same as when she and Lance were together. The winter-white sofa with pink and lime-green throw pillows matched the comfortable lime green easy chairs. One chair in particular still faced the television, the chair where Lance had loved watching the news and sports.

"I have had better days," Riva said, not really wanting to discuss her day. She dropped the mail on the cocktail table and opened the balcony door, careful not to brush against the tall white elephant planter.

"What do you mean, you've had better days? What happened?" Riva heard Lance behind her as she went to the bedroom.

"Daddy is on vacation. Doctor's orders," Riva said. She dropped her purse on the bed and took the headache medicine from the bag, setting the containers on the nightstand. "He needs to rest," Riva said. Going to the closet, she pulled off her dress and began looking for her favorite sleeveless lounger to put on, before she took a shower and went to the spa.

"Well, you know Mason; he works too hard," Riva heard Lance say.

"But I can't tell him anything. My daddy's head is as hard as a rock," Riva complained. "He opened another office in north Florida."

"I know," Lance said, settling down in his favorite chair in front of the bed. "He hired us to investigate the employees he's planning to hire."

"Oh," Riva replied, walking out of the closet into the bedroom. It was just like her father to hire Lance to work for him.

"I think his new company will work, as long as he has another man like Jasper," Lance said.

"Of course, Jasper is being his usual disagreeable self, saving money for the company." Riva didn't mean to complain to Lance about Jasper. "We had an argument today," she said, then immediately wished she hadn't said a word about her and Jasper's disagreement.

"Jasper is doing his job," Lance said.

"Jasper's job is being stingy, and believe me, he's good at his job." Riva took the black slippers she had left in the closet from the second shelf and stuck her feet inside them. She turned and stood inches from Lance.

"Don't worry yourself about Jasper." Lance touched her waist.

Riva shivered from the touch, feeling the warmth of his fingers grazing her skin beneath the thin material. "I'm trying to be optimistic." Riva gave Lance a playful shove. "Get out of here."

How many times had Lance followed her to their bedroom closet when they were together and assisted her, unzipping her dress? Riva couldn't count the times. It almost seemed at that moment that they'd never separated. But they *were* separated and on the verge of finalizing their divorce—all because Lance loved his work.

Riva walked out into the bedroom, noticing that Lance was again relaxing in the chair, his eyes closed. "So tell me about the shoot-out you were involved in a few weeks ago," Riva said, sitting on the edge of the bed.

"Who told you about that?" Lance opened his eyes and looked at Riva.

"Maybe it was a rumor," Riva said. "I'm afraid one day someone is going to tell me that you are injured or dead." She slid farther back on the bed, turned back the comforter, and removed the pillow, throwing it to the side and resting her back against the headboard.

Lance stood, rising to his full six-foot-three height. "That bit of news was not supposed to leave the office." He moved toward her. "So who told you?"

"It doesn't matter," Riva said, not disclosing her source. One of the members of Riva's aunt Udell's kaffeeklatsch had a relative working close to where the shooting took place, and reported to Udell. If the woman hadn't told Udell, Riva would never have known that Lance could have been killed.

"The shoot-out happened a month ago, and it wasn't that bad," Lance said. "No one was hurt. And the good thing about it is that we got the guys."

"It doesn't matter." Riva shook her head. "I'm worried about you."

"Riva, we're not together today because of your worrying," Lance said.

"You're right," Riva replied, getting off the bed and going to the kitchen for a glass of water.

"Riva, it didn't make any sense to tell you." Lance followed her to the kitchen.

"You're right," Riva said, planting her hands on her hips, which made her long dress rise above her ankles. "I don't need to know what happens to you while you're on the job."

"I thought that when we married you understood how much I love my work," Lance said, blocking Riva from moving any farther.

"I thought I understood too," Riva remarked quietly, brushing away the nagging thought entering her mind that her attempt to control Lance hadn't worked. "Soon I won't have to worry about the possibility of identifying your body at the morgue." Lance continued to block her path.

"I could get hit by a bus, crossing the street." Riva noticed that Lance sounded annoyed, and she knew he was getting angry.

"You're right," she agreed reluctantly. She moved around him, taking a glass from the cabinet and filling it with water. Riva left the kitchen headed to her room, with Lance on her heels. Lance was right. He could get hurt anywhere. But working for Samuel Moses investigating crimes had not made Lance any safer. He was determined to get himself killed, Riva thought.

"I can't promise you that I won't get hurt or even killed while I'm working on the street, Riva." Lance seemed frustrated because she still seemed to worry about him. "I'm doing the best that I can to stay safe."

"I am sorry too." Riva swallowed back a rising lump in her throat.

"Are you ever going to forgive me?" Lance asked. "Because I really don't want a divorce."

Although Riva hadn't forgiven Lance, she had softened, realizing that he did love his work. But she had a lot more thinking to do before she could agree not to finalize their divorce. Regardless of their separation, unlike most couples she knew, she and Lance were at least on speaking terms with each other. However, she wasn't certain if, after today, Lance would visit her again, especially after the news she'd heard about him. "If you're so concerned about our not getting a divorce, why have you moved your girlfriend in with you?" Riva asked, determined to know whether the rumor she'd heard from the grapevine was true.

"What?" Lance sounded surprised.

Riva set the glass down on the nightstand with a quick bang. Lance's personal life was not her business. However, if he wanted to reconcile their marriage then it was her concern. "You heard me."

"Babe, Theresa doesn't know what she's talking about."

"How do you know Theresa told me about you and your live-in girlfriend?" Riva asked. In spite of herself, Riva could not control the jealousy crawling around her heart.

"First of all," Lance began, "Vanessa is Samuel's niece. When he left me to run the business and take care of the house while he was away, he asked me if his nieces Vanessa and Tiffany could stay with me and Adam."

"What a nice arrangement. It's too bad the women couldn't find their own apartments."

"Vanessa is recently divorced. Her husband won the house in the divorce settlement. Tiffany and her baby were living with Vanessa after she and her husband divorced."

"It must be wonderful going shopping for groceries with your housemates," Riva said, pictures of Lance sharing his bed with the woman crowding her mind. Riva took the aspirin to the bathroom and placed the bottle in the medicine cabinet.

"Riva, please. Adam, Vanessa, and Tiffany will be moving out soon." Lance sounded positive.

"I thought you had your personal life together and were satisfied," Riva said, still feeling jealous pangs pinching her heart. "So why are your housemates moving?"

"I'm buying Samuel's house." Lance walked over to Riva, stretching his arms toward the ceiling, then locking his fingers behind his head. "Riva, I would like to talk to you about the house."

Riva suspected Lance wanted to know how she felt about his buying a house before their divorce was final. She didn't begrudge him. It was his idea that she keep the apartment they had bought when they were first married.

"I'm glad for you," Riva said, checking the clock on the nightstand beside her bed. "I have to go." She watched Lance unlock his hands from behind his head and start walking toward the door.

"I'll see you soon," he said.

"We'll talk." Riva walked out into the hall, annoyed at herself for being jealous. Lance stopped and turned to her. Gathering her in his arms, he kissed her cheek. "We'll talk again," he said, brushing his lips against hers before he headed to the front door.

"Call me," Riva said, walking beside him and waiting for Lance to leave so she could nurse her regrets in peace. She knew Samuel loved Lance as if he were his son. She imagined that the minute Samuel Moses heard from Lance that she was filing for a divorce, Samuel had hired Lance to work for him. Without hesitation, Samuel left the business for Lance to run while he left town. Riva knew Samuel would do anything to keep Lance happy.

"Do you mean that you don't want me to visit without calling first?" Lance was standing too close to her, and Riva wanted to back away from him, but she felt as if she were rooted to the carpet.

"You're welcome to stop by anytime," she said, hoping that she wasn't sounding like a desperate woman.

Lance opened the door and, without warning, he gathered Riva in his arms, again brushing his lips along the side of her neck until his lips reached hers and the contact deepened into a heart-searching kiss.

Riva knew she should have been running out of

his arms and to the bathroom for her shower, but being close to Lance felt good and right.

Riva threw her worries to the winds, and forgot that she'd filed for divorce, letting herself linger in his arms, tasting the sweetness from his lips. Suddenly the thought of Lance moving on with his life hit her, and she untangled herself from his embrace.

Lance smiled down at her. "Enjoy the spa." He backed out into the corridor, and she watched as he headed to the elevator.

Riva closed the door and slid down to the floor, covering her face with both hands. Every fiber in her body warned her that she was to blame for their problems and that she should move forward. But Riva Dae Cain couldn't move forward. She was stuck. She was still suspicious about Lance's living arrangement. Not only had Samuel left his business and his house to Lance—he'd left Lance a lover.

Riva raised herself from the carpet. She would be fine, because she had her work, and working kept her too busy to think.

Two

Riva pulled herself together and hurried to the bathroom for a quick shower before going to the spa.

Seconds after she stepped out of the shower, the telephone rang.

"Riva." Theresa was on the phone talking before Riva could say hello.

"Yes, Theresa."

"Will you give me a ride to the spa?"

"Where is your car?" Riva asked her cousin.

"It's in the shop," Theresa said.

Riva thought for a second. Giving Theresa a ride to the spa might make her late. "Are you ready?"

"All I have to do is get dressed. Give me ten minutes," Theresa said.

"Theresa, my appointment is in thirty minutes. If you don't hurry I'm leaving you." Riva knew Theresa was on vacation from her job at the courthouse, and had had plenty of time to be ready. Riva also knew Theresa moved at a snail's pace. "Ten minutes. If you're not downstairs, Theresa . . ."

"I know, you're leaving me," Theresa said.

Riva laughed. She knew she would never leave Theresa. "What have you been doing all day?" Riva assumed she knew the answer, but she asked anyway.

"I slept most of the day." Theresa sounded as if she'd just woken up. This information did not surprise Riva. Neither did it contradict the fact that not only was Theresa slow, she was as lazy as a feline on a summer day.

"Theresa, why didn't you call me earlier? You have all of my phone numbers, including my beeper number."

"I told you I slept most of the day," Theresa replied drowsily.

" 'Bye, Theresa." Riva hung up without saying another word to her cousin. She pulled on a white two-piece bathing suit, covering the bottom with a long white wraparound skirt. Riva hurried to her closet and stuck her feet into a pair of black open-toed sandals with two-inch heels, then rushed to the jewelry box, removing a pair of gold bead earrings.

Once her hair was in the usual knot she wore for the spa, Riva checked her purse, making sure she hadn't forgotten her membership card. With that done, she went downstairs, checking her watch with the intention of waiting another minute or two before she went to the third floor to get Theresa.

The elevator door slid open and Theresa walked out into the lobby wearing a pair of blue shorts and a matching pullover blouse. Her smooth milk-chocolate complexion looked free of makeup, and her black shoulder-length hair was twisted into what Riva thought was a makeshift French twist.

"Riva, thanks for waiting." Theresa hurried up to her, long gold earrings dangling from her ears. "I could have used Mommy's car if she would've taken the train to the convention instead of driving," Theresa said. "You know how Mommy enjoys driving herself and her friends to conventions if the meetings are close enough to make the trip in one day."

"Tell me about it," Riva said, pushing the lobby door open and walking to her truck. "But the next time you need a ride, you need to tell me earlier, or I'm not driving you," Riva teased.

"If anything was wrong with the Blue Angel I would give *you* a ride," Theresa said, referring to Riva's blue truck.

"Theresa, the only reason I'm giving you a ride is because you're my cousin. Other than that, you'd be walking or catching the bus to the spa." Riva gave Theresa a devilish grin.

Theresa turned on the radio, filling the cab with music. "So are you and Lance getting back together?"

"What are you asking for?" Riva drove through the gate, passing the guard, then stopped at the end of the street, waiting for the traffic to pass.

"I saw Lance getting off the elevator today," Theresa said, bobbing her head to the music.

"Theresa, just because you saw Lance in the building doesn't mean we're getting back together." Riva drove out into the street, heading toward the spa. She had managed to keep her thoughts free of Lance while she dressed. It was just like Theresa to bring him up.

"So what did Lance say about the lady who was in the supermarket with him?" Theresa inquired.

Riva kept her eyes on the traffic in front of her. When they were children, Theresa had always pried into her personal business, asking questions and keeping her updated on the latest gossip. "It's none of your business," Riva said, and changed lanes to pass a slow driver.

"Come on, Riva, what did he say?" Theresa asked, beaming, eager to listen to any information Riva would give her.

"I don't want to talk about it." Riva flipped her turn signal, changing back into the other lane.

"Mm-hm," Theresa murmured.

Riva ignored Theresa. She needed time to think about Lance's living arrangement before discussing her thoughts with anyone. When Riva was stuck with a problem and didn't know how to solve it, she always talked to her girlfriend Laura. Although at the moment, Riva didn't think she would be discussing Lance with anyone.

Riva drove past mothers walking their children to the nearby park. This was the year she and Lance had planned to start their family. Riva quickly dismissed the tormenting thought. Because of Lance, it would take her years to regain her dreams of having children. First she had to meet a suitable man. After she found Mr. Right, she was going to marry him. Two years later she planned to have a child. By then she would be thirty and would have plenty of time left on her biological clock.

Undermining Riva's perfect plan was a slight problem: she wanted Lance to be the father of her children. Unfortunately that was not going to happen, and from this evening on she was going to control her emotions and stay away from him.

Riva's phone rang. She reached inside her purse and fished around until she located the cellular. "Hello," she answered. Riva smiled when she recognized her father's voice. She was not one bit surprised that he'd taken time out from his rest and relaxation to check on work. "How are you?" she asked him.

"I'm fine. I called to see how everything was going."

"Things are going well, Daddy."

"Are you sure? I spoke to Jasper and he told me about the meeting he had with you at the café."

Riva snaked the truck around a curve. It was just like Jasper to tell her father about their meeting.

"I have a meeting with Isaiah Fuller soon, and I wanted to see if Jasper would make some changes in the project."

"Riva, Jasper is not making any changes," Mason said. "So don't fight with him."

"I understand," Riva said, wishing Jasper would keep some things she said to him to himself.

"All right, Riva. We'll talk when I get back."

Riva listened to the ensuing silence, and she imagined her father was not pleased with her. "Daddy, you should be enjoying yourself instead of worrying." Riva forced herself to sound cheerful.

"I'll see you soon," Mason answered, without telling her that he was enjoying his vacation. The phone clicked, and Riva knew her father was upset. Jasper Wade was not only his friend, but he ran the accounting department with strict determination, hoarding every nickel he could save.

"Is Uncle Mason on vacation?" Theresa asked Riva.

"Yes." Riva dropped the phone inside her purse.

"So what happened between you and Jasper Wade?" Theresa inquired, turning to face Riva.

Riva speeded up, passing through a yellow traffic light. "We had a disagreement."

"You got into an argument," Theresa corrected.

"Theresa, the older you get, the farther you stick your nose into my business." Riva slowed down for a car in front of her.

Theresa shrugged. "You know, Riva, I saw Uncle Mason's fiancée downtown last week, and she walked past me like she didn't know who I was."

"Maybe Alicia was thinking about something," Riva said. It wasn't strange that Alicia Owens didn't speak sometimes. Her mind seemed far away. "Maybe she's thinking about all the things she has do for the wedding."

"Yes, I guess she's thinking about her and Uncle Mason's wedding, and having you as her stepdaughter." Theresa grinned.

Riva gave Theresa a sidelong glance. "Hopefully Aunt Udell will realize that she loves Jasper, marry him, and then you will have a stepfather." Riva laughed.

"Riva, girl, don't even start with that foolishness." Theresa joined Riva in her laughter. "But I'm surprised at Uncle Mason. He's only known Alicia for about six or seven months. Right?" Theresa asked Riva.

"Something like that," Riva replied, thinking that when she had asked her father why he didn't wait a while before he married Alicia, Mason had informed Riva that he loved Alicia and he was going to marry her.

Riva realized her father was stubborn, and more determined than she was to get what he wanted. And most times Mason Dae got exactly what desired. However, he hadn't succeeded in getting Riva's mother, Paula, to stay with him. Their promise to stay married for better or worse and until death did they part was null and void by the time Riva was twelve years old. Riva learned later that it was her father's stubborn determination and strong will that had ended her parents' marriage.

But she didn't understand that at the age of

twelve, when her parents informed her that they were divorcing. All her mother had to do was give up her career as a travel agent, and stay home and wait for her father to come home from work. But Paula wasn't giving up her career. As a result of their divorce, Riva lived with her father and visited her mother one week in the summer and two weeks during the Christmas holidays. Riva's days after school were spent at her aunt Udell's Key Lock center for children and teens whose parents were still at work when they returned from school. Every night before going to bed, Riva wished her parents would remarry. By the time she was fifteen and her wish had not been fulfilled, Riva gave up. Angry and disappointed, knowing her wish was not coming true, Riva promised herself she would never marry and have children. If there was a divorce, she would not want her children to suffer the pain that she'd suffered. But she had met Lance Cain, and her promises vanished. Now she was getting a divorce. There was only one good thing: there were no children who would suffer.

Riva slowed and turned into the spa's well-lighted parking lot. She found a parking space, then cut the engine and lights in her truck.

Inside, the spa was cool and inviting. Soft white lights gave the accommodations a rich ambience. Giant red clay pots supported emerald shrubbery with leaves that appeared to have been waxed and buffed to a perfect shine. Lilies extended from crystal vases, and hot-tub ads sheathed in gold frames tantalized Riva, making her want to move in the direction of the soothing water. Instead she stopped at the desk, greeted the clerk, and signed in for the evening.

"I'll meet you in the lobby at ten-thirty," Riva

said to Theresa. "So don't leave." Riva had several hours to be pampered, and she intended to enjoy every minute. She knew Theresa: if Riva took too long being pampered, Theresa would call a cab.

"Riva, girl, I'm not going anywhere. If I finish before you do, I'll wait in the lobby," Theresa said, going in a different direction from Riva. Headed to the massage room, Riva saw Laura walking ahead of her, swishing her hips as if she were in a rush.

"Where are you racing to?" Riva called out to Laura. She didn't have to see Laura's face to know it was Laura.

Laura turned around, smiling. "Riva, I'm going to the dressing room." Her beige complexion glowed from underneath the thick white turban wrapped around her head.

"Are you leaving already?" Riva asked, hoping she would be able to talk to Laura tonight.

"Riva, I peeked in that room," Laura said, pointing to a nearby massage room.

"Who were you looking for?" Riva was curious. It wasn't like Laura to look behind closed curtains and doors.

"I was looking for my masseuse, and, girl, I saw Foster's behind lying in there." Laura waved her freshly manicured hand.

Riva smothered a chuckle. "Foster?" Riva asked. "Didn't you guys break up a few months ago?"

"Yes, and I'm going home. I don't want to be bothered with him tonight."

Riva laughed.

"Aren't you late tonight?" Laura asked.

"I changed my appointment—and I told you," Riva said to her, knowing that Laura remembered what she wanted to remember. They had been friends since they had met at Aunt Udell's after-school program as children. Neither one of them had wanted to attend the program, but because of the circumstance, they were forced to spend their evenings together. As the weeks passed, Riva and Laura had become best friends.

"That's right, I remember." Laura smiled. "I'll see you tomorrow." Laura gave Riva another smile and headed into the dressing room.

Riva walked out onto the deck, disrobed, and made herself comfortable in the Jacuzzi, allowing the hot, swirling water to massage her body and release her worries and stress from the day. She closed her eyes, not wanting to look into the security cameras that had been installed. Management had become aware of couples in the tub making love. That thought reminded Riva of the times she and Lance had spent together sharing hours of passionate desire. Riva shut out the vision, forcing her mind to quiet. She was unsuccessful, as visions of herself and Lance flitted across her mind like a scene from a romantic movie. As Riva forced her reflections from her mind, she noticed the aroma of male cologne.

"How are you this evening?" The masseuse stood at the edge of the tub and spoke to Riva, pulling her out of her past and back to the present.

"I feel better," Riva said, realizing that the warm water had worked magic on her body, relieving her tense muscles. "I think I'll just have a facial tonight," Riva said.

"You can have whatever you want, Riva." The gentleman smiled down at her.

Minutes later, thick almond and honey cream was being massaged into Riva's skin, draining the lingering tightness in her face, making the last of the problems plaguing her melt and disappear into the night.

While she enjoyed the facial, her mind drifted, and she found herself thinking about Lance again. She dismissed the thoughts, and listened to the music piping through the speakers, filling the room with peace.

After the facial mask had been applied and was tightening against her skin, Riva relaxed even more, and her mind began to wander. Once again she thought about Lance. He had the tendency to kindle smoldering flames within her at the very sight of him, and that was not good. Now she was left with only memories from their past, and the apartment he'd given her.

Riva was successful in keeping herself from living in the past only because she kept herself busy. One night a month she helped out at the after-school program. On Friday nights, she shot pool or played cards with Laura, Theresa, and others from their group, which rented a private club for their parties. With all the things going on in her life, she was certain that she would have forgotten about Lance by now. But she hadn't.

The heat finally chased Jasper out of his black suit coat. He'd stayed at the café longer than he'd intended, and returned to the office around eight o'clock that evening to tie up a few loose ends. While he considered Riva's temper tantrum from earlier that day, he turned off the computer and closed the blinds, shutting out the view. His office was neat, his desk clear except for a Rolodex, a calendar, and a round green leather pencil holder that matched his desk chair, and two chairs were neatly pushed in at the foot of the huge cherry desk. Jasper glanced at the black Nigerian mask on his wall that Riva had given him last Christmas, and wondered if she had calmed down. With all the grief she gave him, he wished she'd find herself a lover.

Jasper picked up his briefcase and headed for the door, flipping off the light as he stepped out into the corridor and pulled the door behind him. Before he could get to the elevator his cell phone rang.

"Yes?" Jasper answered, as he punched the elevator's callbutton. Jasper listened, his eyes squinting, making the bridge of his nose wrinkle. "Riva, I thought we were finished with this conversation. I told you—" Before Jasper could finish telling Riva that his decision was final on Isaiah Fuller's ad, the line went dead. Jasper shook his head. He didn't have the slightest idea why Riva wanted to continue her fight. It was bad enough that she'd invited him to retire. Jasper stepped off the elevator, nodded to the night guard, and walked out to his car, keeping his mind free of anything Riva might have to say to him once he arrived at her apartment.

Ten minutes later Jasper rolled into a parking space in front of Riva's building. Slowly he got out of his car, dreading another argument with his best friend's daughter. He'd known Riva since she was a baby. Right after she was born Mason's father had died, leaving Mason the advertising business. Jasper remembered how when he had first started working with Mason and his father, Dae Advertising wasn't much. Mason's father ran ads for dry-cleaning services, churches, and funeral homes, and designed church fans. Most of the models were hired from the church congregation. But when Mason inherited Dae Advertising, he officially made Jasper account manager. Together he and Mason worked hard gathering clients. Every year Mason added more equipment and staff.

Jasper remembered how he and Mason had struggled to make the company what it was. Mason hadn't gotten where he was by giving in to his clients' every whim. And if Isaiah Fuller thought he could get anything for free, he would do it. Jasper was more than certain that Isaiah knew Mason wasn't in town, and he was pretty sure that Fuller knew Mason hadn't been feeling well. Fuller though he could play on Riva's creativity, get what he wanted, yet take his time paying. Not on his life, Jasper decided. He was the account manager, and he would call the shots. If Riva didn't like it, she could take it up with her daddy, and Jasper knew Mason. At one time Mason had given Riva whatever she asked for. Lately Jasper noticed that Mason had changed, telling Riva he wasn't giving in to her and her whims. To make sure, Jasper had called Mason a few hours ago, letting him know he and Riva had had another meeting. Even though Jasper didn't like disturbing Mason while he was on vacation, he'd rather speak to him before Riva had a chance to talk her father into giving Fuller a break.

Jasper got out and pushed the car door closed with a firm snap. A piercing sharpness ripped through the top of his left shoulder. Jasper tried to turn to see who had shot him, but a sharp, burning pain ripped through his shoulder. Jasper struggled to stay awake, as darkness began to engulf him. He fell, toppling over into a hedge near his parked car.

Three

Later that evening, Lance pushed away from the computer and stretched. Mason had hired Moses Investigations to do a background check on the people he was interested in hiring for his new office. So far everyone Lance had investigated seemed legitimate.

Lance folded his arms across his chest and thought about Riva. She was the only woman he wanted. A vision of Riva played across his mind like a recorded tape. She was tall, with a thick mask of shoulder-length black hair. Riva usually complained about certain parts of her body. Her stomach wasn't flat enough, her hips were too large, and her legs weren't thin enough. He smiled, understanding that those were Riva's views and she was entitled. But as far as he was concerned, nothing was wrong with Riva's body. He loved everything about her. Her round hips were perfect, and he loved slipping his arms around her small waist, drawing her to him, kissing her full lips. Lance locked his hands behind his head. He could almost smell traces of her soft, rich perfume. She was stubborn, feisty, and sometimes she was just hardheaded. But he loved her, and because of a lack of communication on his part, he had lost her.

Lance unfolded his arms and checked the time

on his watch, remembering that it was his evening to buy dinner for his housemates. It was getting late, and if he was going to stop at the restaurant he needed to be on his way, instead of pining over the woman he'd lost.

Lance got up, took his suit jacket from the chair, and walked to the front of the building, stopping next to the receptionist's desk. He pushed his hands into his pockets and stared blankly through the tinted windows, looking at nothing in particular. All Lance could think about was how he wanted to talk Riva into not divorcing him. Maybe on his way home he'd stop by Riva's place and try again, even though she had told him to call her first. But the house was an offer Lance couldn't refuse, and since he was thinking of buying soon, and they were still married, he would need Riva's signature.

Lance stretched his legs into a wider stance and recalled the early part of the evening and his visit with Riva. The last thing he needed to end his day was another altercation with her. How could he justify his reasons for having two women living in the house with him? He was almost convinced that Riva would have nothing more to do with him if she thought he had a lover.

When his mentor and boss, Samuel Moses, learned of his pending divorce and the reasons for Lance's losing his wife, Samuel had offered him the head position at his private-detective firm. Lance accepted his offer, hoping Riva would reconsider going through with the divorce.

Lance visited Riva mostly because he missed her, and when he was with her for a few moments, he looked for some glimmer of hope that she had forgiven him for going undercover when he promised her he would work behind the desk in a safer position. But he had taken the undercover position, telling her only later what he'd done, and he understood Riva's anger.

At one point, Riva seemed to have softened, and their life seemed to have been in order. After a prisoner that he had been responsible for having convicted was released from jail, his and Riva's problems had escalated. The ex-con had succeeded in chasing them off the road one day.

Lance was sorry that he and Riva had ended up in the hospital. But Riva had decided then that she wanted a divorce, and Lance's world had crumbled. Now, thanks to Theresa Hart, the condominium's self-appointed news reporter, who rarely knew what she was talking about, Riva was upset at him again.

Lance freed his thoughts and set the security alarm, before pushing the main switch beside the door, then turned out the lights before he walked out and locked the door to Moses Investigations.

Lance could smell honey-dipped chicken from the fast-food restaurant across the street. He walked to his truck and drove across the street to the restaurant, stopping beside the menu on the drivethrough's board.

Maybe by the time he took the food home, Vanessa and Adam would have finished their assignments. Lance didn't know if Tiffany would be home. She usually took her son Erin to the toy store, or to visit her mother after work. But just in case Tiffany didn't follow her usual schedule, Lance decided to pick up extra food for her.

Lance drove around the curve, heading toward the next window to pick up the order, and stopped. As he waited behind two cars, he forced himself not to think about Riva and the home he could finally afford and wanted to share with her. The price Samuel had quoted to him for the house was low. Lance could have easily paid exactly what the home was worth. A few weeks ago he'd received the trust fund his father had put away for him when he was a baby. After a little over thirty years, the trust fund was now a small fortune.

Lance nodded to the cashier as he took the bags and set them on the seat beside him. If he hurried, he could drop off the food and drive back to Riva's apartment around the same time she arrived home from the spa.

As Lance arrived at the street to Riva's apartment, he noticed fire trucks, police cruisers, and undercover officers with whom he had once worked while on the police force. It looked as if all the neighbors were outside their apartments.

Lance inserted the key card he had kept and let himself inside the gate, driving to the side of building away from the officers and emergency vehicles to an empty parking space. He got out and walked back to the front to where Riva usually parked her truck, noticing that she was not home yet. "What happened?" Lance asked an undercover officer.

"A man was shot. We got an anonymous call a few minutes ago," the officer whom Lance recognized as Bill said. "The caller claims your wife shot the guy."

"You're joking, right?" Lance asked.

"I'm serious," Bill said.

"Riva won't pick up a gun, Bill; you know that," Lance said. Lance remembered when a group of officers had taken their wives to a shooting gallery with plans to teach them how to handle and shoot a pistol. Riva refused to go inside or even look at the tiny pearl-handled gun Lance had bought for her.

"People change." Bill looked at Lance. "She's alone and could've bought herself a gun and learned how to use the thing."

"Was there any identification on the victim?" Lance asked, thinking Riva hadn't changed that much—but maybe she had. However, the idea of Riva shooting anyone didn't make sense. She was tough, but she wasn't a killer.

"The victim's identification tells us his name is Jasper Wade," Bill replied.

"Ah, man," Lance said, groaning.

"What?" Bill asked.

"Riva is not home, or at least she's not supposed to be home," Lance said, taking out his phone. He didn't believe for one minute that Riva had shot Jasper. But the fact that she'd told him she argued with Jasper earlier stuck in his mind.

"Do you know something that we need to know, Cain? Bill asked.

"Riva is at the spa," Lance said.

"You know for a fact that she went to the spa?" Bill questioned.

Lance didn't answer. He believed Riva, and since he didn't see Riva's truck in the parking lot, he assumed she was still at the spa. Lance punched in the numbers to Riva's cellular telephone.

"Riva told me she was going to the spa." Lance waited for Riva to answer her phone.

"Hello?" Riva answered. She sound too relaxed to have just committed a crime.

"Riva, where have you been?" Lance asked.

"Excuse me?" Riva sounded annoyed at him for prying into her personal business.

"Are you at the spa?" Lance asked, equally annoyed at Riva for her defensiveness, when she didn't have the slightest idea that she could be on her way to jail.

"Yes. I was about to leave," Riva answered.

"Riva, you need to call the police station and let Homicide know that you want to come down tonight and speak with a detective," Lance ordered.

"Speak to a homicide detective about what, Lance?" Riva's calm, relaxed voice seemed to have lost its velvet tone. "What happened, Lance?" Lance recognized the tremble in her voice.

"Someone tried to kill Jasper, and you've been blamed for shooting him," Lance said as calmly as he could, but it was hard to stay calm, knowing that Riva must be getting close to hysterics.

"Oh, my God! I didn't shoot Jasper."

"Calm down, and call the station now. And get down there," Lance ordered. He knew she had an alibi.

"I have to take Theresa home first." Lance heard Riva's voice quaver.

"Take Theresa with you, and I'll meet you at the station."

"Lance!" Riva screamed into the receiver. "I have been here all night."

"Riva . . . Riva," Lance called out to her.

"What?"

"Calm down." Lance spoke as calmly as he could. "Let me speak to the manager," Lance said.

"I'm calming down. . . . I can't think straight. . . . Oh, my God." Lance heard the note of panic in Riva's voice.

Lance's heart went out to Riva. He knew she was scared out of her wits. But if she was at the spa all night, she didn't have anything to worry about. "What part of the building are you in now?" Lance asked.

"I'm in the lobby," she answered, sounding more upset.

"Give your phone to the clerk. I want to talk to her."

Lance spoke to the clerk, then waited another second to speak to the supervisor.

The seconds Lance waited seemed like minutes, but he was patient. Finally the woman came on the line. Lance asked the supervisor if she, or anyone who was with Riva that evening, could come down to the police station and verify that Riva had never left the spa.

The supervisor agreed to give Lance all the information the officers needed.

Lance pleaded with the supervisor. If Riva didn't have a witness, she might end up spending the night in jail.

"Babe," Lance said to Riva once she was back on the line.

"I didn't shoot Jasper," Riva said.

"Riva, get your butt down to the station and don't stop until you get there."

"But—"

"Go now." Lance hung up and turned to Bill. "She's on her way to the station."

"Lance, you know she'll be okay as long as she has witnesses."

"You're right. I'll see you at the station, Bill," Lance said, preparing to drive to the station and wait for Riva.

Four

"Theresa, you know I didn't shoot Jasper," Riva said as she drove to the police station. She couldn't remember ever being so afraid in her life. Maybe she had been, but this was a different kind of fear. It was the kind of fear that made her blood run cold, and the thought of going to jail was enough to make her drive at a snail's pace.

"Speed up, Riva—the police will stop us and give you a ticket for driving too slow," Theresa said.

"Theresa, don't talk to me now." Riva pressed the gas pedal, accelerating the speed.

"If we get stopped, the police are going to know it's you, and they'll probably put you in the police car and—"

"Okay, I'm driving faster," Riva said as they sped along the street. It seemed that every traffic light was red. But she didn't dare drive through the red lights; she was already in enough trouble.

Two blocks away from the station Riva slowed down. She wondered who was framing her for shooting Jasper. Riva didn't know if Jasper had enemies. But if he did, why would the person tell the police that Riva had done the shooting?

"Maybe he has a woman friend or a lover who wants him dead," Theresa said as they pulled into the parking lot in front of the station.

"And blamed me?" Riva asked, noticing that Lance was standing next to his truck as she pulled into a parking space beside him. "The only woman I've ever known Jasper to go out with was your mother."

Theresa jerked around, glaring at Riva. "Mommy didn't shoot Jasper."

"I didn't say she shot him. I'm saying that whoever tried to kill Jasper was probably not a lover," Riva snapped. Her fear and anger mingled and settled at the bottom of her stomach, making her realize that she could just as well have put the money she spent at the spa in her savings account. Her headache was back, and her muscles were as tense as ever. "I wonder who shot Jasper and told the police I did it," Riva blinked back a tear.

"I don't know," Theresa said, gathering her purse and preparing to get out. "It seems like you have an enemy."

As far as Riva knew, she didn't have any enemies, at least none who hated her enough to want her in jail.

Riva cut the engine, reached for her purse and got out. She leaned back into the truck and, with trembling fingers, turned off the headlights, then closed and locked the door.

She stepped back, bumping into Lance. "I'm sorry," Riva said, turning and seeing that Lance was now close behind her.

"Let's go inside," Lance said.

"I'm not feeling well at all." Riva leaned against Lance, wishing that the night was over, and that whoever had tried to kill Jasper was in jail. "Is Jasper okay?" Riva asked, just as worried about Jasper as she was about herself.

"I don't know. Bill told me that Jasper was shot

in his shoulder, so probably he'll pull through."
Lance took her hand in his. "The supervisor from
the spa said she would stop by and verify that you
were there all night," Lance said as they walked
toward the station.

"The supervisor?" Riva asked. She didn't think
she needed another witness since Theresa had
been with her all night. She had been in such a
state while Lance was speaking with the spa employees that she hadn't realized Lance had spoken
to the supervisor.

"How are you, Theresa?" Lance asked Riva's
cousin, who was standing at the back of Riva's
truck.

"I'm okay, but Lance, Riva didn't leave the spa.
I can swear to that," Theresa said as they walked
across the parking lot to the station. "You didn't
have to ask the supervisor to come to the station."

"First, you're Riva's cousin."

"So?" Theresa asked defensively.

"The officer is going to want to see a sign-in and
sign-out sheet, and anything else that proves Riva
was at the spa during the time of the shooting."

"There are cameras in the spa," Riva said as they
walked inside the station. "I went to the Jacuzzi
before I had a facial. It's all on film."

"Good," Lance said, opening and holding the
door for Riva and Theresa to go inside.

It had been a while since Riva had visited the
police station. However, nothing had changed except the officer seated behind the information
desk. She walked through the metal detector and
waited for Lance, hearing the buzzer when his gun
was detected. Lance showed the officer his identification and walked inside. When Theresa walked
through the metal detector, Lance asked her to

wait while Riva spoke to the officer at the information desk.

Riva felt as if she were wearing weights as she walked slowly through the lobby to the information desk. She noticed the chairs along the wall in the waiting area, where people waited for identifications to be made. The records room was across from the information desk.

Riva reached the desk, Lance beside her, and told the clerk she wanted to speak to a detective.

Still trembling inside, Riva waited to be escorted to the interrogation room.

"I'll be here when you get back," Riva heard Lance say as another officer led her away.

It wasn't long before Riva was seated in a room with one table and three chairs. She observed the recorder that she was sure would be used to tape her statement. For the first time since she'd learned about the accusation against her, Riva relaxed. She would give her statement because she had nothing to hide. She let that thought skip across her mind as she sat and looked at the only window in the room, realizing that she couldn't see outside. Riva lowered her gaze, thinking that the window was probably designed for witnesses to view the suspect.

It wasn't long before two detectives entered the room and seated themselves behind the table.

"Mrs. Cain, we will be taping this interrogation," one of the men said to Riva as he turned on the recorder.

"Okay," Riva said, and began answering the questions she was asked. When she was asked if she had had a fight with Jasper at the café, she told the truth: she *did* have an argument with Jasper.

Finally the interrogation was over, and Riva was

told she was free to go. She was also informed that until the statement could be verified, she was still a suspect.

The officer escorted Riva back to the lobby, where Theresa and Lance were supposed to have been waiting for her. Instead the family lawyer, Spencer James, was standing at the information desk. When he saw Riva, he walked over to her.

"Riva, why didn't you call me before you answered any questions?" Spencer asked, looking disturbed.

"I didn't call you because I didn't need your services. I have witnesses who can verify that I didn't leave the spa this evening," Riva said, observing Spencer's dark suit and well-groomed appearance. His wavy steel gray hair was combed away from his olive face, and his mustache was neatly trimmed as usual.

Spencer looked as if he'd just walked out of a courtroom. Riva had known the lawyer for years, and it seemed he was a part of the family. He'd spent many evenings at their home with her parents before they were divorced. "Did Lance leave?" Riva asked.

"He'll be back soon." Spencer still looked upset.

"Where's Theresa?" Riva asked.

"She went with a detective." Spencer held Riva's gaze. "If I hadn't been down here with another client, I would never have known that you were here." He looked as if he were studying Riva. "Take care of yourself, Riva."

"Spencer, I'll be fine," Riva assured him, just as Theresa was escorted back to the lobby.

"That goes for you, too, young lady," Spencer said, giving Theresa a tight smile.

"What goes for me?" Theresa looked from the lawyer to Riva.

"Don't worry about it, Theresa," Riva said, chuckling. "I think we should be going."

Riva said good night to Spencer. She and Theresa started out of the building just in time to see Lance about to enter.

"Let's go," Lance said, reaching for Riva's hand. His hand touched hers, and she automatically slipped her hand into his.

"The supervisor stopped by and gave a statement," Lance said.

"I have to thank her," Riva said, wondering why anyone would attempt to set her up.

"I intend to help find the person who shot Jasper, Riva," Lance promised as they walked to her truck.

"I hope you find the person, but be careful Lance," Riva warned.

"I'll be all right," Lance said, sure of himself.

"Riva, are you and Lance going to stand out here and talk all night?" Theresa asked as she stood on the passenger's side of Riva's truck.

"No," Riva said, and unlocked the door. "Thanks, Lance, for everything."

"Oh, I got in touch with Mason," Lance said.

"What did he say?" Riva asked as she opened the door and rested one foot inside. She imagined that her father was upset. He was already angry at her when he had called her while she was on her way to the spa.

"He'll be home in a few hours," Lance said.

She opened her mouth to protest. Lance held up his hand and stopped her. "Mason had to know about Jasper, and he needed to know that you were accused of shooting him."

"Lance, I don't how to thank you," Riva said, knowing that if Lance hadn't told her to call the station, and if he hadn't asked the spa supervisor for her help, she could have spent the night in jail.

"Like this," Lance said, and kissed Riva's cheek.

"Girl, get in the truck," Theresa said. "Gracious, I know I'm on vacation, but I need my rest."

"One second, Theresa." Riva turned back to Lance. "Thanks, Lance," Riva offered her gratitude again, still feeling the effects of Lance's lips against her cheek.

"I have a meeting with Mason"—Lance checked his watch—"this morning," he continued. "I'm going to make sure you get home, and then I'm going home and going to bed."

"We'll be fine," Riva said. "You did enough already."

"I'll see you later." Lance backed away from the truck, and Riva noticed that he waited for her to leave.

"Now, the way I see it," Theresa started as soon as Riva turned the key in the ignition, "I think the woman that Lance lives with tried to kill Jasper and frame you."

"I don't think so." Riva pushed the gearshift into reverse and turned on the headlights.

"See, with you out of the way, she won't have to worry about you and Lance getting back together."

"Theresa, what you're saying does not make sense at all. I doubt the woman you're talking about even knows Jasper."

"She's a private investigator, Riva. And, girl, she probably knows everything about you."

"Theresa, how do you know she's an investigator?"

"Because the night I saw her at the supermarket,

she was telling Lance something about how she was about to wrap up a case she was working on."

"You were close enough to hear her every word, I'm sure," Riva said.

"Uh-huh. I was standing behind her."

Riva didn't say anything. She knew Theresa's ears were like antennae. If a person wanted to speak privately and Theresa was nearby, it was best if the people wrote the message. "You know, Theresa, you have a way of fixing everything."

"It makes sense," Theresa said seriously.

Nonetheless, Theresa did have a point about the woman she had seen with Lance in the supermarket. But what woman would be dense enough to jeopardize her career because of a man? Riva tried to dismiss the nagging thought.

Maybe Lance needed a woman who understood his work, Riva thought, continuing to mull over Theresa's senseless speculation. Riva played with the thought of the woman living with Lance awhile longer as she drove herself and Theresa home, making an attempt to control the green jealousy pricking at her heart. Finally Riva discarded Theresa's ridiculous theory and glanced into her rearview mirror. Lance was behind her. Their life together was over except for the legal technicalities, but Riva realized that, in the darkest hours of her life, she could depend on Lance to stand by her.

Five

Riva woke the next morning to the sound of her clock radio. The station's news reporter was broadcasting news of the shooting at Riva's apartment complex. Riva rolled over and looked at the clock. It was ten minutes past nine. She should have been at work an hour ago, but because she had stayed at the police station until late, she'd overslept.

The light beaming through the half-open spaces in the vertical blinds was almost blinding. Riva scooted to edge of the bed. At least she didn't have a headache. The joy of not having to spend the night in jail seemed to have been all the medicine she needed.

Still, she was tired, she realized as she planted her feet firmly on the carpet. She would have to take the day off; there was no way she could work.

Riva knew her father hadn't planned to return from his vacation so soon and she knew she would have to go to the office to speak to him. She walked to the bathroom for her shower, recalling Theresa's accusations about Lance's housemate. Riva pushed the outlandish thought to the back of her mind and pulled off her gown. What Lance did with his life was his business, she decided as she stepped into the shower and turned the nozzle. She promised herself that she would not listen to any of Theresa's speculations about Lance's house-mate again.

Ten minutes later Riva finished her shower, dried off, slipped the towel around herself, and went to her closet, choosing a dark blue sleeveless dress and blue heels. She combed her hair in her usual style. After applying light makeup and a pair of gold stud earrings, Riva changed purses before she left for Dae Advertising.

It wasn't long before Riva walked into the reception area and stopped at the desk, checking for messages. Her first message was from Alicia, wanting her to stop by Mason's house to see her. Riva slipped the note inside her purse and read the second message.

Within a few months, Alicia and her father were getting married. However, Riva didn't understand why Alicia had moved in with her father before they were married. Nonetheless, Riva figured they were in love and enjoyed each other's company. If her father enjoyed having Alicia living with him, Riva was happy for both of them.

"Good morning." Brenda Clemens, the receptionist, walked in, her light blue suit and navy heels making her look chic.

"Good morning, Brenda," Riva greeted her, then leafed through another batch of messages.

"I, ah . . ." Brenda began. The receptionist appeared uncomfortable.

"Were you about to say something to me?" Riva asked the young woman, noticing that her light skin seemed to darken.

"Oh, I was just thinking about Jasper. You know—"

"You heard what happened to Jasper," Riva said.

"Yes, and I thought . . . well I thought . . ."

"You thought I shot him." Riva completed what she imagined the receptionist was about to say.

Brenda gave Riva a chagrined smile. "Yes, but you know how people gossip around here."

"I am aware," Riva said, moving away from the desk. She wasn't surprised that it had been only hours since she'd left the police department, gone home, and slept for a few hours, and already the gossips at Dae Advertising were churning the rumor mill. "Is my father in his office?" Riva asked, changing the subject. The receptionist was known for gathering bits and pieces of information and adding her personal spin before spreading the tales among the other employees.

"Yes," Brenda said.

Riva snapped her purse shut. "Brenda, take messages for me today," she said, before heading out to the corridor. As she turned the corner, she was almost knocked down by two typists who had their heads together talking.

"Good morning." One woman spoke and gave Riva a frozen smile.

"Good morning," Riva greeted them as she headed toward the elevator. Riva couldn't be certain, but she imagined the women were whispering about her. She pushed the annoying thought to the back of her mind. With everything going on in her life this was not the time to become paranoid

Riva pressed the fourth button on the elevator's panel. While she waited for her stop, Riva called the hospital to check on Jasper. The nurse informed her that Jasper was out of surgery, and his operation had gone well. However, shortly after his surgery, Jasper's blood pressure had needed stabilizing. He was recovering in the intensive-care unit.

The elevator bell rang, alerting Riva that she had

arrived on the fourth floor. Riva walked to her office, wondering what Alicia wanted to talk to her about. She and Alicia didn't talk much, but since she'd been engaged to her father, Alicia seemed to be friendlier than usual.

Riva stopped at Laura's door, peeking in and hoping to find her. When Riva didn't see Laura in her office, she headed down the hall to her own office.

"Hi, Riva," she heard Phillip Davis speaking in his nasal voice. "You look exhausted this morning." He grinned, showing her a set of uneven short teeth.

"Thanks, Phillip. I'm glad you noticed." He was inquisitive and had a habit of sticking his nose where it didn't belong. Phillip had recently been hired to work with the creative team, coming up with ideas and slogans for the clients' advertisements.

Since Phillip's arrival at Dae Advertising, Riva was never surprised to find him lurking around office doors or slinking around a corner as if hoping to hear another employee sharing the latest gossip.

"Let's have lunch today?" Phillip asked.

"I can't go to lunch with you, Phillip."

"Ah, come on, Riva. I'm treating."

Treating or not, Riva never wanted to socialize with Phillip. She understood that he was probably lonely. Phillip had mentioned to her and Laura once that he was new in the city and wanted to make friends. Riva remembered telling Phillip that he should go out more and meet people other than the employees.

"No, thank you, Phillip." Riva walked around him, only to have him block her path. "I'm going to lunch in about four hours." He snaked out his bony wrist and looked at his watch.

"You know, Phillip, I feel exactly like I look—I'm tired," Riva said, not wanting to sound rude.

"You women in this town know how to make a man feel unwelcome," Phillip complained, spreading his palm wide.

"If you haven't noticed, Phillip, this is an office, and there are other women in this town who would probably love to have lunch with you." Riva headed down the hall.

"Good, be that way," Riva heard him call out to her. She didn't stop to respond. Her energy was needed elsewhere—like defending herself to her father on why she fought with Jasper on a decision she should've known she couldn't win.

"You see, Riva, I'm trying to be nice to you." Phillip's voice rose. "The problem with you is that you're stuck-up and . . ." Riva continued to walk, noticing two doors opening and a pair of well-groomed female employees sticking their heads out of their offices.

Sometimes Riva didn't know what to think of Phillip, and she'd stopped trying to figure out why or how he was hired. She dismissed him and his actions from her mind and went to her office before she headed down to visit with her father.

"All right, Mason, I'll need the names of all your employees." Lance pressed the receiver against his ear as he checked off the list of items he needed to find Jasper's attacker. He listened to Mason for a while. "Yeah, I need Social Security numbers." Listening to Mason, Lance knew Mason thought that someone working at Dae Advertising shot Jasper. "What do you mean, when do I need the information? I need it as soon as possible. And Mason, I need to send Adam over to work with you." Lance paused. "He's going to be your personal assistant." Lance leaned back in his chair and let out a long sigh.

"Mason, Adam is not really going to be your personal assistant," Lance said when Mason told him he didn't need an assistant. "I need him there to eavesdrop, plant bugs, and install surveillance— stuff like that." Lance listened to Mason awhile longer before he ended their conversation.

Until last night, Lance had worked mostly behind the scenes in Moses Investigations, supervising and reviewing reports. Samuel Moses assigned other investigators to the streets, trenches, and alleys. These were all the jobs that Lance loved; however, when Samuel left six months ago, saying he was taking care of family business in New Orleans, Lance didn't bother to make changes in any of the employees' positions.

But Mason seemed certain that someone from Dae Advertising had shot Jasper. Mason's reason was valid: if anyone knew Riva was constantly disagreeing with Jasper, the person had a perfect opportunity to set Riva up.

Lance promised himself and Samuel that he would learn to love working behind a desk, but even though he didn't hate the job, he preferred working in the field.

Now that Riva was accused of a crime she didn't commit, his plans were to find the person. For him to be successful, he would get the job done himself, which meant going undercover and working the alleyways, dinky bars, and wherever else his leads took him.

Lance pushed the intercom and called for Adam. If any two men could find Jasper's attacker it was him and Adam. "You're working for Mason," Lance said when Adam answered.

Two minutes later Adam was standing in his doorway. Adam was tall, and his biceps were proof that he worked out at the gym at least four times a week. His light skin was smooth, complementing his short black hair.

"Someone shot Jasper Wade last night," Lance said, giving Adam the details on what had happened to Jasper, and how Riva was accused of the shooting.

"What do you want me to do?" Adam moved into the room and sat on the table against the wall facing Lance.

"Mason seems to think that someone working for him shot Jasper," Lance said. "I would like for you to get inside and find out everything you can."

"What is my job description?" Adam asked.

"You'll be Mason's assistant." Lance grinned.

"Was Jasper Mason's assistant?"

"No, Jasper was the account manager," Lance replied.

"I understand that being Mason's assistant, I get the chance to mingle with the employees without being suspicious." Adam folded his arms across his chest.

"And eavesdrop, plant bugs and do other surveillance." Lance winked.

"When do I start?" Adam got off the table.

"I would like for you to meet with Mason as soon as possible."

"I'll get over there today."

"We need to solve this case as soon as possible,"

Lance stated. He didn't like that Riva was being set up.

"You know I'm not finished with the assignment Vanessa and I are working on," Adam said to Lance.

"I'll get someone to help Vanessa." Lance was satisfied that the case that Adam and Vanessa were working on was almost solved. Only a few more details needed attention, and then he could give his findings to the police.

Adam walked over and stood at the front of Lance's desk. "I would think that you wanted to work on the inside with Mason." He grinned.

"I think I can do a better job if I stayed out of Mason's company." The only people who knew he was a private detective were Riva, Mason, Jasper, and Laura. If he worked inside with Mason, he knew he could keep a low profile, but Lance thought it was best if he didn't take the chance.

"Are you saying that you don't want to work with Riva?" Adam said.

"No, that's not exactly the reason I'm asking you to take the job," Lance said. "I'm going to help you out with employee background checks, but I can find out more if I work on the outside."

"I thought you might want to be close to Riva."

"I'm not sure if Riva wants to be around me now," Lance said.

"She is upset with you about your work." Adam looked as if he felt sorry for Lance.

"Yes. Plus the latest gossip she heard," Lance replied, and stood up to walk around and sit on the edge of the desk. "Riva thinks that Vanessa and I are together."

"Well?" Adam chuckled.

"Man, come on," Lance said, wishing he'd never

brought up the subject. It seemed to do Adam good to watch his reactions when Vanessa made a pass at him.

"I hope Riva believes you." Adam chuckled dryly. "Because Vanessa has the hots for you, man." Adam shook his head, as if he felt a chill run over his body.

Lance realized that Riva probably found it hard to believe him, especially since he had lied to her before they separated, about quitting the police force. His intentions were to give up his undercover cop position and take a desk job. But when his supervisor asked him to take one more job, he couldn't refuse. He didn't bother to tell Riva that he'd taken the assignment. She found out he was still working undercover when he stopped by their apartment one day and she had come home from work early. She accused him of lying to her and told him she couldn't stay married to him.

"I don't know if Riva believes me or not. She thinks I'm a liar anyway." Lance wanted to drop the subject. He didn't think Riva cared who he shared his life with, since it was she who had wanted him out of her life. However, having Vanessa for a housemate didn't matter to him. His relationship with Vanessa was business.

Lance rubbed the back of his neck, a habit he had when he was thinking, especially when things weren't going exactly the way he wanted them to. He wasn't a liar; he just loved his work.

"Yeah, you've got yourself in a jam."

Vanessa was like a thorn in Lance's side; it was as if she wanted the world to think that they had a hot, sizzling love affair, when all he wanted was to stay married to Riva—even though Riva seemed comfortable with her life as it was. Maybe it would be better for both of them if he forgot about reconciling their relationship. He wasn't going to change careers. Taking the job Samuel offered him was as much as he was going to change about his work. Once he helped find the person who had shot Jasper, he was beginning to think that he should forget about his relationship with Riva. A small voice reminded him that he loved his work, but he loved Riva more. "I don't know if it matters to Riva what I do, or who I see. She seems content with her life since she doesn't have to worry about me," Lance finally replied, acknowledging to himself that Adam was right: he was in a jam.

"I don't know, Lance. Maybe you need to talk to Riva," Adam said.

Lance knew Adam wished he'd put up a fight to save his marriage. Lance realized from talking to him that Adam hadn't fought hard enough to save his own relationship. His ex-wife was remarried, and Adam didn't want Lance to make the same mistake.

Lance's problem with Riva was different from Adam's with his ex-wide. Adam's wife at the time didn't mind if he loved his work, so Adam worked all the time. Their problem was that Adam didn't spend enough time at home. He ex-wife was now the wife of another detective and, according to her, her new husband spent more than enough time with her.

"I don't know if talking will do any good," Lance said, picking up a sheet of paper off his desk and crumpling it into a tight ball. He'd spent time with Riva yesterday and last night, and in spite of himself he couldn't keep his hands off her. "I don't know, Adam; I think Riva would rather we went our separate ways."

"All right," Adam changing the subject. "I'll meet with Mason." Adam walked to the door. "Are you sure you don't want to help Vanessa finish the case?" Adam seemed to be camouflaging a smile with his serious expression.

"Get out of here." Lance threw the crumpled ball of paper at Adam.

Adam laughed. "When Vanessa botches the job on purpose just to get your attention, don't come complaining to me."

Lance pushed his hands into his pockets. If it were his decision, Vanessa wouldn't work for Moses Investigations. "Vanessa knows better than to play with me." Vanessa's unscrupulous behavior toward him knew no boundaries, regarding her feelings for him.

"I'll see you later, Lance," Adam said. "I think it'll be safe for me to plant a few wiretaps after I speak to Mason."

"Yeah." Lance ignored Adam's chuckle as his friend walked out of the office and down the hall.

The fax machine rang, and seconds later the information that Lance needed from Mason slid from the machine into the tray.

Lance looked over the list of Dae Advertising employees, remembering why he had chosen criminal justice as his career.

He was thirteen years old when his father was robbed and murdered. Lance remembered being angry, hurt, and confused. After the funeral he attended school, but he might as well not have been in the classroom. His thoughts were centered around revenge on the teenage boy who had caused him the greatest loss of his life. After school, instead of going home, Lance often visited the street where his father had died. The deserted building on the corner was where the teenage gangs loitered, spending their time robbing and killing innocent, hardworking people like his father.

One of Lance's classmates who lived near the area where his father was murdered had told Lance that he'd heard that one of the boys on that particular corner had robbed and killed his father. He also learned from his classmate how the boy caught his victims off guard. The unsuspected person was beaten and robbed, and sometimes murdered.

The ringing fax machine drew Lance back to his work, alerting him that he was probably receiving more information he'd requested from Mason. Lance gathered the report, then sank back down at the computer next to his desk and began thinking about the past again.

Shortly after his father's funeral, a detective spoke to his mother, informing her that he and other officers were continuing to search for the young man known as Hank. The detective had received a call from an eyewitness, telling him the name of the teenage boy who'd murdered his father. According to the officer, this was not Hank's first offense. The officer suspected Hank had left the area. He was on the most-wanted list, not only for his father's murder, but for other crimes as well.

Lance overheard the detective speaking to his mother, and decided after seeing Hank's picture on the evening news one night that he would find the young man himself. Every day after school, Lance stood near a store that wasn't far from the abandoned building, and watched to see if the young man who had murdered his father had returned to the area. Lance figured that if he could get inside the abandoned building, he could see for himself whether Hank was hiding out. But before he could get inside, he had to make friends with Hank's gang. Lance hadn't figured out exactly what he was going to do to Hank once he found him, but he intended to do whatever was necessary to avenge his father's death.

The second week, Lance rounded the corner and headed inside the store. As he walked out of the store and onto the sidewalk, some guys from the gang Hank hung out with blocked his path. One of the guys stated that he'd watched him for a couple of weeks. They needed another guy for their group until one of their men returned. The young man told Lance to snatch the purse of an old lady who was standing near the store. If Lance could carry out the order, he would have proved himself worthy to hang out with the boys.

If Lance didn't follow orders, one of the young men promised that he would take whatever money Lance had in his pocket and beat him senseless. Fear gripped Lance, and he realized that what he was about to do was wrong. But if he could get inside, he had a chance to find Hank, or at least he would find out where he was hiding.

The elderly woman stopped halfway down the sidewalk, examining whatever she'd purchased from the store in her bag. Lance headed in the woman's direction. When he was a few feet away from her, he reached out for the purse. Just as he did, a strong hand grasped his shoulder, forcing him around and giving him a good hard shake. "Come here, boy!" Lance could still hear Samuel Moses's growl now, as he sat in his office mulling over the past. Lance remembered the mean, serious expression on the detective's face, and how his complexion had darkened as he gripped Lance's shoulder with one wide, thick hand, jerking him around to face him.

Samuel had asked what he thought he was doing, then grabbed the front of his shirt collar, raising him up. His big feet dangled above the concrete sidewalk. Lance peered over the detective's shoulder and saw that the other boys had disappeared.

Lance remembered the dreadful pang that settled in his stomach as he tried to avoid making eye contact with the detective. Every time Lance looked away, Detective Moses jerked him around, barking out how he'd been watching the area and had noticed him two weeks ago. Finally the detective lowered him to the sidewalk.

Lance remembered being frightened out of his wits. He never had any trouble with the law. So, when Detective Moses asked him why was he hanging out in the area, Lance told him he was looking for the boy who had killed his father. It was then that the detective dragged him off to his unmarked patrol car, telling him that he had too much time on his hands.

With Lance's mother's permission, Detective Moses wanted to sign him up for a weekend program. At least once a month the children went camping. There were also many other events, like sports, for the children. Moses hoped that keeping Lance busy would take his mind off finding his father's killer.

As he was driven to the station, Lance was warned that Samuel was calling his mother. Tears settled in Lance's eyes and rolled down his face. He'd been too angry and hurt to cry when his father died. Lance remembered his father once telling him that if anything happened to him, he would have to help his mother. To Lance, taking his father's place meant he would be a man, with a man's responsibilities. And according to his father, men didn't cry. But that day in the back of Samuel Moses's unmarked patrol car, Lance cried. He wept for his father's untimely death and for the punishment he knew he was going to get once his mother found him at the police station.

Once they were inside the station and he was seated in a chair across from the detective's desk, Lance held his head down. He was ashamed of himself and knew that he was wrong to try to steal an old lady's purse, but at the time he had only been doing what he thought he had to do to find his father's killer.

Lance remembered the lecture Detective Samuel Moses had given him as if it were yesterday.

"I know you're upset because your father is dead. But hanging out on street corners, trying to join a gang of thugs who will kill you and think nothing of your death, is not the path to take, son." Lance remembered watching Detective Moses pick up the telephone. "What's your mother's name?" he asked, and Lance told him. "Where is she employed?" Lance gave him the name of the company. He didn't wait for the detective to ask for the phone number; Lance gave it to him. The pang that had settled in his stomach earlier was back, stronger than ever.

While he waited for his mother to arrive at the station, Lance listened to Detective Moses give him the spill on the program.

"Is the program in the detention center, sir?" Lance remembered asking the officer.

"No, but if you keep up this foolishness, that's exactly where you're going to end up. So I'm going to save your behind now." Lance drew himself out the past and shook his head. If it hadn't been for Samuel Moses he would probably be in jail or dead by now.

Lance locked his hands behind his head and leaned back as pictures of his past continued to click across his mind like pictures from a View-Master. He didn't have to look to know his mother was in the building. "Where is that boy?" He saw her headed in his direction as Samuel rose from his chair and went to calm her down. All Lance could hear from Grace Cain was, "Boy, are you trying to run my blood sky-high and give me a heart attack? I'm out here working hard trying to make ends meet, and you're out in the streets getting hauled off to jail!"

Grace calmed down long enough to listen to the reason Lance was at the station. However, the detective's explanation brought on another tirade.

Once the detective explained that he was recommending a program for him, Lance's mother calmed down. Lance was instructed to meet with the group every day after school. He would complete his homework, and join in on other activities. On the weekend he and other children his age would be accompanied by Detective Moses and other officers and members on camping trips or to sports games and other activities.

The last part of Lance's day at the police station ended when Detective Moses gave him a tour of the jail cells. The sound of iron doors slamming was enough to make Lance's flesh crawl. After that day, Lance promised himself that he would never again do anything to get in trouble, and he would never again upset his mother. That day was the beginning of Lance's new life. Samuel Moses was his mentor, and often treated him as if he were his own son.

As the years passed, Lance was mentored by Samuel Moses. By the time he graduated high school, Lance knew he wanted to be a detective. His goal was to find and put away the bad guys.

He was a private detective now. He understood the dangers of working the streets. But as with everything, there was a price. Other than the fact that he loved being a private investigator, Lance had the scalding reminder that Riva wanted to finalize their divorce as a result of the work he loved.

However, too late, he'd found a position in his career that he could work with. Now that he suspected someone was trying to frame Riva, Lance was determined to find the person, and if going undercover meant searching alleys, and all the other places that Riva feared, he didn't care anymore if Riva knew what he was doing or not.

Lance went back to his work, with thoughts of Riva trickling through his mind. He loved her, and he would do anything to protect her.

Six

From the entrance of her father's office, Riva observed Mason Dae talking on the telephone. The lights in the ceiling cast an extra shine onto his steel gray waves, which complemented the light gray suit he was wearing.

As always his office was neat. The cherry desk was polished to a perfect shine. The only clutter gracing Mason's desktop was the yellow pad he was writing on, a Rolodex, and a gold-framed picture of his fiancée, Alicia.

Hi." Riva walked inside as soon as Mason finished his telephone conversation.

"Hi," Mason greeted her, and she observed the crow's-feet in the corners of his eyes when he flashed her a white smile.

Riva crossed over to the sofa and sat, making herself comfortable. "You look rested." She crossed one leg over the other, observing her father, who had appeared exhausted before the doctor had recommended that he take out time to rest.

"I was completely lazy for two weeks." Mason's smile turned serious, as he turned his gaze toward the window. For a moment he looked as if his thoughts were in the past.

"Riva, how many times have I told you about arguing with Jasper about his job?" Mason picked up a pencil and tapped the eraser against the desk-top.

"I was just—" Riva started, but Mason inter-rupted her.

"Why can't you listen to me?" Mason asked, sounding even more annoyed.

Riva glanced at the walls, as if the answer to her father's question hid among the gold-framed pic-tures and awards and the Bantu mask. He was right; she never listened to him the way she should have listened. If she had, she would never have married Lance. She understood it wasn't because her father didn't like Lance. He thought Lance was a good man. But he warned her: Lance's work was danger-ous, and he wouldn't have the time to spend with her that she wanted. On top of that, Lance was good at his work, and there was always someone looking for revenge. "I wanted Jasper to give Mr. Fuller a break," Riva finally answered.

"Well, that's too bad. Fuller can't have a break," Mason replied."

"I thought the idea to have a limousine and a model for the lipstick ad was a good one," Riva said, knowing she had no right to fight with Jasper over a project that he felt the client wouldn't pay for on time. Besides, she hadn't known that the company had had problems with Isaiah's paying in the past,

"It's a good idea, but you're the traffic control-ler, Riva. Your job is to organize the flow of work and make sure everything gets done on time." Ma-son's forehead creased into lines. "I'm surprised at you. You should've agreed with Jasper on saving money and choosing who would and who wouldn't get a break with this business."

"I know." Riva was aware of her position, but sending out a tacky ad was not what she wanted.

"Well, at least you didn't shoot Jasper," Mason said, pushing away from the desk. "I hope you learned a lesson from having a disagreement in public. I've told you about your attitude, too."

"I didn't want to meet with Jasper in his office. The café is usually quiet that time of the day. At least no one from the office or no one I knew was in the café."

"I think that maybe someone who knew you and Jasper usually have disagreements may have heard you arguing with him," Mason said, rolling the pencil between his finger and thumb.

Riva still didn't know what to make of the false allegation that had been made against her. "I don't know why anyone would want to set me up for something I didn't do."

"You provided the person with all the ammunition. But Lance promised to work for me."

Riva scooted to the side, sitting on one hip, hoping Lance didn't get hurt while working on Jasper's case. "Couldn't you have hired another agency?" She braced her elbow on the sofa's arm, resting her chin on the heel of her fist, worrying that the person who had shot Jasper might try to kill Lance.

"Lance is good at what he does. Why are you worried about him working for me?" Mason inquired, studying Riva.

"I'm hoping that Lance will stay safe." Riva lowered her gaze.

"What difference does it make if Lance works on this case? You are divorcing him, aren't you?"

"Yes, we're getting a divorce, but why wouldn't I want Lance to stay safe?" Riva replied.

"I don't want him hurt either. But you knew

when you married him that he was a detective. Your mother and I both spoke to you about the choice you were making."

I know," Riva said, remembering clearly the evening her parents reminded her that Lance's work was dangerous. But she was in love. Riva mulled over the idea. And she still loved him.

"But as always, you did exactly what you wanted, because you had to have your way." Riva watched her father's steel gray brows furrow. "Lance is a good man. "It's too bad you won't reconsider the divorce and try to make your marriage work."

Riva realized her father was right, but it was possible that Lance had moved on, and she wasn't feeding her imagination any ideas about a man she couldn't have. She was trying to make peace with the fact that soon she and Lance wouldn't share a legal tie to each other's lives.

"Are you still marrying Alicia?" Riva asked.

"I plan to marry her," Mason said. "Do you have any objections?"

"No." Riva smiled. It was good to see her father happy, with his mind on other things beside work. Mason had met Alicia a month after Riva and Lance had separated and Riva had filed for a divorce.

"Well, I spoke to Adam, and starting tomorrow morning he'll be working as my assistant." Mason seemed pleased that Lance wasn't hesitating about getting the job done.

Riva settled back on the sofa. "I guess Lance will do the reports on the case," Riva said, her worries beginning to ease.

"I'm not sure, but I think he prefers working outside," Mason said, and Riva watched her father studying her again, as if he was looking for a special reaction.

"Outside?" Riva started to vent her frustrations and stopped. She hadn't spoken to Lance since the night before, and he'd already told her he was going to find the person who had shot Jasper. But she assumed Lance would assign the task to other detectives.

Riva cut off her musings. She had no right to ask Lance to choose how he worked. It felt like rocks had settled at the bottom of her stomach. Riva knew from experience that Lance loved the streets. It seemed that he enjoyed being surrounded by danger, masquerading as someone other than himself. Riva stopped herself from worrying. Lance was no longer hers to worry about.

Riva uncrossed her legs and stood, rising to her full five feet, ten inches. "I'll see you tomorrow. I didn't get to bed until early this morning." Riva realized that no matter what she did or said, nothing was going to keep Lance out the alleyways and streets of south Florida.

"I'm sorry I wasn't with you last night," Mason said, joining her as she moved toward the door. "Riva, when you meet with Fuller, don't give him any breaks. If you do, I won't approve the ad."

Riva didn't attempt a confrontation with her father. She knew she wouldn't win. Her only choice was to come up with a simple, eye-catching solution that would fit Fuller's budget.

Riva stopped in at her office to return Alicia's call. Riva was certain her message had something to do with the wedding. Riva punched the numbers into the phone's pad, noticing that the receptionist had left a message from Lance on her desk: *Call me—Lance.*

When Alicia didn't answer, Riva left a message telling her that she would speak to her soon. Then she returned Lance's call. A detective answered and told Riva that Lance was not in. Riva walked to the elevator, wondering what Lance wanted to talk to her about, and made a mental note to call him later that evening. It seemed too soon for him to have found the person who had shot Jasper. Even if he had, Lance would inform her father first.

The elevator's door opened, and Riva waited while a group of young women wearing business suits that looked as if they were fresh from a steam iron walked off the elevator and into the corridor. Their hairstyles were neat and styled to perfection, and their black pumps shone, as if their shoes were freshly buffed. Riva recognized a few of them from the clerical pool.

"Did you see the guy in the lobby?" one woman asked.

"Yes, I saw him, and he is fine."

"I hope he's here for Jasper's job." One of the women giggled.

"If he is and he's hired, neither one of you had better speak to him, because he belongs to me."

"He probably has a few guy friends," another young woman said.

Riva pushed the button for the lobby, and listened to the giggles floating through the closing elevator door.

Riva couldn't help but smile. It seemed that all the women liked Adam and wanted to know if he had a buddy. Of course Adam had a buddy, Riva thought, as visions of Lance cradling her in his arms before she had gone to the spa last evening infiltrated her memory.

"Hi, Riva," Adam said when she walked off the elevator into the lobby.

Riva couldn't help but admire how nice Adam looked in his dark suit. "Hello." Riva almost felt sorry for him. He'd barely made it inside the building and the women had already sharpened, buffed, and polished their romantic claws, ready to pounce on him with hopes of getting him committed to a date. Riva smiled. Seeing Adam triggered another batch of memories in her, reminding her of Lance, and she pushed the vision to the deep crevices of her mind.

Seven

Riva got into her truck and pulled the door shut. She sat for a moment, thinking about the promises she had made to herself to forget Lance. Keeping her promise would not be easy. But at least she was willing to try until her feelings for him vanished. She started the truck and drove out onto the street into traffic.

Riva kept her mind free for a while as she drove past buildings sitting behind spindly palms, weathering the warm Florida sun.

The promise Riva made minutes ago broke as she observed the scenery, which brought to mind the lunch breaks she and Lance had enjoyed on his days off, when he worked for the police force.

Riva honked her horn at a biker snaking his way in and out of traffic, missing her truck by inches. She let out a string of profanity while pressing the brakes. Her heart pumped in her chest as she clutched the steering wheel. "I'll be all right," Riva said aloud as she pressed the accelerator and sped up. Her near-collision with the biker brought to life old memories. The vivid details of her and Lance's car smashing into a cement wall, nearly killing them, sent her reeling back to the last drive she and Lance had taken together on a Sunday afternoon before she filed for the divorce.

When Riva had learned later, after she was out of the hospital, that the driver who had forced her and Lance off the road was a man Lance had helped put in jail years before, she was sure the man had every intention of killing them. The next day Riva called her lawyer and set up an appointment to file for a divorce. Lance had pleaded with her not to file, but she had been afraid.

Riva felt tears burn her eyes, but she refused to cry. She pulled up to the guard gate and inserted her key card into the bar, thinking that whoever it was who had shot Jasper had to have been walking. There was no way the person could gain entry to the property without a key, she mused. Unless the pedestrian gate was unlocked. Riva decided to think about how Jasper's attacker had entered the property later, after she took a nap.

Minutes later Riva unlocked the door to her apartment and walked inside. She didn't remember leaving the balcony door open. Riva crossed the living room and closed the door. She'd been tired from the night before when she woke up this morning; it was a wonder she remembered to lock the front door to her apartment. Being overtired and not getting the right amount of sleep always made her crazy. Added to that was her fear from being accused of trying to kill Jasper Wade, which was enough to make the average person lose their good sense.

On her way out of the living room, Riva passed the winged chair that was once Lance's favorite. She noticed a magazine lying on the cushion. Lance had stopped by late yesterday, but he didn't sit in the chair—or did he? Riva couldn't remember.

Looking at Lance's chair brought back old

memories of how happy they had been. Riva went to her room, discarding the thought along with her clothes. Nevertheless, the reminders found their way to the front of her mind, reminding her how Lance had loved his work and because of her fear, they were separated with plans to divorce.

Riva pulled on a pair of shorts and a comfortable oversize T-shirt and headed back to the living room, taking a sheet from the linen closet to cover the sofa, where she planned to sleep for the rest of the day.

As she settled down on the sofa, Riva fought to forget. It had never occurred to her that she and Lance could have worked out their problems. He was still a private detective, now working for a privately owned company. It was too bad he hadn't thought to smooth out the rough edges of his career earlier. He still preferred danger. Right now he was probably searching for Jasper's attacker in a dark, dinky hole.

Another fearful thought clutched Riva's heart: what if Jasper's attacker found out Lance was investigating the crime? Riva forced her fears back into hiding and settled down on the sofa, wrapping herself comfortably in the covers before drifting off into an exhausting slumber.

Her laughter rang out, echoing against the ocean waves smashing against the sandy golden beach. "Come here, woman," she heard Lance say behind her as she darted into the water, dodging a wave rolling to shore. Riva squealed, swimming out of Lance's reach, until he finally grabbed her and pulled her to him. They walked out of the ocean to their towels, stopping only to share a kiss. His kiss was firm, hard, and unrelenting. "We promised, Riva—no matter what happens we'll always be together." Lance reminded her of their promise as they walked toward their towels. When they reached the colorful terry they stretched out under the warm late-afternoon sun, snuggling against each other.

Riva closed her eyes and relaxed close to Lance. Suddenly she couldn't feel his muscular body against her. She called out to him. When Lance didn't answer, Riva opened her eyes and watched helplessly as he walked down the beach near the edge of the ocean, while gentle waves splashed and washed against his ankles.

"Lance," Riva called out to him. He turned, looked at her and faded out of her sight.

The screeching sound of automobile tires and the honking of horns slipped through the opening of Riva's living room window. She sprang up to a sitting position, her heart pounding in her chest from the noise on the street and her horrible dream.

Riva composed herself and sat quietly on the sofa, watching patches of the early evening full moon peek through the huge oaks outside her apartment window. In the distance whining sirens permeated the air, mingling with melodies from her neighbor's stereo.

Riva got up and went to her bedroom, stuck her feet into a pair of black leather thongs and went down to get her mail. The lobby was empty except for a guard making his rounds. Riva unlocked the box and took her mail, which consisted of a letter from her lawyer, an advertisement from the supermarket, and a catalog from her favorite store. On her way to her apartment she started to open the letter addressed to her and Lance, but then decided to read it later.

Just as she laid the mail on her nightstand and was about to take a bath before getting into bed, the doorbell rang.

Riva peeked through the glass opening in the door, and then opened the door for Laura.

"Girl, you look like death warmed over." Laura walked past Riva into the living room. "Your eyes are swollen, and your hair is standing up on your head.

"Thanks a lot, Laura," Riva said. "I'm doing okay. How are you?"

"Riva, why didn't you call me last night and tell me about Jasper?" Laura didn't wait for Riva to ask her to sit; she dropped her purse on the sofa and flopped down.

"Laura, by the time I left the police station, after clearing myself of being accused of shooting Jasper, and I got home, it was too late to call you."

"I wish someone would've told me before I went to the old coot's office."

"Were you supposed to meet Jasper today?" Riva asked, sitting in the chair across from the sofa.

"I wanted to know what I was to do about Isaiah's ad, since I couldn't find you and you weren't answering your phone," Laura said.

"I didn't work today."

Laura spread her hands. "I knew something was wrong. Every time I walked up to a group of people, they would stop talking. I knew those sisters were gossiping about something that wasn't their business."

"I'm sorry I didn't call you last night." Riva smiled.

"You know I would've stayed with you," Laura said.

"Laura, I have never been that afraid in my life." Riva chuckled. "If I hadn't had proof that I was not at the spa . . ." Riva stopped. "I don't know, I probably would've been locked up."

"Make me understand. Who would want to hurt Jasper?"

"I don't know," Riva said. "But you never know these days. Jasper could have looked at someone the wrong way."

"Are you sure you're all right?" Laura looked over at Riva, checking to make sure she was okay.

"I'll be much better tomorrow, I'm sure." Riva smiled and ran her hand over her tangled curls.

"I'll see you tomorrow at work?" Laura asked.

"Sure." Riva didn't like staying home; it gave her too much time to think about her problems.

"Riva, I met with Foster."

Riva noticed that Laura didn't look upset. "You were running from Foster last night at the spa. Why would you meet with him?"

"If I had known he was going to pay me, I wouldn't have dodged him. I loaned Foster some money a few months before we broke up. Today he paid me." Laura smiled as if she was pleased.

"The next time Foster calls, he'll want you to take him back." Riva laughed.

"This money was my last connection to Foster." Laura patted her purse. "If I see him next year, it'll be too soon." She chuckled.

"I have a meeting with Isaiah Fuller in the morning. Let me warn you: the car and the model are not happening." Riva got up off the chair and walked with Laura to the door. "I tried. Daddy agrees with Jasper."

"So you did speak to Jasper about the ad," Laura asked.

"We had a heated discussion at the café," Riva said, telling Laura how it looked as though someone who knew her and Jasper had framed her for shooting him.

"It sounds like someone wants to get rid of you and Jasper." Laura opened the door.

"Well, their scheme didn't work," Riva said. "I'll see you at work tomorrow, but I'm not going to the staff meeting."

"Okay, Riva, take care." Laura walked out into the hallway.

Riva closed the door, deciding that Laura's suggestion that maybe someone wanted to get rid of her and Jasper didn't make sense. But then, nothing that had happened in her life the last day or two made sense.

Riva went to the kitchen and opened the refrigerator, realizing she had to go grocery shopping. The only food in her refrigerator was a dozen eggs, and a gallon of water, and half a head of lettuce. Riva was never much of a domestic, and cooking was not one of her favorite chores. It wasn't that she couldn't cook—her mother and especially her aunt Udell had taught her how to cook a variety of foods. However, once she and Lance were married, she left the cooking to him when he wasn't working. Back then their small pantry and freezer were well stocked. But these days Riva ate most of her meals at her favorite restaurant, and when possible, she walked up the hall and ate dinner with Udell, which was usually a lively, old-fashioned supper, since Udell often cooked enough for herself, Theresa, and one other person.

Riva didn't feel like eating tonight. She closed

the refrigerator door, went to the bathroom, and filled the tub for a bath, remembering that she hadn't returned Lance's phone call. She would call Lance tomorrow, Riva promised herself while squeezing strawberry bubble bath into the warm water. She pulled off her T-shirt and shorts, discarding the clothes in the hamper, and stepped into the tub, allowing the warm water to soothe her.

In Riva's relaxed state, she reflected on her dream. She didn't understand why it had frightened her. Riva assured herself it was the noise outside that had woken her, sending her into a state of near-shock.

She slid farther underneath the bubbles, considering her social life. It wasn't bad, if she considered it sufficient to share her meals with clients and spend time every Friday night enjoying herself with friends and coworkers at the private club, where she was a member. She shot pool, played cards, and danced. Her plans were not to date until her divorce was final, though she shared many of her lunches with Dylan. She'd known him for years, and their relationship was simple: Dylan was a client and a friend. After his father retired from his car dealership, Dylan took over the business and continued to work with Dae Advertising. Mostly while they ate lunch their conversation was centered around Dylan's automobile business—how many new cars he sold, and anything related to car sales. Other times Riva listened to Dylan while he discussed his problems, allowing him to use her as a sounding board. After Dylan's divorce, Riva fixed him up with blind dates at his request. When his love affairs didn't work out, Riva would listen without making any comments. She decided that Dylan was more interested in his business than he was in his dates.

Riva finished her bath and went to bed, but was unable to sleep. She pulled the sheet up around her neck and stared at the dimly lit white ceiling, allowing her mind to swirl back in time. She could almost smell Lance's heady cologne, like the first time she had met Lance at the billiard hall, years ago. Riva remembered looking back and noticing the tall, brown-skinned man who was emanating the aroma of soft, masculine cologne. Not only did he smell good, he looked good.

Finally, when Riva was finished with her game, she passed her pool stick to a waiting pool player and backed away from the table. By mistake, Riva backed into Lance. She apologized profusely for stepping on his shoes. But when she looked into Lance's light brown eyes, it was as if his gaze drank her into his soul. She could almost feel his energy. His electric vibration stunned her, and she was speechless. Never had a man succeeded in drawing her to him in a first encounter. Nevertheless, their encounter was a silent one. Words were not spoken, but his eyes spoke volumes.

When Lance finally had spoken to her, he had sounded as if he were reprimanding her for being inside the billiard hall. Riva recalled being insulted, and asked Lance who he thought he was, telling her what she should do. She thought Lance was rude, and she told him what she thought about him. After an almost heated argument outside the billiard hall, Riva learned that Lance Cain was a detective working on a case in the area. Lance didn't think it was safe for her to stay out late, especially in an unsafe area. Riva didn't think the area was that bad; she and Laura and the other young women never had any problems.

Lance promised Riva that he didn't mean to sound as if he were telling her where to have fun. But to make up for interfering in her life, he asked her to have dinner with him. Riva told Lance she would think about accepting his dinner invitation. Before he left her that evening, he asked for her telephone number. Riva gave her number to him, not expecting him to call her. But when Lance called her the following Thursday evening and asked her if he could pick her up at seven Saturday night for dinner, Riva agreed.

After their date, Riva and Lance became a couple. Riva usually found herself worrying about Lance, especially when she didn't hear from him for days. She constantly forced herself not to think that Lance was hurt. Several times she wanted to end their relationship, but by then she was in love.

Six months into their relationship, Lance asked Riva to marry him, and she agreed, even after her father warned her that being Lance's wife was not going to be easy. Riva told herself that she would adjust.

The next year she and Lance were married. Three years later she filed for a divorce, because she couldn't adjust.

Riva pulled the sheet over her head. *One day I'll forget Lance Cain.*

Eight

The next morning Riva was rested and ready for a good day's work. She showered and dressed in an oyster shell–colored suit, with matching heels and purse, accenting the jacket with a silver pin, a gift from Lance last Christmas.

Riva took her purse from the nightstand drawer and called the hospital to check on Jasper. "Good morning," Riva said when her call was transferred to a nurse in the intensive-care unit. She knew Jasper was not allowed phone calls, so she asked about his condition.

"I'm only allowed to give information on Mr. Wade's condition to family members," the nurse said.

Besides, as far as Riva knew, Jasper didn't have any family. "Mr. Wade works for Dae Advertising, and I wanted to know if he was doing all right, and if there were any improvements in his condition," Riva said to the nurse.

"May I have your name?" the nurse asked.

"Yes. My name is Riva," Riva replied.

Riva waited, listening to the tapping sounds from the computer keys.

"You are on the list of visitors once Mr. Wade is moved into a private room," the nurse informed Riva. "We're still monitoring his blood pressure."

"When will he be assigned to a room?" Riva asked.

"Today or tomorrow. Moving him depends on what the doctor thinks of his condition."

"Thanks," Riva said, hanging up and deciding that she would stop by the florist's later to pick out a plant for Jasper. The last time she had flowers sent from the florist's, the arrangement hadn't been what she'd ordered and she'd paid more money for an inexpensive arrangement.

Riva had one more call to make before she forgot. She dialed the spa. "Susan, hi," Riva said to the desk clerk, and asked for the supervisor's extension. "Hello, this Riva Dae Cain. I wanted to thank you for taking time out to come down to the station night before last."

"You're welcome." The supervisor laughed. "We can't have our clients in jail for a crime they didn't commit."

Riva thanked the supervisor, and made an appointment for the following week before she ended her call. She picked up her purse, and headed out to her truck.

Riva's truck looked as if it were unbalanced, its weight resting on the passenger side. "Damn!" Riva lamented, looking at the flat tire. Changing the tire was not a problem. Mason made sure he had taught her the basic mechanics of automobiles. However, this morning Riva had no plans to indulge in minor mechanics while wearing her suit and heels; besides, she was already pressed for time.

Riva kicked the flat black rubber, taking out her phone to call a cab. She was so engrossed in dialing the cab's telephone number that she didn't notice the truck driving up. The thump of a vehicle door closing caused Riva to look up from dialing. Lance was walking around the front of his truck.

"Good morning," he greeted her, looking at the tire.

"Hi," Riva disconnected the call. It was as if an angel had sent Lance to help her. "I am glad to see you." Riva spoke the words evenly and with pleasure, observing that Lance's faded jeans, black T-shirt, and black high-top sneakers suggested that he wasn't dressed for work.

"It's a good thing I stopped by to see how you were doing," Lance said. "When you didn't return my call, I thought I'd better check on you." He knelt down and swept his palm against the top and sides of the tire, probing the grooves in the black rubber to find the problem that had caused the flat. "This tire is new." Lance rose from his kneeling position.

"I know; that's why I'm surprised it's flat," Riva said.

"You probably drove over a nail," Lance said, walking around to the back of Riva's truck. "How are you?"

"I'm fine now," Riva said, not mentioning to Lance that she'd been so tired she'd left her balcony door open.

"What do you mean, you're fine now?" Lance squatted and looked underneath her truck.

"I slept well last night. I'm all rested and ready to work." Riva moved to the back of her truck. "I got your message. I'm sorry I didn't return your call."

"We can talk later." Lance sat back on his heels. "Riva, look in my glove compartment and give me the pliers."

Riva opened the driver's side of Lance's truck,

inhaling the scent of leather and the last traces of
Lance's cologne while opening the compartment
and taking out the pliers. She walked back to
Lance, handing him the tool.

Lance lay on the pavement and scooted back underneath the truck, unscrewing the bolts on the
rack that held Riva's spare tire in place.

While she waited for Lance to change the truck's
tire, she wondered what was so important that he
wanted to talk to her about it. She had already told
him she wouldn't stand in his way if he wanted to
buy a house, but still, Riva was anxious to know
what Lance wanted.

Lance removed the spare tire. In a minimum
amount time he had also removed the flat. "I'll
drop the tire off at the station and have it repaired," Lance said.

"Thanks, Lance." Riva smiled, glad that she
didn't have to take a cab to work.

"I'll drop the spare off to you tonight." Lance
rose from his squatting position and put away the
jack and wrench.

"Let me know how much the repair cost, and
I'll pay you," Riva said, realizing that Lance no
longer had to be generous to her.

"I'll take care of the bill," Lance offered, brushing his hands together after putting the jack away.
"Drive carefully."

"I'll try to drive carefully, I'm already late," Riva
said.

"If I get a chance I'll call you later," Lance said.
"I've started working on Jasper's case."

Riva looked at Lance again. He wasn't wearing
a suit, which meant he was going to dig around,
searching for clues to solve the case. A pulse of
apprehension wormed through her and settled

near her heart. "So, what . . . you're on your way
to search for clues to the case now?"

Lance chuckled. "No."

Riva relaxed and checked her watch. She was already late for work, and to top that off she had a
meeting with Isaiah Fuller.

On her way to work, Riva stopped and picked
up a box of cheese Danishes, then made a call to
the office. "Brenda, this is Riva. I'll be a few minutes late. Please have Mr. Fuller wait for me."

She pressed the gas pedal, accelerating the
truck's speed. Remembering Lance's warning to
her to drive carefully, Riva then slowed. Her curiosity was getting the best of her, and she decided
that around noon, she would stop by Lance's office
and hear what he had to say. She needed to order
Jasper's flowers. The florist was located in the same
area as Moses Investigations, giving her the opportunity to get two things done at once.

Nine

Lance dropped Riva's tire off at the mechanic's, then drove home with the intention of working some more on the list of names from Dae Advertising's employee roster. Lance walked into the study, taking from his attaché case the list of employees' Social Security numbers and birthdays that Mason had faxed to him.

Lance checked the clock on the study's wall, noticing that it was close to ten. He knew he would spend the remainder of the morning checking out the lives of the people employed at Dae Advertising, and decided that he would spend the whole day working at home. He didn't want to delay any more time checking the employees' backgrounds, trying to find a lead that would connect anyone working for Mason to Jasper's case. So far the police hadn't found any information that would capture the suspect, who Lance was more than certain was the person who had called the police accusing Riva of shooting Jasper.

Lance carried the laptop and the information he had received from Mason into the kitchen. He set the computer on the island kitchen counter, and turned it on before making a pot of strong black coffee, which was a perfect remedy to keep him alert.

While the coffee brewed, filling the quiet house with a hearty aroma, Lance logged on to the search system, then got up and took a mug Riva had given him from the mug tree, waiting a few more minutes for the coffee to finish brewing. The coffee-maker's red light flashed, and Lance filled the mug with sugarless black coffee. He pulled a stool to the counter, just close enough to work comfortably.

Lance lifted his coffee, preparing to take a sip, and squinted, drawing his eyes half-closed as he noticed the name Alicia Owens among the list of names on the employee list. Mason had told him that he was getting married to Alicia. Lance studied the name on the list for another second, then picked up the phone.

"Mason." Lance didn't bother to make small talk when Mason answered his call.

"Talk fast, Lance; I'm going to a staff meeting."

"The woman you're engaged to marry . . . her name is Alicia Owens?"

"Yes," Mason said, slowly. "Why?"

"Does she work for you now?" Lance realized he could have been off base, but he needed to know if this was the same woman Mason was engaged to marry.

"Alicia was hired to work as my personal assistant. She helped out in areas that my secretary was unable to assist me with. She traveled with me, she went on errands, and finally she worked out of my home." Mason gave Lance a quick brief on Alicia's position. "She worked for about two months before she quit and opened the cosmetic boutique," Mason said, satisfying Lance's curiosity.

"I was asking because her name is on the list of employees," Lance replied.

"I'll have to take her name out of the system," Mason said.

"I would think Alicia takes care of many of your personal details now." Lance's curiosity flared again.

"Well, yes. But she doesn't get paid by the company." Mason chuckled.

"I understand." Lance tapped the top of the counter with his finger and hung up. He and Riva had already been separated when Riva had mentioned her father's engagement to him one evening while he was visiting her. It appeared to Lance that Mason was really ready to get married, since he and Alicia would be marrying so soon after they had met. Lance dismissed his wandering recollection. He had his own marital problems to worry about, with Riva getting ready to divorce him. With that thought in mind, Lance went back to work. However, his curiosity got the better of him once more, and he decided to check out the woman that his soon-to-be ex-father-in-law was about to marry.

Lance began his search on Alicia Owens. She was from New Orleans, and she had no children. Her credit was okay, but not good enough for her to open a business. Lance figured Mason probably gave Alicia the money for the cosmetic business. Lance also learned that she'd been married twice before. Her first husband was deceased, and she and her second husband were divorced.

Lance folded his arms across his chest. "Riva . . . Alicia and Mason . . . uh." Lance groaned. He and Mason had gotten pretty close when he and Riva were together. Mason explained to him while they were at one of Mason's barbecues that when he died, Riva would own everything. Even after he retired, Riva would own Dae Advertising.

"Hmm," Lance murmured. "Riva, Mason, Alicia,

and Jasper." The combination didn't make sense because the café was a small establishment. If Alicia had been in the café the afternoon Riva and Jasper met, Riva would have seen her. Lance considered his suspicions. *Maybe Riva wouldn't have seen Alicia*, Lance mused, and went back to work, checking Social Security numbers and other information on the employees who were on the roster. Most of the employees were in good standing. Their degrees and schools matched, except for two people. Lance put a check beside the names of those employees, then added a check beside Alicia's name to remind himself to investigate her further. In the meantime he needed to set up a meeting with Mason.

Lance had just reached back and removed the telephone receiver from the cradle on the kitchen wall when he heard someone open the front door.

"Lance," Vanessa called out. He heard her heels striking against the tile floor as she crossed the foyer onto the living room carpet, which silenced her steps.

"Yeah?" Lance asked, annoyed that he was being disturbed. If Vanessa wanted to talk to him about the case she was working on, or if she'd found an apartment and was moving tonight, she could have called him.

"Gosh, you don't have be so grumpy," Vanessa said as she walked into the kitchen.

"What do you need, Vanessa?" Lance took the first sip of the coffee, which had cooled since he had filled his cup earlier.

"I had to come home for something I forgot this morning," Vanessa said, walking around the counter and stopping next to where Lance was working. "I found the woman we were looking for," she said, leaning close to him. Her shirtwaist dress was unbuttoned, exposing too much cleavage.

"Good." Lance wasn't surprised that Vanessa had found the woman. She was an excellent investigator.

"Is that all you have to say—good?" Vanessa asked, as if she had been expecting more praise for her work.

Lance looked up from the screen and the information he was reading. "Have you found an apartment?" He studied Vanessa. Her smooth ebony complexion seemed to darken.

"No, I haven't." Vanessa pushed a hand over her thick black hair. "You know, if you weren't so busy disliking me, we could be very good friends." She gave him a seductive smile.

Instead of responding to her accusation and her smile, Lance returned to his work. Vanessa wasn't serious about finding a place to live. Lance imagined that Adam's speculation on Vanessa's feelings for him was true. Adam often teased Lance, telling him that Vanessa had a fantasy that one day Lance would fall in love with her, and that they would marry and start a family.

"Vanessa, I am very busy," Lance said, not stopping to look at her.

"You know I am telling the truth, Lance," Vanessa replied.

Not wanting to be rude, Lance leaned up from his work, interrupting his search. "Your work is excellent, and I think you're a nice person, Vanessa." Lance paused, giving Vanessa time to respond. When she didn't speak, Lance continued: "Samuel asked me if I would mind your staying here until you found a place, or until I bought this house."

"Are you buying this house?" Vanessa asked, as if she was surprised.

"That's my intention," Lance replied.

"I understand." Vanessa straightened. "If you weren't still hung up on your wife I could probably stay here forever."

Lance ignored her. For once Vanessa was right—at least about his feelings for Riva.

"Lance." Vanessa leaned against the counter.

"I'm listening," he said, gathering the employee list he was trying to complete.

"I haven't found an apartment. I need more time."

In the time he'd lived in Samuel's house, Vanessa and the others had lived with him for six months, which was enough time for her to find an apartment. Vanessa certainly could afford to buy an apartment if she chose to, Lance mused. He didn't understand Vanessa. Tiffany had a baby, and she was in the process of buying an apartment.

"Well?" Vanessa seemed to have been waiting for an answer.

Lance raised his head and gave Vanessa a cool gaze.

"Gosh, your eyes are like ice," Vanessa snapped. "Okay, I'm moving!"

Lance didn't say anything. He didn't mind Vanessa sharing the house with him and the others. Lance mulled over their living arrangement. If he had, he would have mentioned his misgivings to Samuel in the first place. But it was Vanessa who wanted everyone to think that he shared her bed at night. Thanks to Theresa, Riva was thinking he and Vanessa were lovers. "Vanessa, make that move happen as quickly as possible," Lance remarked firmly, and went back to work.

Ten

"It's the best I can do," Riva said, surveying Isaiah Fuller, studying his shrewd expression. Fuller was average height. He appeared to be in his late fifties, with a mixture of black and gray hair growing in a horseshoe pattern atop his head.

"Jasper and Mason know my situation. And they know I'm good for the money." Fuller crossed one leg over his knee, exposing brown socks that matched the color of his suit.

"If you have questions, or want to discuss this matter further, I suggest that you call Mr. Dae and set up an appointment," Riva offered.

"The best you can do is give me a gold tube of lipstick on a half-page ad?"

Riva gave him a flavorless smile. "I'm sorry, but neither Mr. Dae nor Mr. Wade would agree to the terms you offered."

Fuller ran a finger across his jaw. "Well, I guess I'll have to take that," he finally said, rising from his seat.

"I'll call you as soon as I have the layout drawn up," Riva replied. She hated that Fuller couldn't have the ad he wanted. She'd tried to help, speaking out for him and getting herself in trouble.

"I can't have the model?" Isaiah asked.

"No, Mr. Fuller, you can't have a professional

model, but Jasper suggested that we could hire a young woman—" Riva started.

"I know. I'll need more money for a professional model." Fuller cut Riva off.

"This way you can have an ad at a lower price with no problem paying." Riva said.

"All right. Give me a call as soon as you complete the draft, and we'll go from there."

"Fine." Riva rose from her chair, extending her hand, giving Fuller a firm handshake. She waited until he left the room before she settled back into her chair.

As soon as he walked out of her office, Riva took a pencil from the container on her desk, ripped a sheet of paper from the notepad, and began sketching a lipstick tube, wondering what Lance wanted to speak to her about. Riva brushed all thoughts of Lance and what he wanted to talk to her about out of her mind, and went on with her work.

While Riva drew the simple artwork, she mulled over a slogan for the inexpensive advertisement. She sketched an open tube with just a touch of lipstick peeking from the opening. She sat back visualizing the gold tube filled with icy pink lipstick, and began thinking of a slogan to sell the cosmetics: *Make your life click with icy pink lipstick.* "No," Riva said aloud, and crumpled the paper, pitching it into the garbage container beside her desk. She began again, attempting to come up with a better slogan.

"Good morning." Laura entered without knocking.

Riva looked up. Laura was her usual attractive self, wearing a tan pantsuit, her hair pulled back in a ponytail, exposing gold earrings that looked as if they were growing out of the pierced holes in her ears.

"Hi," Riva greeted her girlfriend.

"Tell me that Adam divorced his wife." Laura sank down onto the chair in front of Riva's desk.

"He's divorced." Riva rolled the pencil between her fingers and studied Laura. Since Adam was the newest employee in the building, Riva suspected he was at the meeting this morning.

"No!" Laura laughed.

"Are you interested in him?" Riva giggled, realizing from the expression on Laura's face that her friend was interested in Adam.

"Girl . . ." Laura started, then suddenly seemed to give up, shaking her head. "I am interested."

Riva laughed. All Laura could think about was a man.

"He's a free man," Riva said, remembering that Lance had told her about Adam's situation when he moved in with him. At any rate, her answer to Laura's question appeared to satisfy Laura's curiosity.

"Divorced . . . hmm?" Laura murmured, as if she were overwhelmed.

"Yes." Riva smiled, remembering that Laura had met Adam and his wife at her and Lance's wedding.

"Riva, are you serious about Adam being divorced? Because I was kidding when I asked you if he was still with his wife."

"I'm absolutely positive. Have I ever lied to you?" Riva grinned.

"Let me think. Adam is a detective. Maybe someone working here did shoot Jasper. But you know everybody in the meeting believes Adam is Mason's assistant." Laura smiled.

"That's the idea, making everyone think he's here for a regular job."

"I like him." Laura's smile returned.

"Well, you'd better work fast, because these women around here are out to get him." Riva couldn't help but laugh, recalling the conversation she'd overheard from the women when she walked off the elevator.

"He looks good," Laura said seriously. "When I met him a few years ago, he was tall and thin."

"He looks all right," Riva said, casting a glance at the blank paper in front of her.

"You're prejudiced. The only man who looks worth anything to you is Lance. It's a shame you guys are getting a divorce," Laura said, looking at Riva as if studying her reaction.

All Riva could think about was Lance lately. She was supposed to have been making plans to move on with her life. But she hadn't, and Riva suspected that, whether she liked it or not, she was never going to find another man comparable to Lance Cain. Riva didn't comment or respond to Laura's probing.

"The thing is, I never would have known Adam was in the building until I heard those cackling little typists discussing the new employee," Laura said, changing the subject.

"So you went to the meeting to see the man the women were talking about?" Riva rolled the pencil between her fingers.

"Yes, girl, and there he was sitting in the conference room with Mr. Dae, looking good." Laura smiled.

"Did you get a chance to talk to Adam after the meeting?" Riva asked.

"Nope, he stayed behind with Mr. Dae. But I'll

get a chance to talk to him." Laura was still smiling. "And those little chickens had better stay out of Adam's face."

Riva dropped the pencil and joined Laura's laughter. "This is the first time I've heard you openly admire a man in a long time."

Laura wasn't dating Foster anymore and was finally looking for a new man.

"Gentleman," Laura corrected her.

"Whatever. How was the meeting?" Riva hadn't gone to the meeting because of her meeting with Isaiah Fuller. But she knew that her father was introducing Adam to the staff.

"Except for Adam's introduction, the meeting was the usual stuff." Laura got up and took a cheese Danish from the tray on the table near the window, then returned to her seat.

"You mean my father didn't go into the long, drawn-out story of how he built this business up after his daddy died?"

"Yes, it wouldn't have been a meeting if we didn't hear about the church-fan era." Laura giggled.

"And how parents paid them to photograph their children for church fans." Riva added, puffing out her chest, imitating Mason.

"Riva, you know Mr. Dae talked about all of the hard work he put into building the company. I was so bored, I didn't know what to do. If I hadn't been interested in Adam, I probably would have nodded off."

"Do you think we'll ever have another conversation without you talking about Adam?" Riva asked, knowing that once Laura was interested in a man, she would never hear the end of him.

"I think in the near future we may be able to

have a reasonable conversation without mentioning Adam." Laura was still smiling, and Riva was happy that Laura was thinking of someone other than Foster. Riva realized that since Foster had paid Laura the money he owed her, Laura had had no need to mention him again.

"Anything else interesting happen in the meeting today?" Riva was curious.

"Well, I guess it was somewhat different. Mr. Dae said he was determined to find the person who shot Jasper, and that when he did, he would have them prosecuted to the full extent of the law."

"He's determined to do that," Riva said, watching her girlfriend pinch the pastry and eat tiny pieces of it. "We're changing Fuller's ad," she said, switching the subject.

"Sounds like Mr. Dae agrees with Jasper."

"He did, and it didn't make any sense for me to argue with him. It would have been like banging my head against a brick wall." Riva got up and broke a cheese Danish in half and ate a small piece. "Um, these are good." She returned to her chair. "I have to remind myself to lock the door when I leave. Because Phillip will come in here and eat . . ." Riva started.

". . . all of the pastries." Laura finished Riva's sentence. "He'll swear someone else ate them." Laura broke off another piece of the sweet breakfast treat and popped it into her mouth.

"Right," Riva agreed. "I caught him one day enjoying my apples, and he pretended he had brought it from home," Riva said.

"He's such a liar," Laura replied.

"And so disgusting." Riva added. "I wonder where he got his advertising degree from, because he doesn't know what he's doing most of the time."

"He probably bought the darn thing." Laura laughed.

"I wouldn't put it past him." Riva joined in her friend's joviality.

"Thanks for the pastry." Laura got up and went over to the table, pouring herself a cup of coffee before she left Riva to her work.

"You're welcome, and we'll talk later," Riva said as Laura left her office.

"Yes, because we have to figure out a way to beat Theresa at the card game Friday night."

"Tell me about it." Riva grinned. "My cousin and her partner put a whipping on us last week."

When Laura was gone, Riva went back to her work, finishing the simple sketch and slogan for Isaiah Fuller. Then she checked files to make sure ads were completed for the upcoming month.

Riva stopped checking one of the files and rested her chin in her palm. Without warning her mind wandered to Lance, and she decided that since it was so close to lunch, she'd drive to the florist's, pick out the flowers she was sending to Jasper, and, when she finished, stop in and speak to Lance. That way she would find out exactly what Lance intended to tell her.

Before she left for the florist's, Riva walked down to the graphic-art department, taking the sketch and the slogan to the graphic artist. As she made her way down the corridor she almost passed the artist. "Hi." Riva stopped him. "I have some extra work for you." She held out the sketch to him. "I need a gold tube and icy pink lipstick." Riva waited for the young man to take the rough sketch.

"My computer is broken, but as soon as the repairman gets here, I'll work on it." He took the sketch and studied it for a moment.

"Thanks," Riva said, glad she'd met the young man in the hall, saving herself a trip to the floor above her. Riva checked her watch; it was almost noon. She decided that if she wanted to talk to Lance, she'd better get across town. Riva headed down to the ground floor. She passed the mirror in the lobby, noticing that her lipstick was fading and a few strands of her hair were straying. She went to the rest room off the receptionist area and brushed her hair and applied lipstick before hurrying out of the building to her truck.

Keeping her mind free of Lance wasn't easy as she drove across town through the thick noon traffic. She noticed mothers pushing their babies in strollers, going to fast-food restaurants.

Seeing the mothers with their children reminded Riva of the children she wished she and Lance could have had together. Riva brushed the thought aside and slowed the truck before she turned off onto the street that led to Lance's building.

Even so, it was too late for them. Riva drove into the shopping center's lot driving slowly, searching for a parking space. Finally she found a spot and got out, inhaling the aroma of fried chicken wafting over from a nearby fast-food restaurant.

Riva walked across the parking lot, stepping onto the walkway in front of the stores and passing a convenience store near the florist's. She walked inside the florist's, and studied the flower arrangements. Riva purchased a gold kettle with a green plant. She gave the clerk the correct floor of the hospital to which she wanted to send the plant, and Jasper's name and any other information that she thought would help the plant arrive at its destination. When she was satisfied that the correct plant would arrive at the hospital for Jasper undamaged, Riva left the shop and headed to Lance's office.

Riva moved toward the building, recalling how Lance had stopped by her apartment one day telling her that he'd stopped working as a detective at the precinct and had taken a job with his mentor, Samuel Moses. Lance seemed to think that she needed the address and phone number to his new job.

Riva dismissed her recollections, and read the engraving on the dark-tinted window that read MOSES INVESTIGATIONS.

Riva entered the average-size room. A petite young lady appearing to be in her early twenties stood behind a mahogany counter. A mahogany nameplate perched in the center of the counter read TIFFANY in gold letters. "May I help you?"

"I would like to speak to Lance." Riva waited while the receptionist checked the computer, as if she were checking to see if Lance had a noon appointment with a client.

"No, I don't have an appointment. I'm his . . ." Riva corrected herself. "My name is Riva . . . Cain."

"You're Lance's wife," Tiffany said, smiling at Riva. "I don't think he's here today. But I'll check," the receptionist said, punching two numbers on the telephone keypad. "Sometimes he uses the back entrance."

"Thanks," Riva said, realizing that the woman could be one of Lance's housemates, while allowing the woman's statement that she was Lance's wife to slip through her mind. *Soon to be ex-wife,* Riva thought, wondering if Lance had discussed their pending divorce with his coworkers.

While the woman waited for an answer, she looked up at Riva. "I'm Tiffany, one of Lance's housemates. It's nice to meet you."

"It's nice to meet you too," Riva said, noticing Tiffany's cheerful demeanor. Tiffany's short brown hair was streaked with soft golden tones. "If Lance is not in, I'll call him later," Riva said. If she hadn't been anxious, she could've waited until Lance stopped by that evening to drop off the tire he'd taken to be repaired, Riva thought as she studied the waiting area. The room was neat, with a fresh, airy ambience that reminded Riva of Lance.

One magazine catering to female clients and one magazine catering to male clients lay on each side of the coffee table, which was placed in front of a royal blue sofa. A lamp towered at the far end of the sofa in the corner. Riva was about to leave when Tiffany got her attention.

"Lance is not in." Tiffany set the receiver down on the cradle.

"I'll talk to him later," Riva replied, preparing to leave.

"Is there anything I can help you with?"

Riva turned around to face a dark-skinned woman with thick black hair who was walking toward her. Her shirtwaist dress fit tight across her hips, rising with her movement.

"No," Riva answered, moving toward the door.

"So you're Riva." The woman gave her a smirk.

"Yes," Riva said, glancing at her watch. While she was out she wanted to stop by her father's and see what was going on with Alicia.

"I'm Vanessa, and I'll tell Lance you stopped in to see him when I get home tonight."

"Do that," Riva said, wheeling on her heels and leaving the room, realizing she'd finally met the woman with whom she thought Lance was sharing his bed. She walked to her truck, vowing to dismiss any feelings of passion she had for Lance. It was obvious he had gone on with his life, while she was living in the past and regretting that it was she who had insisted they get a divorce.

Jealousy sliced at Riva's heart. If she hadn't made a public scene and almost ended up in jail a few days ago, she might have considered thinning Vanessa's thick black hair.

Riva decided to return to work. She would talk to Alicia later. She needed something to do. Working seemed to free her mind of her problems, and thoughts of the dreary, loveless, passionless future she was facing.

Seeing Alicia would only remind her of how lonely she was. And she didn't want to think about romance, marriages, relationships, and weddings.

Riva knew it had taken her too long to forgive Lance even after she had filed for the divorce. She understood now that he couldn't help if he was chased by a person who hadn't liked being caught and sent to prison. However, she'd once blamed Lance for the car chase, the accident, and the crash that had resulted in both of them ending up in the hospital for a few days.

Tears stung her eyes, and she blinked them back. The only cure for her broken heart and the disaster she'd created in her life was time, and the desire to move on with her life.

It didn't make any sense to mentally beat herself up over the mistake she'd made. First she'd blamed her immaturity; now she realized her behavior had simply been absurd.

Riva was back at work before she realized it. It was a wonder she hadn't had an accident, she thought as she slowed the truck after glancing down at the speedometer as she wheeled into the parking lot at almost ten miles per hour.

Riva parked and went inside the cool building. She passed the receptionist and hurried to the elevator, taking it to her floor.

Riva stepped out into the hallway, greeted by the sound of raucous conversation filtering out from the room where the creative team held their meetings. She stopped at the door, listening as Laura and the others busily sorted ideas for a new ad campaign. Riva stopped at the door and half listened to the discussion of an idea that had just been presented to the group. If she hadn't been thinking about Vanessa, she would have listened carefully, Riva mused. It wasn't that Vanessa had *said* she and Lance were lovers. It was the authoritative way she presented herself, as if she held a claim to Riva's soon-to-be ex-husband.

"What do you think, Riva?" a man asked, after she'd vaguely listened to him speak on an advertisement he thought was perfect for a billboard.

"The part I heard sounds good. But don't take my word for it, because I wasn't listening closely," Riva said, and noticed Laura watching her from across the room.

"I thought you were listening to him," Phillip remarked.

"Not really," Riva said. "I didn't mean to interrupt," she apologized, as a vision entered her mind of Lance and Vanessa cradled in each other's arms that evening when he returned home from work.

"Come on, Riva. We can use a good suggestion."

Phillip made an attempt to coax Riva into the room.

"Phillip, I couldn't think of a single suitable idea if I tried," Riva replied, thinking how just this morning she'd had a hard time coming up with a slogan for Isaiah Fuller's lipstick ad.

Riva left the room and went to her office. Just as she was about to close the door behind her, she felt a tug on it.

"What is wrong with you?" Laura asked, and settled down in a chair.

Riva sat and turned her attention to the window, avoiding Laura's gaze. "I don't want to talk about it."

"Is there anything I can do to help?" Laura asked.

"I don't think so." Riva spun herself around in the chair.

"Well, I'm listening, if you want to talk," Laura offered.

"I am stronger than this." Riva got up and walked to the door, then turned around and walked back to the window. "I have made mistakes in my life, and I've gotten over them . . . like this!" Riva snapped her fingers. "But when I saw Vanessa . . . I almost lost control."

"Okay. Who's Vanessa?" Laura asked, rising from the chair.

"One of Lance's housemates." Riva replied. "Other than Adam, Vanessa and Tiffany also share the house with Lance."

"There are more people than Adam sharing Lance's house?" Laura asked.

"Vanessa wants Lance," Riva said, telling Laura about Theresa's gossip. Riva couldn't hold the information in any longer. If she kept her feelings pent up inside her, she felt she would explode. Riva explained to Laura her innermost fears. She could always talk to Laura about her problems.

"Are you sure, Riva?" Laura asked, sounding concerned.

"Theresa told me she saw Lance and Vanessa in the supermarket one evening." Riva went on to explain all that Theresa had told her about seeing Lance and Vanessa.

"Riva, you know Theresa talks all the time. She's your cousin, but she is a gossip."

"I know," Riva remarked. Theresa loved to carry tales, true or untrue. As long as the other person's business was juicy enough, she was bound to inform her listeners. Riva crossed over to her chair and sat.

"Lance told you that he and Vanessa were in a serious relationship?" Laura pried.

"No. He said they were housemates."

"I would believe Lance, and forget about that foolishness Vanessa is trying to make you believe," Laura said.

"Believe me, Laura, what Lance do is none of my business. But every time I think about how I could have waited before I filed for the divorce . . ." Riva's voice faded.

"Girl, it's never too late." Laura shifted in her chair as if she was getting comfortable.

"It's too late." Riva said. Trying to convince herself that what Lance did with his personal life was a waste of her time, even though she knew she cared. Riva changed the subject. "Did you get a chance to speak to Adam?"

"No, but I need to speak to him and kind of find out if he's involved with anyone." Laura winked. "Because I did not know all those women lived in the house with Adam and Lance."

"Now, do you believe me when I tell you that Lance and Vanessa are lovers?"

"No, I don't know," Laura said. "I am inviting Adam to lunch one day soon. When lunch is over, I'll know all I need to know about Adam Johnson." Laura chuckled softly.

Riva shook her head and smiled. "I believe you."

"Anyway, it's nice to see that you're jealous and a little angry." Laura stroked the arms of the chair with her fingers. "I never thought I would see the day that you would be jealous. I was always the one in a tizzy."

"I'm angry at myself, because this is all my fault. The ridiculous part of it all is, I have no right to be jealous." Riva couldn't help but laugh at herself, if she were honest. "Do you think I'm crazy?"

"Yes, I thought you were crazy when you filed for the divorce," Laura remarked seriously.

"At the time, getting Lance out of my life seemed to be the best thing to do. I had good reasons. After the accident I was really afraid," Riva confessed.

"I can understand your point, but remember, Lance was chased by a man he'd help put behind bars. I wouldn't think that type of accident would happen every year," Laura said.

"I wasn't thinking straight," Riva replied.

"So what are you going to do about it?" Laura asked.

Riva didn't know what to do. She was hardly ever without a solution to a problem. "Nothing," she replied, getting up and pacing to the window, memories of the kiss she'd shared with Lance a couple of days ago running through her mind. "He had the nerve to visit me a few days ago and he . . ." She let the words trail off. Laura didn't have to know about the affection they had shared. "This whole thing is driving me nuts," Riva said instead.

"I can see." Laura gave Riva an evil smile.

"Stop smiling." Riva glanced at Laura. "You're supposed to be my friend."

"I have a suggestion." Laura tilted her head to one side. "Go to Lance's house and throw that Vanessa out." Laura chuckled.

Riva laughed. "I can't remember how many years it has been since you, Theresa, and I pulled a stunt like that." Riva smiled, remembering how crazy they were. "I think I'll pass on throwing Vanessa out of Lance's house." She chuckled at the way Laura managed to make her remember the crazy things they'd done years ago. Riva picked up a folder she'd worked on before lunch. It wasn't much to work on; however, the work would keep her busy enough to keep her mind off her problems.

"Yes," Laura said. "But if you get the urge to throw her out, call me and I'll help you." Laura stood and walked toward the door.

Riva raised her head, trying not to smile at Laura. "Out!" She pointed to the door.

Laura pulled the door closed behind her, smothering her giggles.

As Riva worked, she remembered one of the ridiculous things she and Laura had done while they were juniors in college. Their motto was, never let another woman take your man. Some motto, Riva mused, as her reflections wandered to the past and she recalled how young and immature she was. Nevertheless, when Riva realized that her two-timing boyfriend was dating another girl, she and Laura had gone to his apartment on campus and knocked on his door. When he opened the door, she and Laura walked past him to the bedroom and dragged the girl, sheets and all, off the bed. It was a wonder they didn't go to jail for all the disturbance they caused in the neighborhood that Saturday night.

She was a woman now, and it was important that she control her emotions, especially since she and Lance were no longer together. Riva turned her thoughts back to her work, but it wasn't long before her mind wandered again. It was as if an imp stood on the desk in front of her, daring her to commit a crazy act. Riva shook her head. Those days were over. Lance Cain was free to love who he wanted, which had nothing to do with her feelings for him.

At exactly six o'clock in the evening, Riva finished her work and decided to stop by and speak with Alicia. She parked in front of her father's house behind Alicia's red automobile and got out in the sinking sunlight, crossing the driveway and brushing against a small green hedge resting against the base of the house.

A soft golden glow shone from the living room window behind a pair of thin white drapes. Riva rang the doorbell and waited for Alicia to open the door. She couldn't understand why Alicia wanted to live with her father before they were married. Riva concluded that maybe her aunt Udell was right: Alicia could have been marrying for security. Unable to make up her mind whether Alicia was marrying for love or money, Riva dismissed the thought. She had her own problems she couldn't solve.

"Come in, Riva," Alicia said as she swung the door open, stepping aside for Riva to enter.

Riva moved inside the foyer and stood under the crystal chandelier. "How are you?" she asked, moving farther into the house.

"I'm fine," Alicia said. She could have told Riva about the party she was planning for Mason over the phone when she left a message for her to stop by. But Riva didn't seem to like her, not that she had ever said anything rude to her. It was the way Riva looked at her, as if she thought she didn't love Mason and was marrying him for financial security.

She invited Riva over hoping that after she asked for advice, they would have a friendly conversation. That way she would have a chance to convince Riva that she was a nice person and not out to get Mason's money.

As always, Alicia was cheerful and well groomed. Her short black hair lay close to her head, with wisps of curls feathered against her forehead. Her makeup looked as if she'd just applied it. "I got your message," Riva said. "I wanted to visit sooner, but I was busy." She didn't bother to explain her reason for not stopping by sooner. She was sure her father had filled Alicia in on her problem. "Is this urgent?"

"If you can call Mason's birthday party urgent, I suppose it is." Alicia pressed her manicured hands over her light-colored sundress and followed Riva to the kitchen.

"Giving Daddy a birthday party is simple." Riva slid onto a stool at the island kitchen counter and crossed her legs. "He'll be happy with a cake and a few of his favorite dishes."

"That's the problem; I don't know many of Mason's favorite dishes." Alicia's smile was chagrined.

Riva turned her attention to the French doors leading to the patio, where an array of pink, orange, and purple carnations sprang from clay pots sitting on a black iron stand. Alicia was in her forties, a mature woman who Riva would think had the ability to learn every detail about the man she was about to marry and hopefully spend the rest of her life with. "Are you saying that you never cooked Daddy a meal?" Riva studied Alicia.

"I've made him vegetable salads and sandwiches," Alicia said. "We usually eat our meals in restaurants."

"He likes down-home food," Riva stated seriously. "Collards, potato salad, potato pies, potatoes and steak smothered in gravy, chicken cooked any way your heart desires. And if this is a problem for you, I suggest that you make reservations at a restaurant, or call a catering company." Riva couldn't believe that Alicia had made her take time out of her day to find out what foods her father loved to eat.

"I wanted the party here at the house, and I intended to invite people from the company, especially those people from the creative team." Alicia paused for a moment, as if she were envisioning a grand ball. "I don't know what to serve."

"If the food is edible and the drinks are cold, you don't need to worry about anyone from Dae Advertising turning down an invitation to a party," Riva said, realizing how friendly Alicia had been with many of the creative team members when she had worked for a short time at the agency. Even now, when she came by to visit with her father, Alicia often stopped in to speak to a few of the

employees. Phillip and a few others seemed to have
been her favorite people to visit.

"Riva, you know what everyone likes, so I'll take
your suggestions." Alicia seemed pleased that Riva
was helping her.

"I suggest making a reservation at a restaurant."

"Thanks, Riva," Alicia said. "I think I'll make
reservations."

"You're welcome," Riva said, not understanding
the woman her father was planning on marrying.
It was clear that her father loved Alicia. He probably didn't mind whether she could prepare a meal
or not.

The phone rang, and Alicia rushed to answer it.
"I am expecting a call." She seemed to be apolo-
gizing.

"I'll talk to you before the party," Riva said, walking out of the kitchen and toward the front door.
The house was quiet except for Alicia's low voice.

Riva walked out into the warm air, got into her
car, and drove home. Later she would see Lance.
He was returning her truck tire. Riva planned to
keep in mind that she and Lance were friends now,
and she would keep her feelings for him under
control.

Eleven

Riva drove home and parked, wondering when anyone was ever going to remove the eerie yellow crime tape that surrounded the area where Jasper had been shot. She got out of the truck and walked toward her home, remembering how comforting it was to have had Lance at her side the night she was accused of shooting Jasper. Lance had assured her that she was going to be fine. Riva knew she was going to miss Lance Cain.

Riva dispelled her recollections and made another attempt to dissolve images of Lance from her mind. Their relationship was nothing more than mere friendship. But nevertheless her rambling thoughts of Lance returned as usual, and again Riva wished they were still together, even after she promised herself she would keep her feelings under control.

Riva walked into the quiet apartment lobby, savoring the crisp air. She stopped to check her mailbox for the day's mail before taking the elevator to her sixth-floor apartment.

The sixth floor was unusually quiet. Her neighbor's teenage son was not blasting his music, and her aunt Udell's pooch, Misty, was not barking to go out for her walk, which meant Aunt Udell had probably returned from her trip and was walking the dog. Riva moved down to her apartment with intentions of reading the letter she'd been too tired to read days ago.

She was about to the unlock the door to her apartment, when she noticed that it was open just enough for her to see a strip of light from the inside of her living room. Icy fear crept through Riva, provoking a fresh batch of fears. Riva felt as if the cartilage in her knees had turned to rubber. She gathered her draining strength, attempting to move, but she felt as if she were rooted to the floor.

Finally she mustered enough strength to move away from the entrance, but before she stepped backward and rushed to the elevator, out of curiosity, Riva pushed the door open with the tip of her key.

With the door standing ajar, she could see the open balcony door. Several plants lay on the balcony floor, black soil scattered against the edge of the cream-colored carpet at the edge of the living room leading out to the balcony.

Slowly Riva backed away from the front door. Apprehension coursed through her, making her heart thump hard in her chest. Something was wrong, and it wasn't just that someone had broken into her home. First someone had tried to kill Jasper and blame her for the botched attempt to end his life. Now, as she backed away from her door, she couldn't be sure whether her continuing adversities were connected to Jasper.

The slender skirt to her suit, in addition to her high heels, made it difficult to run to the elevator as fast as she wanted to. She pressed the button, turning her attention back to her apartment, afraid to take her eyes off the door for fear someone was still inside and might come out.

While Riva waited for the elevator, she fished around in her purse for her telephone. Her trembling fingers made it hard for her to push the numbers as she called security at the guard gate.

The elevator door slid open. Without further hesitation Riva hurried inside, quickly sending it to the lobby. As she reached the ground floor, she called the police.

From the glass door of the lobby she spotted the guard, dressed in a blue uniform, riding on his white cart headed in the direction of her building. It seemed that he could have driven faster, Riva mused, wanting to rush out and drag him inside the building.

"Did you say the sixth floor?" the guard asked, when he finally arrived.

"Yes," she answered, repeating her apartment number to the guard for the second time. "I've already called the police," Riva said.

"I called the police too," the guard said, walking toward the elevator. "You stay here and wait."

That was Riva's intention, to wait in the lobby until she learned whether or not someone was hiding inside her home. "Yes, I'll wait," Riva said, her voice sounding as though it belonged to someone else.

"Did you see anyone inside of your place?" the guard asked.

"No," Riva said. If she had stayed and watched the apartment until the guard arrived, she could have been attacked if the intruder was still inside the apartment.

"Did you go inside?" the guard asked.

Riva knew the questions were important, although she wished the guard would skip the interrogation and check the apartment. "No, I didn't go inside.

Why don't you go up and take a look," Riva said, trying not to sound like a hysterical woman.

She was surprised the guard had answered the telephone when she called him. It seemed that most of the time the guards were never around or didn't answer the phone when a resident needed assistance.

The night that Jasper was shot, Riva learned later that the guard had not been at the gate.

"What's your name?" the guard asked.

"Riva," she said, her fears mingled with annoyance at the guard's unenthusiastic attitude toward her predicament. Instead of going to her place, he acted and sounded as if he were about to retrieve a cat from a tree.

"I'll take a look." The guard headed toward the elevator.

Not more than ten minutes past before the guard was back. "There's a lot of stuff strewn around up there, but I didn't see anyone." The guard stood next to Riva. "The person probably used the back stairs to leave the building.

Riva figured as much. She walked to the lobby door, nervously waiting with the guard for the police. At least she would get a written report from the officer, one that she could give to the apartment's association. To sue for having better protection. And if a tenant or resident had broken into her apartment, maybe she could hold the association responsible for not screening tenants carefully. Maybe the officers would dust for fingerprints and learn who had entered her home. Riva anxiously paced the lobby's floor. "Where are the police?" She addressed the question to herself more than to the guard. Riva tried to remain calm. But she was not known for her calm demeanor when facing a crisis. The equanimity she did manage to maintain threatened to vanish into thin air.

"Calm down," the guard said.

"Calm down?" Riva wheeled around on her heels. It was clear that the guard didn't know the problems that had followed her around over the last few days. "Did you see any strangers on the property today?"

"No, I haven't been on duty all day, but I didn't see any reports of trouble from the guard who was on duty."

As much as Riva wanted to blame the guard, she couldn't. If the person had been walking, he or she could have easily waited for someone to enter the pedestrian gate and gained access to the property that way. Riva decided she would have to check with the security guard working the day shift tomorrow.

Riva's battle to keep her tears from falling was beginning to wear her down. She was determined to stay strong. She felt violated, knowing that someone had gone into her apartment and handled her possessions, spilled her plants, and walked out, leaving her door open as if they wanted her to know she had no control over their comings and goings.

Finally Riva saw the police officer walking toward the building. She ran out to meet him, not giving the officer time to get inside before she told him her problem. "Officer, my apartment was broken into and—" The guard stepped in front of her and finished reporting the crime to the officer.

Riva didn't like being interrupted, but the guard had searched the apartment and could give a better report as to what he'd found.

The police officer and the guard headed inside and Riva followed them.

"Riva." Riva heard her aunt Udell calling her while she was waiting with the officers near the elevator.

"Aunt Udell," Riva said, glad to see a familiar face. Udell Hart looked as if she'd just stepped out of the beauty salon, instead of coming from walking Misty. Udell's black hair was twisted into a glamorous style. The small white strands streaking the side of her hair lay smooth as a sheet of silver. Her makeup and red, medium-length fingernails appeared freshly done.

"What happened?" Udell asked, drawing Misty to her while holding the door for two other tenants who were pulling a cart filled with groceries.

"Aunt Udell, someone broke into my apartment." Riva told her aunt all that had happened.

"What? Riva, are you all right?" Udell Hart asked, setting the tiny white pooch on the floor and holding on to the leash.

"No, I'm not all right. I haven't gone inside, but the guard said my things are strewn all over," Riva said, willing herself not to cry. "I was on my way up. Are you coming?" Riva asked her aunt.

"Yes, I'll go with you." Udell lifted the dog into her arms as another group of people entered the building and stood waiting for the elevator.

"When did you get back from your trip?" Riva asked as they waited.

"I got back around noon today. Theresa told me what happened to Jasper, so I went by to see him and took him some flowers. He didn't have a room, so I had to leave the flowers at the nurses' station. I hope those nurses give them to him when he's moved to his room tomorrow."

In spite of herself, Riva laughed. "Aunt Udell, Jasper will get his flowers. I spoke to the nurse this morning too," Riva said, thankful that her aunt always had the ability to make her laugh, even when she didn't feel like smiling.

"You know Jasper has hypertension," Udell said.

"I know, but he'll be fine," Riva assured Udell. Riva knew her aunt had a soft spot in her heart for Jasper.

"Yes," Udell said, and looked past Riva out to the front of the building.

"I'll stop by and see him tomorrow." Riva turned to see what was holding Udell's attention. Several plainclothes police officers Riva recognized from when Lance worked on the force entered the lobby.

The elevator door opened, and Riva stepped inside with Udell and Misty, along with the officers and the other tenants.

Riva stood quietly as they rode to the sixth floor. The more she thought about her home being entered without her permission and trashed, the more she had to fight back the urge to cry.

They arrived on the sixth floor. Riva waited for the officers to walk out before she and Udell followed them to her apartment. "I'll be right back," Udell said to Riva, and went toward her apartment.

"Why don't you wait out in the hall until we're finished?" an officer said to Riva when another officer walked into her apartment.

"Does anyone other than the management have a key to your apartment?" an officer Riva didn't recognize asked her.

"Yes," Riva said, telling the man that her father and her aunt Udell each had one, and then she remembered that Lance had never returned his key after he moved. "Are you saying that the person who entered my apartment used a key?"

"Not necessarily. There are several ways a person could've entered. But you have a double lock on this door." The office pointed to the door.

"My relatives have a key, and I don't think any of them would do this," Riva said, looking at the plants strewn around the balcony.

The officer didn't say anything before he walked back inside.

"Riva," Udell said, returning from her apartment with two lightweight chairs from her balcony. "Here." Udell set two chairs down across the hall from Riva's apartment. "Sit down."

"Thanks," Riva said, taking a seat.

"Child, I don't know what's going on with you." Udell sat beside Riva and lifted Misty onto her lap. "Theresa told me that you were accused of shooting Jasper."

Riva nodded. "I was mad at Jasper, but not mad enough to hurt him."

"If it's not one thing, it's another," Udell murmured.

The tears Riva had held in check since she'd learned that her apartment had been broken into rose from within her and spilled over. She had never hated anyone, but this week she was beginning to think that she could hate with no problem. Riva opened her purse and snatched a small white tissue from a tiny container, then wiped the tears. "This place is supposed to be secure," Riva said, noticing her aunt's girlfriend Esther walking toward them and stopping in front of Udell.

"What happened?" Esther asked Udell, then looked at Riva.

Esther was short and dark, and wore a friendly smile most times. But today a frown creased her smooth, wrinkle-free dark brown skin.

"Riva's apartment was broken into, Esther," Udell said before Riva could compose herself enough to speak.

"Riva, honey, if I believed it, I'd think someone had a hex on you. You have had more trouble this week than I've had in years." Esther shook her head.

"Esther, please." Udell said to her girlfriend. "Don't you see Riva is upset?"

"Aren't you getting a divorce?" Esther asked Riva.

"Yes." Riva looked at Udell, thinking there were not many people who knew that she and Lance were divorcing.

"I told Esther about the divorce," Udell said, as if she'd read Riva's mind.

"I didn't see your husband around here anymore, so I asked Udell."

Riva stared blindly at the tissue she was holding. She had learned long ago that her aunt kept no information from her girlfriends.

"Maybe it's your husband who's doing this to you," Esther suggested.

Riva didn't bother to consider Esther's suggestion. "Lance wouldn't vandalize my apartment."

"You never know," Esther said, turning to Udell. "Udell, you remember when Marilyn's husband tried to—"

"Esther, why don't you stop making a bad situation worse. That boy Riva is divorcing wouldn't hurt her."

"I don't know what's going on around here, because I heard that you were the woman who shot that man the other night."

"Esther, my niece did not shoot anyone," Udell defended Riva.

"I'm just telling you what I heard," Esther said.

"What is this place coming to?" Udell asked. Riva heard the concern in her aunt's voice, and she wondered why someone was trying to destroy her life. Her life was complicated enough without someone making matters worse.

"I knew I shouldn't have gone to the convention." Udell shifted the dog in her lap as if making Misty more comfortable.

"There was nothing you could do," Riva said, noticing that Esther was listening closely to her and Udell's conversation.

"Well, I guess you're right, but at least I could've been with you and Theresa and Jasper."

Riva observed the frown that creased her aunt's forehead. The fine lines between Udell's brows accented the worried look in her eyes.

"I know that after all of this, Mason is not still on vacation," Udell said.

"Daddy is home now," Riva replied.

"Udell, is Mason still getting married?" Esther asked, leaning toward Udell as if she didn't want anyone else to hear her question.

"Esther, we do not have time to gossip; I have to see about Riva," Udell said, patting Riva's hand. "Riva, you're going to be all right. Everything happens for the best."

"Udell, I was just asking if Mason was still getting married," Esther said, as if she was offended, "and you're telling Riva everything happens for the best. I don't think so."

"I agree," Riva said. Riva understood that her aunt was trying to comfort her. But she didn't like having her home entered without her permission, and as far as Riva was concerned, all the things happening to her were *not* for the best.

"I'm selling my apartment and moving if this trouble continues," Esther said to Udell. "It makes no sense to live where a person can walk into your house whenever they feel like visiting without being invited."

Riva didn't respond. She noticed that the officers seemed to be finishing their work in her apartment.

"Esther, this condo is not that bad. This is the first break-in we've had since I moved here, and you and I have both lived here for years," Udell defended.

"It *was* safe," Esther corrected Udell. "Riva, tell me . . . why are you and your husband divorcing?"

Riva held her head down and smiled. She was not answering the question. "Miss Esther . . ." Riva started. Respecting her elders was what she had been taught to do. However, her neighbor was getting too personal.

"Can I talk to my niece in peace?" Udell said to Esther. "You're so nosy!"

The hallway began to fill with tenants walking off the elevator and going to their apartments after a day of work.

"I'm going inside," Riva said, getting up, and Udell joined her. Riva wanted to see what the intruder had done to her apartment. She'd seen the toppled plants, picture, and pillows. But she had to go inside and take a look at the shambles the guard had told her about. "Can I go inside?" Riva asked a policeman who walked out of her apartment with the guard.

"Sure," the officer said.

"If these guards didn't waste their time flirting with the ladies they might get their jobs done properly," Udell spoke loud enough for the guard to hear her, and Riva noticed that her aunt seemed to have been waiting for a reply from the guard. When the man didn't say anything, Udell bundled Misty closer to her.

"Aunt Udell . . ." Riva spoke in a low voice, hoping her aunt wouldn't make a scene.

"If the association doesn't get decent protection around here, I'm selling, and buying where it's safe." Udell picked up a chair to take back to her apartment, and asked Esther to take the other chair.

Riva silently agreed. The safe apartment she and Lance had bought a few years ago was no longer safe, and she intended to get out as soon as she could.

Just as Riva was about to go into her apartment, Bill Lee—an officer she'd known from Lance's days on the force—and another officer walked off the elevator.

"Hello, Bill," " Riva spoke, then went inside her apartment to see the damage. The throw pillows that Riva had had in the corner of her sofa were scattered. The magazine rack lay on the floor. Riva checked the kitchen. As far as she could tell, not much damage was done. Then she went to her bedroom and wanted to scream. The dresser and chest drawers were opened, and clothes were scattered on the floor. Riva did scream when she saw her closet.

Suits cluttered the floor. Her comfortable sleeping gowns and cotton housecoats lay in a pile. A few pairs of shoes were out of their plastic boxes, covered with several of her purses. Riva walked out of the closet and headed to the living room.

"Mrs. Cain." An officer stopped Riva, telling her that they had dusted for fingerprints. Then he warned Riva to change the locks, and walked out into the hall. She noticed that all the officers had left her apartment except for Bill Lee. He stood on the balcony talking on his wireless phone.

Riva felt an even more unsettling fear creep through her insides near her heart. She was scared. Her stomach felt as if butterflies nested at the bottom. She could remember only before when she'd been as afraid as she was now, and that was when she and Lance had been chased and then crashed.

It couldn't be happening again. Did someone think that she and Lance were still together and was out for more revenge? Another icy shiver coursed through Riva. She pressed her lips together as if the action would comfort her ailing spirit.

Twelve

"Riva." She turned around at the sound of Lance's voice, his presence drawing her out of the past few hours. For a moment she forgot about her problems and her reasons for not wanting him in her life.

"Hi," Riva said. He was as handsome as ever, dressed in a dark suit instead of the jeans and sneakers he had been wearing this morning when he changed the flat tire on her truck.

"What's going on?" Lance asked.

Riva studied the shocked expression crossing his face, remembering that he had offered to bring the truck tire to her that evening.

Riva stretched out her hands. "Someone broke into my apartment."

"What?" Lance sounded surprised.

"Maybe one of your victims was released from prison and decided to pay us a visit." Riva kept her voice low so the officer who had stayed behind couldn't hear her.

"I'm not sure if that's the case," Lance said.

"Really?" she questioned him. "First Jasper and now this." She held his gaze, paying attention to the calmness in his eyes. At any rate, Riva had to blame someone for the disaster taking place in her life, and Lance and the hoodlums he had been responsible for sending behind bars were convenient bystanders.

"I'll find the person who did this to you." Lance moved closer to her.

"I hope you find the person soon. I do not like someone coming into my home when I'm not home." Riva turned her attention to the balcony, where Bill was still talking on the telephone. She recalled the day she had come home and the balcony door was open.

"What is it, babe?" Lance's gaze followed Riva's to the balcony.

"You know, this may not be the first time someone was in my apartment. I think someone was here the day after Jasper was shot."

"Are you sure?" Lance urged Riva to tell him more about the open balcony door, but there wasn't much to tell, since nothing had been disturbed, as it was now. Riva was still exhausted after staying up until the early-morning hours the last time she'd dealt with the police, proving to the authorities that she was innocent of any crime.

"I promise you, Riva, I will find who's doing this to you," Lance said, moving even closer behind her, and Riva wished he would keep his distance. Being too close to him ignited warmth in her heart that she didn't need.

Riva felt Lance's hand touch her waist, and she backed away. She had no intention of allowing herself to get caught up in his affections. Riva struggled against her desire to have Lance back in her life.

"You'll be fine, Riva." Lance drew her to him, and this time she didn't struggle to free herself from him. She stood close to him, ignoring the warning inside her to untangle herself from his embrace. But Riva refused to listen, and she knew she was never going to get over Lance. Just seeing him sparked passion that should have been dead months ago. But her feelings for Lance seemed to have been growing stronger instead of subsiding.

"Where would you look?" Riva asked. She didn't doubt that he would find whoever had infringed on her space. It was just that looking for the criminal sounded dangerous.

"We'll talk later," Lance said, moving toward the balcony to join Bill Lee just as the officer was headed back into the living room.

"Riva, give us a call if you have any more trouble," Bill said as he walked through her living room.

Riva nodded, and checked her watch. The locksmith was closed, and she wouldn't be able to request a lock change from the association until tomorrow. Riva went to the phone and dialed the association's answering service, leaving a message that she needed her locks changed. She set the receiver back on the cradle and listened in on part of the conversation Lance was having with Bill in the living room.

"I hear you're working the Jasper Wade case, Cain," Riva heard Bill say to Lance as they walked out of the room and into the corridor.

Riva didn't listen to Lance's response. She made herself busy picking up the scattered pillows off the floor and inspecting a picture that lay near a corner.

At last her apartment was free of police officers, the two plainclothes detectives, and Lance. She went to her bedroom closet to pick up the scattered suits and other clothes strewn on the closet floor. Straightening her apartment usually calmed her down, but today Riva could hardly contain herself as she checked to make sure none of her jewelry had been stolen. The engagement ring Lance had given her was scattered outside of her jewelry box along with other pieces of jewelry.

Riva stopped and buried her face in her hands. Other than being physically attacked, she couldn't imagine how she could possibly feel more violated.

Nevertheless, there was nothing she could do but wait until the person was captured, if he ever was.

Riva began picking up the clothes off the floor, checking to make sure there was no dirt or marks from the soles of the intruder's shoes just in case the person had stepped on them. When she didn't see any stains she began putting the panty hose and underwear in the drawer.

Riva brushed the exasperating thought away. She and Lance had bought the apartment because it promised safety. In that case, the association should take care of changing the lock on her door. Riva knew she would also have to buy her own locks.

"Riva." Riva looked up from putting a pair of panties in the drawer and saw her aunt Udell standing near her bedroom door.

"I'm calling Mason," Udell fussed.

Riva grabbed a handful of panty hose and stuffed them into the drawer. She didn't respond to her aunt.

"Riva?" She heard her aunt call her again.

"Yes, Aunt Udell." Riva grabbed a handful of matching panties and bras and packed them in the drawer with the panties.

"Aunt Udell, I'll tell Daddy myself. Tomorrow," Riva said. She wasn't a little girl who needed to run to her father every time something happened to her. Besides, he had enough to think about. His stress level was too high, and he was only just beginning to feel better after his vacation.

"Fine, tell Mason. But I know you're not staying in this apartment with that person wandering around in the streets. So you can stay with me and Misty," Udell remarked firmly.

Riva stopped stuffing clothes. Staying with her aunt or any of her relatives hadn't crossed her mind. If she was going to stay anywhere other than her home it would be a hotel. "I'll be fine," Riva said to her aunt, putting more clothes in the drawer.

"Child, have you lost your mind?" Riva heard Udell scolding her from across the room. With all the things happening to her, Riva wasn't sure if she'd lost her mind or not. But living with her aunt while she waited for the encroacher to be caught didn't seem like a good idea to her.

"I'm thinking of going to a hotel," Riva said. "Or maybe I'll place a chair underneath the doorknob."

"A chair?" Udell asked, sounding annoyed at Riva's decision.

"Aunt Udell, you worry too much," Riva said, going back to checking the clothes still in the dresser drawers.

"You can do what you want, but I'm calling Mason." Udell pulled out her phone and started dialing. "Maybe he can talk some sense into that hard head of yours." Riva watched her aunt as she began dialing her father's number.

"Aunt Udell, please."

"Well, he needs to know about his family, instead of getting ready to marry some woman none of us know anything about."

"Don't call Mason," Riva heard Lance say from the doorway. "I'm staying with Riva tonight."

"Well, thank you. At least there's one other sane person in this room besides me." Udell shut the phone off and pushed it inside her pocket, then picking up one of the bags Riva had brought in from the kitchen.

"Let me help you," Udell said. She began picking up a suit that was lying on the closet floor.

"The suits on the floor in the closet need packing for the cleaners," Riva said, not looking up.

Riva didn't allow herself to focus on her aunt's comment about her being crazy. She was too busy digesting Lance's decision to spend the night with her.

Riva finished putting clothes away and closed the dresser drawers. "I don't think staying the night with me is a good idea, Lance," she said, taking a moment to study Lance's tall, muscular frame. She had been tortured enough for one week. Having Lance around would rack every passionate nerve in her body.

"I'm staying with you," Lance said.

"I can manage alone," Riva stated, determined to keep Lance at a distance.

"Are you getting the locks changed tonight?" Lance asked Riva.

"No."

"Then it's settled. I'm not leaving you," Lance replied firmly, taking off his suit jacket and tossing it on the chair at the foot of the bed.

Riva noticed the black revolver strapped to his shoulder, like a dangerous third arm. "No, you're not staying with me. I don't need a bodyguard." Riva packed a sock laying on the floor next to the dresser inside the bag.

"One way or another, Riva, we're going to be together until this problem is solved," Lance said, fingering the knot in his tie.

Riva stood up and looked at Lance as he undid several buttons on his shirt, exposing a section of his wide chest.

She decided that arguing with Lance was useless; once his mind was made up, she was no match for him. However, Lance's strong determination and willpower were more reasons she loved him. He knew what he wanted, and Riva knew Lance Cain didn't stop trying until his mission was complete. "You can stay tonight." Riva wagged one finger at him, placing her free hand on her hip. She had to put up a good fight. After all, she had rights too. She had the right not to have her emotions disturbed for a few evenings as she pined over the man she loved and was about to divorce.

"I will live with you as long as I have to," Lance stated, planting both hands on his narrow hips.

"Have you forgotten that we are no longer together?" Riva asked, recalling her meeting with Vanessa earlier in the day.

"Our separation has nothing to do with what's going on here," Lance stated. "And just in case you've forgotten, our divorce is not final."

"As far as I'm concerned, we're no longer married." Riva made a final attempt to defend herself.

"I think I'm in the way. Let me find Misty, and I'll talk to you tomorrow, Riva," Udell said, tying two open ends of the bag that she'd filled together, while she was in the closet. She began dragging the bag of clothes out to the living room, leaving Riva arguing with Lance.

"No longer married?" Lance asked, moving closer to her.

She had heard her aunt and observed her leaving the bedroom with the garbage bags filled with clothes, but she had a few things to straighten out with Lance.

"Yes, it's not your duty anymore to stay with me," Riva remarked flatly.

"So that's what you thought of our marriage—a duty?" Lance asked her.

"You know what I mean," Riva yelled, knowing she'd already lost the battle.

"No. I don't know what you mean. Explain it to me," Lance replied hotly.

Riva had no explanation except that she was giving up a man she loved because of her fears, and she feared what would happen if he stayed with her tonight. She placed the other hand on her hips, and paced to the window to avoid being close to him.

"I'm listening." She heard Lance speaking, his voice almost a whisper.

What Riva wanted to explain to Lance was her anger at how he'd found happiness with his housemate. But she didn't have the right to let her fury out on him; she'd made her choice.

"You can sleep in the other bedroom tonight," Riva finally said, crossing the room to her bags of clothes. She tied the open ends of the bags together and began dragging one to the living room. Dragging bags of clothes to the living room was better than giving Lance the explanation he was waiting for. When she returned to the bedroom for another bag of clothes, Lance was dialing numbers on his cellular phone.

"Mason," Lance spoke to Riva's father, taking one of the bags from Riva and going to the living room. "I'm okay."

Riva set the bag down beside the others in the living room and returned to her bedroom, waiting for Lance.

"*I* wanted to tell him about the break-in," Riva said when Lance returned to the bedroom.

"I thought he needed to hear what happened from me," Lance said, holding the phone and looking as if he was about to make another call.

Riva knew that telling her father about her expanding problems would probably upset him. "Lance, my father has just began to feel better," Riva remarked, wishing that Lance had waited before he mentioned her problems to her father.

"Mason told me he felt much better after his vacation," Lance said, punching numbers into his phone. "In the meantime, I need to get surveillance over here just in case the person returns before you get the locks changed."

Riva listened as Lance made the call, speaking in a low tone and ordering diminutive cameras designed to tape anyone inside her apartment while she took a suit off the rack Udell had just hung. She had been planning to drop the suit off at the cleaners on her way to work for the last few days and had forgotten.

When Riva returned to her room, she began placing the scattered earrings and necklaces inside the jewelry box. "This whole thing is strange," Riva said to Lance.

"What's strange?" Lance asked her.

"The person didn't take anything." Riva held up an expensive gold chain.

"I think the person knows you, Riva," Lance said.

"Knows me?" Riva repeated, and her mind went back to Esther, who had insisted that it was Lance who might have entered her apartment. However, Riva knew her neighbor was speculating as she did with everything else that happened in their building.

"Yes," Lance said, pacing the room.

Riva didn't know anyone who wanted to harm her, but then again, she didn't know anyone who wanted to accuse her of Jasper's shooting either.

Riva decided the best way to calm her frazzled nerves was to soak in a hot tub of bubbles. She was hot, tired, and aggravated. Her next remedy was to go to bed.

"Riva, I'm serious. I think after tonight you should stay with me until the person who shot Jasper and who broke into this apartment is found." Lance looked around the bedroom. Riva heard Lance, but she didn't believe him.

She was having problems allowing Lance to sleep across the hall from her tonight. Just knowing that he was there made her doubt that she would get any sleep.

Riva didn't bother to comment on Lance's suggestion that she live with him. She went to the closet and pulled off her suit and heels, then slipped on a thick white terry bathrobe before she headed to the bathroom and began filling the tub for her bath.

"Riva, I'm serious. I think after tonight you should stay with me until this is solved." Lance sat on the edge of the bathtub, watching while she waited for the right amount of water to fill the tub before she poured in the bubble bath.

"I don't think that's a good idea," Riva said, allowing Lance's presence to give her a sense of unwanted pleasure.

"Think about my offer before you refuse," Lance

said, getting up off the edge of the tub and moving to the bathroom door.

"Lance, I really do appreciate your concern, but why would I want to stay with you?" Riva got up and walked to him. She placed a finger on the open space in his shirt that displayed a small section of his muscular chest, giving him playful shove before she tried to move around him.

"Are you telling me that you have become braver over the last few months?" Lance asked, blocking the door, keeping her from moving around him.

At that moment Riva was determined not to show Lance her fear. Tomorrow it would be over because new locks were being installed.

"I'm brave enough," Riva said, thankful for locksmiths. She pushed past Lance to go to the closet to get one of the nightgowns that hadn't ended up on the floor.

"Oh, yeah. You're brave enough," Lance said, following her into the closet.

Riva sorted through the rack of silk gowns and chose one. "Excuse me." She gave Lance another playful shove, pushing past him and heading back to the bathroom, only to be stopped when Lance caught her wrist, pressing her hand against his chest.

"Are you saying that you're not afraid?" Lance pried playfully, his smile reaching his eyes.

"Of course I'm afraid of people walking around in my home looking into my things. But that's no excuse for living with you." Riva was still determined. She couldn't exactly tell Lance that she was jealous of his new relationship and give him a speech on how inappropriate it was for him to invite her to live with him and his girlfriend. "When did you become so unscrupulous?" Riva asked Lance instead of giving him her speech on morals.

"What are you talking about, unscrupulous?"

Riva pushed against him, moving him out of her way. "If we spend the rest of the evening discussing the people you have living with you, I'll never get my bath." Riva moved to the bathroom, turned off the water, and shut the door.

"Riva. Babe, wait—don't lock the door."

Riva heard Lance calling her. It seemed strange that he might have changed his beliefs and values in less than a year. Riva suspected that Lance needed someone in his life.

She locked the bathroom door, something she had never done before she and Lance separated. Just thinking that Lance was sharing his bed with Vanessa or any woman made her act irrational. He could have at least waited until the divorce was final before he found a lover. The nagging thoughts threatened to drain her of her remaining energy. Riva pulled off the bathrobe and sank into her bath.

Thirteen

Lance picked up his suit jacket from the chair and headed to his bedroom across the hall as he finished unbuttoning his shirt. He slipped the holster and gun off his shoulder, placing it on the top shelf in the closet. It was a habit he'd acquired since he lived with his housemates who included Tiffany's two-year-old son.

Unscrupulous? Lance played with the word Riva had used to describe his personality. He'd never given Riva reason to think he was a disrespectful man. He reached inside his pants pocket and took out the receipt for Riva's truck tire he'd paid for and dropped the paper in the small garbage can near the bed.

If Riva thought he was dating . . . Lance smothered the thought and continued taking things from his pockets—his wallet, telephone, and a few quarters he used for parking meters—and lay the contents on the nightstand.

Lance doubted that Riva wanted any more to do with him, but he was hopeful. He pulled off his shirt and dropped it on the chair. At any rate, he wasn't leaving her tonight. Lance went to the telephone beside the bed, lifted the receiver from the cradle, and dialed his home number.

The telephone rang several times before anyone

answered. When Tiffany finally picked up he could hear her baby crying, the television playing, and Vanessa and Adam arguing in the background.

"Cain's nut house," Tiffany answered.

"You got that right," Lance said.

"Wait a minute," Tiffany said.

It was Tiffany's night to pick up dinner. Even if he didn't leave money with her for his dinner, she would buy and he paid her when he got home. He hoped he hadn't called too late.

"Vanessa and Adam, be quiet. I can hardly hear myself speak!" Tiffany yelled over the loud argument.

Lance heard them in the background and didn't bother to ask what the argument was about. "Tiffany, I'm staying at home tonight."

"All right, Lance, we'll see you tomorrow," Tiffany said.

"I'll be coming over to get some clothes tonight," he said. "I didn't want you to buy dinner for me."

"Thanks for telling me," Tiffany said. "See you later."

Lance dropped down on the edge of the bed and lay back, contemplating Riva's reaction if he suggested that she discontinue the divorce proceedings. Riva was determined, headstrong, and more stubborn than she'd been when they were living together. Lance stared at the white ceiling. Maybe he and Riva were never meant to be together.

He closed his eyes, considering the thought. However, the fact remained that he wanted Riva, and it wasn't because of his starving libido—cold showers froze any sexual ideas his body managed to drum up in the middle of the night.

He had no intentions of dating. At this point the

only women Lance shared his dinners with were the clients. Before he considered dating seriously, he would first have to be divorced from Riva. Only then would he move forward, and for him, that process would take time. First he'd have to make sure his date was safe. He wasn't looking for a death sentence. Connected to the health check, a background check wouldn't hurt. With that thought marching to the front of his mind, taking center position in his consciousness, Lance wondered if Riva had become serious with anyone. He pushed the thought out of his mind. He didn't know what his reaction would be if he found out Riva was in a relationship.

Once they had been happy. Nevertheless, it all ended the day Hank got out of prison and chose to run him down with his car. Once Hank had been released the last time, he'd come after Lance.

The terrible memories of that day pulled Lance back to the past. He closed out the thought. It was still too painful to think about, and he assumed Riva would never forget. It was over for them, but still, he held a glimmer of hope for their future.

Lance drew himself up off the bed, put on his shirt, and crossed the hall to Riva's bedroom door. "Riva." He knocked on the closed door. When she didn't answer, he let himself in. Riva was out of the bathroom, smelling like strawberry bubble bath. Her face was covered with white cream. "Riva."

"Uh," she said.

"I have to go home for a minute; would you like to come with me?" he asked Riva, watching her smooth the cream into her skin.

"No," Riva said.

"I don't want you to stay here alone." Lance was

hoping Riva would come home with him; that way he knew she would be safe.

"I'll visit with Aunt Udell until you get back," Riva said.

"Okay." Lance leaned against the back of his favorite chair at the foot of the bed he had once shared with Riva. "I'll wait for you to get dressed." He settled down and waited until she finished massaging the face cream into her skin, and finally went to the closet to get dressed for her trip down the hall.

A few minutes later, Lance rose from the chair as Riva emerged from the walk-in closet fully dressed and picked up her purse. Lance didn't know why Riva was taking a purse, but he didn't ask. He'd learned long ago that Riva had her own reasons for doing everything.

However, he was satisfied that she wouldn't be alone until he returned. "I won't be long," Lance said, giving Riva a tight squeeze as they walked out of her bedroom together. He couldn't resist touching her; she smelled good, like strawberries and subtle sweet powders. Lance moved his hand from Riva's waist. That was another problem he had; he couldn't keep his hands off her. "Be careful," Lance said, once Riva locked the door and they were walking to Udell's apartment three doors down from Riva's place.

"Believe me, Lance, no harm can come to me at Aunt Udell's," Riva said, and Lance chuckled. He had to admit that Udell Hart was a tough woman. He had a feeling that if she'd seen the intruder leaving Riva's apartment, she might have held the person for the police.

Lance waited until Riva knocked on her aunt's

door. A few minutes later Udell was standing before them, holding a large spoon.

"Riva, I hope you and Lance are here for dinner, because I have enough food to feed a small army." Lance watched Udell eyeing him and Riva carefully, remembering how Riva's aunt had tried to be a mediator, talking Riva out of filing for their divorce.

"Lance has to go home for a while, so I decided to visit with you," Lance heard Riva say, and he couldn't help but observe her smile.

"Come in." Udell moved back enough so that Riva could enter. "And by the time you get back," Udell said, pointing a spoon at Lance, "dinner will be ready."

Lance laughed when Udell shook the spoon at him. "I will return." Lance took a step closer to the door, brushing Riva's hand. What he really wanted to do was hold her. "I'll see you in a little while." Lance moved away from Riva before he broke his promise. The last time he had held Riva, he'd kissed her. He had promised himself that he would not kiss her again until he knew whether or not he and Riva were finalizing their divorce. Clinging to that thought as he left for his home was how he was going to stay with Riva tonight without kissing her. His night was not going to be easy, but he would manage.

Fourteen

Lance parked in the driveway and sat in his truck for a few minutes before going inside the house. For reasons that didn't make sense to him, he had an annoying inkling that Alicia was behind the problems Riva was encountering. When he had first checked her out, Lance had found several people with the same name as Alicia. Some had the same Social Security number, but different last names. The last two names he'd checked had different Social Security numbers, but the same birth dates.

Lance stared out the windshield of his truck at red roses decorating the yard. Was Alicia going into Riva's home? Lance didn't have an answer. He allowed his thoughts to slip away from Alicia while he stared in front of him, allowing his thoughts to return to Riva. Riva was like the roses in his yard; she was beautiful, but handled without care, she pricked with penetrating spurs. Like the palms perched at the edge of his driveway, Riva was strong and determined, and every star sprinkled against the velvet sky reminded him of how her eyes sparkled when she was happy. Lance couldn't deny that Riva was tough in her own way. Thinking about Riva's character brought his previous question to mind: Did Alicia set Riva up for the crime committed against Jasper?

Lance's questions were hard to answer, but he intended to put the pieces of the puzzle together. Lance was not sure, but he wouldn't put his money on Alicia's not having anything to do with the case. He didn't know why, but he did know that he didn't trust Alicia Owens.

Lance unhooked his phone from the waist of jeans and started to dial the station. He decided to wait; it was too soon for the fingerprint verification. Instead he dialed Mason's cellular number, just in case Alicia was eavesdropping. He didn't want her to hear anything he had to say to Mason.

Mason answered the phone. "Are you alone?"

"No. Alicia is upstairs."

"Okay. Don't say my name, or repeat anything I'm saying to you. Just answer yes or no, and don't discuss what I'm about to tell you with anyone," Lance said. Just in case Alicia was in the room and listening, he didn't want her to know about the place he wanted to meet Mason.

"What's wrong?" Mason asked.

"I need to meet with you around noon tomorrow," Lance said, giving Mason directions to a secluded place to meet where he knew they could talk without being interrupted by anyone they knew. "I'll explain everything to you when we talk." He closed the phone, noticing Tiffany's car pulling up to the curb. Lance got out of the truck and walked to the house, holding the door open for Tiffany, Erin, and Vanessa. Vanessa pushed the door farther open, carrying Tiffany's baby with Tiffany close behind.

Lance dropped the phone into his pocket. "Hey, little man." He plucked the baby's cheek, and watched his smile display several tiny white teeth. "Hi, Tiffany," Lance said, giving her a smile.

"Hi," Tiffany said, adjusting the blue plastic bag she was carrying from the drive-through convenience store down the street.

Lance was about to speak to Vanessa when she started in on him.

"You don't have to be impolite; you could speak." Vanessa moved down the foyer and to the sitting room, still carrying Tiffany's son Erin.

"Good evening, Vanessa."

Vanessa set the baby on the sofa and gave him a toy. "Your wife was in looking for you today."

"And you told her what?" Lance asked, realizing that Riva didn't mention that she had stopped by Moses Investigations to see him.

"I told her I would tell you that she stopped by when I got home tonight," Vanessa said, and smiled. "She looked upset when she left."

Lance opened the refrigerator and took out a bottle of water. Lying was one of the main reasons he didn't like Vanessa. "You knew I was home, Vanessa."

"If your soon-to-be ex-wife wanted to see you, she would have waited until I told her you were working at home today."

Lance turned around just in time to see Vanessa perch herself on a stool at the counter, as he reflected on Riva's attitude toward him this evening. If Riva thought he and Vanessa were lovers, his chance to mending their broken marriage was over. "Damn!"

"What's wrong, Lance, Riva wants you back?" Vanessa smiled.

Lance set the water bottle on the counter, unable to miss Vanessa's seductive smile. He didn't like Vanessa in the least bit. He could imagine the act she must have put on for Riva today. Lance was determined that Vanessa was not going to ruin the small chance he thought he had with Riva. He didn't care if she was Samuel's niece. He glanced back at Vanessa leaning over the counter, noticing that the buttons on her dress were still undone, exposing too much cleavage.

"If I were Riva, I'd give up," Vanessa said.

"Did you look for a place to live today?" Lance unscrewed the top off the water bottle and dropped it in the small recycling container for plastic.

"How could I look for an apartment when I had to work?" Vanessa snapped.

"Easy—buy a newspaper and use the telephone." Lance tried unsuccessfully to keep his voice low.

"Hey, hey!" Adam walked in carrying two bags of take-out food and interrupting the fight. "I thought you were staying with Riva tonight?"

"I forgot to pack my gym stuff." Lance turned the bottle up, taking a long swig.

"Food." Tiffany grinned, going around the kitchen's counter, pushing Lance aside, opening the refrigerator, and taking out Erin's favorite baby food.

"I hope you didn't forget my crab cakes." Tiffany unwrapped the soft chicken sticks and sweet peas. "You didn't forget, did you, Adam?" Tiffany asked while getting the baby's booster chair from underneath the counter.

"Crab cakes, what crab cakes?" Adam joked, taking the container from the bag.

"All right, Adam, don't play with me," Tiffany said, setting the booster seat in the chair at the breakfast table.

"Vanessa, you ordered grilled chicken." Adam took the white container from the bag and set it on the table.

"I don't want it; I'm going out!" Vanessa picked up the phone and started punching in numbers.

"Vanessa, don't yell at me again tonight," Adam said, and turned to Lance. "What were you guys arguing about?"

Lance shrugged. "Vanessa has issues."

"What issue is it now?" Adam asked Lance.

"Her panties pinch," Lance replied.

Adam chuckled and pulled another white container from the bag. "All right. The little man can eat Vanessa's dinner," Adam said, referring to Tiffany's son Erin, and winked at Lance.

"Uh-uh. You're not feeding my baby that greasy, salty chicken." Tiffany took Erin's small blue plate and spoon from the cabinet and filled its two sections with bland chicken sticks and sweet peas, heating the food in the microwave oven for a couple of minutes before she set the food in front of Erin.

Lance watched the two-year-old struggle with his food, missing his mouth a few times, and he wondered what would it have been like if he and Riva had had a child.

"I'll see you guys tomorrow." Lance moved from behind the counter, dropping the empty bottle in the recycling container.

"You're not eating with us tonight?" Tiffany took the crab cakes from the counter and joined her son.

"No," Lance said, getting ready to leave the kitchen and go upstairs for his gym clothes and shoes.

"I'll eat with you, Tiffany." Adam grinned, opening the refrigerator, taking out a gallon of orange juice, and filling a glass.

Lance couldn't help but notice that Adam was

in a jovial mood this evening, after Lance had heard him arguing with Vanessa earlier.

"I have a date." Vanessa dropped the receiver down on the cradle and walked across the room to sit at the table with Tiffany and Erin.

"Promise us that you'll enjoy yourself," Adam said.

"Is that supposed to be a snide remark?" Vanessa asked.

"No. Hey, Lance, man, you'd better eat with us," Adam said. Setting the glass down, he sat on a stool at the counter, opened his container, and prepared to eat dinner.

"Udell invited Riva and me to dinner." Lance left his housemates and went to his room for his gym clothes and shoes.

"I should've known." Lance heard Vanessa and chose not to respond. He was sure something was wrong with her. It seemed to have happened when she got a divorce. Lance prayed that if Riva divorced him, as she planned to, he would not turn into a grouch.

Lance remembered that he and Adam had introduced Vanessa to at least two men they knew well. Vanessa didn't like any of them. Finally Lance gave up. Vanessa didn't seem interested in dating. It seemed that she enjoyed spending her evenings at home when she was not working on a case with him or Adam. Trying to figure out Vanessa's moods was exhausting. Lance was sure Vanessa was going through a cycle. Maybe she was having those flashes he'd once heard his mother complaining to her girlfriend about. Lance decided that Vanessa was too young for menopause. Lance shook his head and took his gym shoes and sweats from the closet, thinking that Vanessa would probably have to take a pill every other day.

A few minutes later, Lance was back downstairs, carrying his case. "I'll see you guys later," he said, stopping at the kitchen entrance.

"It's too bad Riva needs a guard tonight," Vanessa said to Lance.

Lance pretended not to hear Vanessa's comment. He moved over to Erin, who was about to dip his spoon into the sweet peas, refusing any help from Tiffany. "Hey, man, you got to handle your spoon better than that." Lance grinned. "You got green hair." He gave Erin's round cheeks a playful pluck, making the little boy laugh, before he headed out of the room.

"He is the rudest man I've seen in a long time. And you are too, Adam," Lance heard Vanessa say. He didn't turn back to give a comment. If he and Adam appeared rude to Vanessa, they had valid reasons.

When Lance's father was alive, he had taught him to respect women. His mother continued to teach him well after his father's death. When Lance finally met Samuel, who was like a father to him, Samuel taught Lance to stay out of the path of women who made themselves readily available.

As Lance climbed into his truck, he doubted that Samuel had had his niece Vanessa in mind when he had advised him on the ways of some women. Lance closed the truck's door, stuck the key in the ignition, and started the motor. When he went to work for Samuel's detective firm, Lance had met Vanessa and Tiffany, and he and Adam had decided that they would befriend the women. After all, they worked and lived together. However, it seemed that Vanessa had other thoughts in mind concerning her friendship with him and Adam. Lance mulled over the night Vanessa had proceeded to apply another one of her tacky tricks to get his and Adam's attention.

Early one evening, he and Adam had come home from dinner with clients. Vanessa greeted them both looking as if she had stepped off the page of a negligee catalog, wearing a skimpy black lace teddy and black heels, and fully made up. Seeing Vanessa half-nude didn't bother him. Lance understood that Vanessa had gone undercover to find a person at a negligee fashion show. But when she insisted on modeling the skimpy lace outfit for him and Adam, Lance realized that Adam was as surprised as he was.

Vanessa also didn't seemed to mind flirting with both of them. It was like a game to her. It was then that Lance had decided to introduce Vanessa to a man he knew. It wasn't long before Vanessa explained her wants and needs to him and Adam.

With that thought in mind, Lance headed home to Riva.

As soon as Lance pulled out of the driveway, he called Mason again.

"Mason, someone broke into Riva's apartment today," Lance said.

"Is she all right?" Mason asked.

"About as well as can be expected," Lance said, taking notice to how groggy Mason sounded.

"I would like to visit her tonight, but I'm so tired," Mason said.

"I'm staying with Riva tonight, so don't worry," Lance said. "I don't want you to say anything about the break-in or discuss the shooting with anyone, and that includes Alicia."

"I did mention to Alicia that Jasper had been shot," Mason said, sounding as if he was yawning.

"Don't mention it again, and I would also like to meet with you concerning Jasper's case."

"I won't," Mason agreed.

Lance made a mental note to remind himself to repeat his message to Mason at their meeting. Mason sounded as if he were half-asleep.

Fifteen

Mason pushed the off button on his phone, and stretched his long legs out in front of him. His eyes were half closed as he watched the evening news and sipped the icy rum drink Alicia had made for him. Mason didn't understand why Lance wanted him to keep secrets from Alicia. However, he agreed to keep his meeting concerning Jasper a secret and he wouldn't mention that someone broke into Riva's apartment. Mason forced his groggy mind to try to remember. However, Mason had agreed to keep his and Lance's meetings a secret, though he wasn't sure why he couldn't tell Alicia. When he and Paula were married, Mason had to admit, he had been overbearing at times, but he never kept a secret from Paula. He and Alicia weren't married yet, and he was already making plans with Lance not to tell Alicia what their meeting was about. However, Alicia was not like Paula. And even though he'd asked Alicia to marry him after meeting and dating her shortly after she began working for him, from that point on, he often found himself comparing her to Paula. His head began to throb. Mason figured his drink was too strong, not to mention all the stress he'd been under lately, what with the trouble with Jasper and having Riva accused of the crime. The fact that she was now free of the accusation didn't help much.

Mason set the drink down and wondered in his drowsy state what was so important that Lance wanted to speak to him in an isolated place. The room seemed to spin slowly in front of him. Mason felt that something was wrong with him. It couldn't have been the rum. He'd taken only two drinks. Maybe the doctor would have an explanation for his lethargy. He was always tired and wanted to sleep, especially since he'd returned from his vacation. Mason pushed himself up in the recliner and forced himself to stay awake to watch the evening news.

Still, he could barely keep his eyes open. It was if his vacation made him more exhausted than rested and relaxed. He would change doctors, maybe, and take more vitamins. He would do just about anything to rid himself of the sick, dizzy feeling that swept over him after he'd had one drink.

"Mason," he heard Alicia call out to him as he drifted, struggling to stay awake.

"Um?" Mason answered her, and considered that he would be in no condition to marry if his sick feeling continued. The consideration of calling off the wedding entered his groggy mind, and it didn't seem like a bad idea. It was unfair to marry Alicia and burden her with a sick husband.

"I heard you talking to someone on your cellular. You aren't keeping secrets from me, are you?" He could almost hear the teasing smile in Alicia's voice as she spoke to him from the doorway.

"Secrets," Mason murmured, trying to gather his composure and match his voice to her cheerful demeanor, but the drink made him tired. "No, Alicia."

"Who called you?" Mason heard her as he drifted off, and forced himself back awake.

"We'll talk tomorrow, Alicia. I'm tired," he replied, and wondered if Lance had told him to keep their phone conversation and private meeting to himself. He had thought Lance had told him to do that. Now he wasn't sure. He closed his eyes again. If his exhaustion continued he would immediately have to train Riva to take over the company, and he hoped he would live long enough to make sure she was cable of handling it. He had worked long hours for many years to build Dae Advertising. He couldn't allow Riva to lose the company.

"Mason, I'm going to bed," Alicia said, and Mason forced his eyes open again and watched as Alicia left him to doze in his easy chair. He drifted in and out of sleep until finally he dozed off.

Sixteen

Udell's apartment was just as warm and cozy as Riva remembered her house had been years ago. The smell of a cake or pie baking usually was a familiar aroma at Udell Hart's residence. Tonight the scent of frying chicken floated out to greet Riva.

Udell's apartment was large, giving her aunt the pleasure, Riva assumed, of furnishing the living room with a large blue circular sofa, and white chairs that sat next to the faux fireplace. On the mantel were pictures of Riva and Theresa when they were little girls and teenagers, and next to those was a picture of Misty. A silver collar circled the dog's neck, and a tuft of white fur was tied in a pink bow on her tiny head. There was also a picture of Udell and her late husband, Fred, sitting on the bookshelf near the balcony door.

"Aunt Udell, I don't know why you wasted good money having this little mutt's picture taken," Riva teased her aunt as Misty ran out of the room and pranced around Riva's legs as she followed her aunt to her bright yellow kitchen.

"Because she deserved to have her picture taken," Udell said, laying the spoon down beside the sink and going to the powder room outside the kitchen.

"Misty deserves to go to bed. Come here, Misty," Riva saw Theresa entering the kitchen and began to shepherd the dog out of the room while Udell ripped a towel from the roll on the wall next to the sink and wiped her hands, then discarded the paper towel in the garbage container.

Riva walked through the kitchen and sat at the dining room table, laying her purse in the chair beside her, while Udell battered another piece of chicken and dropped it inside the countertop deep fryer.

"Theresa, is Misty all right?" Udell asked from the adjoining kitchen when Theresa returned from putting the dog in her basket next to the closet, which Udell had designated as Misty's space in her bedroom.

"She's fine," Theresa said, taking her purse off the buffet, taking out her checkbook, and writing a check.

Riva smiled as she inhaled the familiar scent of down-home cooking. "If I didn't know better," Riva said, "I would think Misty was a person."

"Don't talk about Misty like I can't hear you," Udell said to Riva from the kitchen.

"She's thinks that dog is human." Theresa looked up from writing a check for the rent on the club she, Riva, and a few other women they knew rented for parties and just to have a place to hang out.

"Riva, are you all right? Mommy told me someone broke into your apartment today." Theresa ripped the check from the checkbook

"I'm fine, Theresa. But it almost makes me sick to talk about it."

"I can feel that. But I wonder who broke in," Theresa asked Riva.

"Your guess is as good as mine," Riva replied.

"If you don't mind, I would like to forget about the break-in—at least until after I eat."

"I saw Dylan today," Theresa said, placing her checkbook inside her purse.

"And?" Riva asked nonchalantly, taking out her own checkbook and writing a check for the club. She was surprised that Theresa remembered Dylan. She had pointed Dylan out to Theresa several months ago.

"Riva, I don't know why you pretend you don't like Dylan." Theresa got up and laid her purse on the buffet, then sat back down at the table.

"I personally think he'd make a good friend for *you*." Riva dropped her checkbook back into her purse.

"Me?" Theresa asked Riva, her eyes seeming to gleam with a special spark. "I thought you and Dylan were dating."

"Dylan is a client. He invites me to lunch, and I accept," Riva said, laughing lightly, wishing her aunt would finish cooking so she could eat dinner.

"Oh, well," Theresa said, getting up and leaving the room, then quickly returning with a pack of cards. Theresa shuffled the cards and started dealing back and forth between herself and Riva. "Let's play."

"What're we playing?" Riva picked up the cards and looked at the hand her cousin had dealt her.

"Go Fish." Theresa giggled.

"Girl, you're crazy." Riva laughed. She hadn't played Go Fish since she and Theresa and Laura had spent their after-school hours at Udell's after-school program, Key Lock.

"Riva, why didn't you tell me Dylan Edwards was a client? I could've asked him out."

"Why don't you ask him?" Riva pulled a card

from the extra pile in the center of the table and matched it to a card in her hand. "Go fish."

"Are you sure?" Theresa snatched a card from the pile.

"I told you once before, I don't like Dylan like that," Riva replied, waiting while Theresa searched her hand for a card.

"I forgot—you're still in love with Lance," Theresa said, matching a card. "But if you're not cool, someone is going to snatch Lance up."

Riva dropped the cards in her hand. She didn't exactly want to play their childhood game anyway, and Theresa's reminding her of the man she'd lost didn't add further interest to her dwindling excitement for the card game. "Theresa, shut up."

"It's just a warning." Theresa dropped her handful of cards on the table. "It's bad enough Lance lives in the house with that woman."

"Who's Lance living with?" Udell called out from the kitchen.

"He has a housemate," Riva said, looking at Theresa. "You talk too much and too loud." Riva lowered her own voice. She didn't mind her aunt knowing some things about her life, but now that she knew Lance had a female living in the house with him, Riva was sure her aunt would never stop reminding her of how she should rethink the divorce.

"See, you get upset at the mention of his name," Theresa replied.

"Because every time we get together you have to remind me that Lance and I are not together—just be quiet," Riva said, annoyed at her cousin.

"You're just mad because you know you made a mistake, filing for a divorce."

"I'm angry at you," Riva snapped.

"That's why you got bent out shape when I told you about that woman who moved in with him."

"Did I look upset?" Riva asked her cousin, thinking Theresa should have been minding her own business.

"Just as upset as you are now," Theresa remarked firmly.

"Ah, shut up!" Riva was tired of hearing about the mistake she'd made. After meeting Vanessa at Lance's office she was certain that she was right in her decision to finalize her and Lance's divorce.

"The two of you still argue like children." Udell took four plates from the cabinet and set them on the table.

Riva agreed with her aunt. She and Theresa had spent a lot of time in their childhood days arguing over mostly nothing. But this time Theresa's argument might be valid.

"Riva, you know I'm telling the truth." Theresa pushed away from the table and went to get wine-glasses.

Riva couldn't deny that she didn't love Lance, but loving him was a waste of time. She found her energy was better spent forgetting about him. However, after the trouble she'd found herself involved in, Riva knew she would never be able to resist Lance if he continued to live with her. It was going to be impossible for her to sleep tonight, knowing he would be across the hall from her bedroom, sleeping in the next room.

"Theresa, mind your business," Udell said to her daughter.

"Thank you, Aunt Udell," Riva said, getting up, going to the refrigerator, and taking out the homemade white wine her aunt made from store-bought white grapes.

"Mama, you know I'm telling the truth. Riva is divorcing Lance because . . ."

Riva gave her cousin a cool glance. She knew her own reasons. She'd made a mistake in marrying Lance. She had allowed her emotions to triumph over her common sense, believing that love conquered all, including her fears that one day Lance's job might be the cause of his death. Riva realized that she'd also thought Lance would change his career.

"Okay. I won't mention your problem again, Riva." Theresa set a glass down beside her plate.

"Great." Riva sat, filling her glass with homemade wine. Udell set platters of golden brown chicken, potato salad, and string beans on the table, then went back for a pan of hot bakery croissants.

"Theresa, I don't know why you're drinking wine tonight. The same goes for you, Riva." Udell took a chocolate frosted cake from the refrigerator and set it on the table.

"Gosh, Aunt Udell, it's one glass of wine." Riva held the glass to her nose and inhaled the rich aroma. Riva's aunt was old-fashioned; she didn't believe in drinking alcoholic beverages on weeknights. However, Riva knew the other reason for Udell's warning; the wine was potent. One glass of her homemade wine was enough for Riva. She took a sip of the wine and rolled the stem of the glass between her fingers. "Uh-huh." She smiled, closing her eyes and savoring the taste.

"I'm telling both of you right now, I'm not calling either one you in the morning to get your behinds out of bed, " Udell said, and from the tone of her voice Riva knew she wasn't joking.

"Yeah, Mommy, it's just a little wine," Theresa

said, waving her hand before she drank from her glass.

"Aunt Udell, my alarm clock works." Riva chuckled.

"The clock is useful only if the owner is not too drunk to hear it." Udell took forks, knives, and spoons from the flatware drawer. "Where is that boy?"

"Aunt Udell, you worry too much." Riva chuckled, taking another sip of wine. "Lance will be here."

"Yeah, Mommy, you know Lance don't miss no meals." Theresa joined Riva's laughter.

The doorbell rang. "I'll take this," Udell said, taking the wine off the table and setting it on the kitchen counter before opening the door.

"Come in, Lance; I was beginning to think you weren't coming back." Riva heard her aunt inviting Lance inside.

"I wouldn't miss dinner," Lance said.

Riva heard Lance, and the sound of his voice made her smile. She composed herself. Her aunt's wine had always had a special effect on her. But this time it wasn't the wine that made her smile. Lance's presence usually had the same effect on her.

"You can put that bag over there," Riva heard her aunt instructing Lance. "And go eat dinner."

"I'm starving." Lance said. For a moment things were quiet, and Riva assumed he'd gone to wash his hands. She finally saw him following Udell out of the kitchen and into the dining room.

Udell set the wine in front of Lance once he was seated at the other end of the table, close to Riva.

"Lance, do you have any leads on who could've shot Jasper?" Udell asked, shaking her head sadly.

"No, and we're not going to discuss the case tonight," Lance said, filling his plate with potato salad, chicken, and string beans.

Udell didn't seem to mind that Lance didn't give any speculations on who might have tried to kill Jasper. Instead the conversation changed, and who won the lottery became the main topic at the dinner table, and finally Mason's upcoming wedding to Alicia Owens.

"I still can't believe my brother is getting married," Udell said. "He's only known Alicia for a few months."

"He's happy." Riva stuck her fork into a string bean.

"Mommy, Uncle Mason and Aunt Paula are never getting back together, so get over it." Theresa dug her fork into the potato salad.

"That's true," Riva said, remembering how she'd wanted her parents to remarry years ago. She soon realized after she was older that they would never reunite. The pattern was repeating itself—her and Lance's marriage was over. Riva had one thing to be thankful for: they had no children who would be hurt from the break in their marital union.

"You never know." Udell looked at Lance as if she were waiting for his views on Mason's choice to marry Alicia Owens. "I guess Mason seems happy to you too," Udell said to Lance.

"I don't know, " Lance said, filling his glass with wine. "There's nothing wrong with a man being happy," Lance said, and Riva noticed the swift gaze Lance sent her.

"At least Daddy will have someone to share his time with," Riva said, and bit into the chicken.

The conversation changed from one subject to the next while Riva mostly just listened to Udell,

Lance, and Theresa discuss the news and sports for at least ten minutes after they finished eating.

"Aunt Udell, thanks for dinner," Riva said, pushing away from the table and rising from the chair, feeling a little lightheaded from the wine.

"You and Lance are always welcome." Udell smiled. "Such a nice couple—it's too bad you're getting a divorce."

"Yes, it is," Theresa agreed with her mother.

Riva noticed Lance looking in her direction and she looked away.

Lance pushed away from the table. "If I continue to eat like this, I'll gain twenty pounds, Mrs. Hart."

"There is nothing wrong with a chunky man," Udell said, then looked at Riva and Theresa as if she wondered why they were laughing.

Riva and Lance headed to the living room with Theresa tailing them. "What do we have here, a bag?" Theresa tugged at the black leather handle before Lance lifted the black bag from the carpet.

"He's spending the night with me. Do you mind?" Riva moved toward the door and opened it. She didn't want to hear any more of Theresa's teasing.

"Uh-huh, I knew it." Theresa let out a giggle.

"You know what?" Riva asked Theresa, who was beaming with satisfaction, as if her suspicions of whatever she knew were finally confirmed.

"That you and Lance weren't getting a divorce." Theresa stopped laughing.

Riva glanced at Lance. He didn't seem to mind Theresa's comment. "He's staying the night with me." Riva opened the door.

"Of course he is. Right, Lance?" Theresa gave Lance a playful punch on his shoulder.

"Yeah, Theresa. I'm staying the night with Riva."

He paused. "Do you have a problem with the arrangements?"

Even though Riva kept her eyes on the front door and the empty hallway in front of Udell's apartment, she could feel Lance's eyes on her.

"No, I don't have a problem, but Riva might, later on tonight." Theresa's chuckling floated out, bouncing against the corridor's wall.

"Come on, Lance, let's go." Riva reached for Lance's hand, pulling him through the doorway. "And Theresa, this is the last time I'm telling you to stay out of my business. Good night."

"Good night, cousin." Theresa was still grinning when Riva looked back at her.

Riva allowed Lance to slip his arms around her waist as they walked the short trek down the corridor to her apartment. His arms felt good around her, making her feel warm and safe, and for a second the thought that Theresa might have been correct about her sleepless night played across her mind. Riva shoved the thought of Lance sharing her bed away. Lance was no longer interested in her, and she knew it.

Not even a minute later, she and Lance stood at the threshold of her door. Riva took her key from her purse and started to insert it into the door's lock.

"I got it," Lance said, taking his door key from his pocket. But instead of unlocking the door right away, Lance slipped both arms around her waist, pulling her close to him. A warm feeling settled over her, and she longed for more.

"I think we should go inside," Riva said, freeing herself from being pressed against Lance strong body. She felt Lance's arm slide from her waist and brush against her hips before he unlocked the door.

"Wait here," Lance said as he unlocked the door to her apartment and flipped the light switch near the door before he walked inside. "Stay near the door while I check things out."

Riva stood near the door and waited for Lance to return. It wasn't long before he was back. "I don't think anyone would take a chance on coming here again." Riva said, closing the front door and going to the kitchen.

"You never can tell." Lance walked to the kitchen.

"You have a point," Riva said, opening her refrigerator, taking a survey of the nearly empty racks. Riva wasn't sure if any of the food and water in the refrigerator had been tampered with.

"I'll check the cabinets," Lance said, going to sort through the items in the cabinet.

"I'll get rid of this stuff," Riva said, and began taking and throwing out the half gallon of water, the half head of lettuce, and the dozen eggs, because several of them were cracked.

"Everything in the cabinets looks all right," Lance said, handing Riva a sealed gallon of water.

Riva put the water on the counter. "Lance, will you get a paper cup from that cabinet?" Riva asked. All the glasses would have to be washed. Riva wasn't taking any chances. There was no telling what her intruder had taken the liberty of doing to her things. Those thoughts clicked across Riva's mind as she waited for Lance to open a new pack of cups.

Lance's hand brushed against Riva's as he gave her the paper cup. Riva ignored the pleasant feeling crawling through her and reminded herself that she was going to stay as far away from Lance tonight as possible. As it was, she could still feel the effects of Udell's wine. Riva pushed the ice button, filling the cup with ice, then opened the water and poured a small amount in the cup. Riva quenched her thirst, keeping in mind that the combination of her, Lance, and homemade wine usually ended with a night of passionate lovemaking.

Riva set the jug inside the refrigerator and pushed the door closed, then dropped the cup into the garbage. "See you in the morning," Riva said, moving past Lance and going to her bedroom.

"Riva."

"Yes." Riva stopped.

He gathered her in his arms and smothered her with a long, lingering kiss.

She should've kept walking. But no. She had to stop, and as a result, found herself enjoying the kiss, and the weight of Lance's arms around her. Riva threw her concerns to the wind, savoring his sweetness and enjoying the kiss that filled her with a special sense of reckless satisfaction and rising passion.

Finally, after she returned Lance's kiss for the second time, she came to her senses and backed out of his embrace. "Behave yourself," Riva said to Lance, forcing her voice to sound light and undisturbed, as if taking the liberty of satisfying her craving had had no effect on her. But who was she fooling? Riva reflected, her passion and emotions surging with desire. No one but herself. Riva realized that if she thought her feelings for Lance would retreat quietly to the far corners of her heart, she had been mistaken.

Seventeen

As soon as Riva was free and going toward her room again, Lance pulled her back to him, showering her with irresistible kisses. She was about to push him away again, but he kissed her neck, and any hope of setting herself free of him now was useless.

"Stop," Riva heard herself whisper, which only seemed to make Lance find another tender spot to touch with his lips—the hollow of her neck this time—and finally he brushed his lips against hers.

It was a struggle, but Riva managed to get herself away from him, and quickly went toward her room as he headed to the kitchen. Just because they were staying together did not mean she and Lance were going to make love. The thought of Vanessa sharing his bed wobbled recklessly across Riva's mind, and again she entertained the idea of snatching Vanessa's hair out by handfuls.

Riva dismissed the thought of Vanessa's hair, and allowed her thoughts to wander back to Lance. If he thought he was going to protect her from some vicious intruder and make love to her all in the same night, he was clearly mistaken.

She realized she had finally come to terms with her mistake about the divorce. Even though the divorce was not final, it didn't matter. She would soon forget the shared kisses, and she wouldn't dare hope that Lance still loved her.

The best antidote for her was to stop thinking about Lance in sensual ways. For a moment Riva stood in the hallway and looked inside Lance's room. From the dim light in the hall, she could see the light blue bedspread, rumpled as if he'd lain on it. The sleeve of his suit jacket dangled over the edge of the chair. *Lance,* Riva mused. *Will he ever stop throwing his clothes on the chairs?*

Riva heard Lance whistling in the kitchen and hurried to her room. If he saw her standing outside his bedroom, he might get ideas, thinking she wanted to share his bed tonight.

Riva slipped into her dim room, which was lit only by a streetlight outside the building. She flipped the switch on the lamp on the nightstand next to her bed. The light from the lamp cast an inviting yellow glow over her room, giving her a placid sense of security. Or maybe her feeling of security came from the realization that Lance was just a room away. Or maybe she was just still feeling the effects of the wine she drank earlier.

Riva closed the blinds in her bedroom and headed to the bathroom. She brushed her teeth and rinsed her mouth as if she could rinse away memories of the lingering sweetness Lance's kiss left her with. Nothing seemed to work, so she splashed her face with cold water as if it would rinse away the small voice whispering to her that fate had played a hand in her and Lance's reunion tonight.

Soon her troubles would be over, Riva Dae Cain considered, patting her face with the towel and going to get a nightgown. Tomorrow her home would be safely secured with cameras, just in case the intruder decided to break and enter again. There would be no need for Lance to spend his nights with her. He could spend his evenings at home, or hunting criminals, placing them behind bars, and making the city safe again.

Riva took out a long black silk nightgown she used to wear to bed when she and Lance were still living together, since her soft cotton comfortable sleepwear was packed away in garbage bags in the living room. *Much too sexy,* Riva mused, searching through the row of red, yellow, white, and blue gowns for the housecoat that would cover the tempting lingerie she was forced to wear to bed tonight. Finding the housecoat would not have mattered if she were alone, but Lance was in the apartment, and he had a habit of walking into her bedroom.

It wasn't that she was afraid of what Lance might do to her if he took the liberty of visiting her room. Riva was afraid of what she might do to him.

Riva finally located the housecoat and pulled it over her gown. As she covered herself, she heard the second bedroom door close with a soft thump, a sure indication that Lance was going to bed.

Good, Riva thought, going into her bedroom to comb and brush her hair and twist it into a bun before getting into bed with the intentions of reading a magazine she'd been planning to get to for a month.

Riva leaned over and opened the nightstand drawer; then she remembered that she had left the magazine in the living room. Just as she was walking to the living room, the doorbell rang. Riva didn't know who could be visiting her at that time of night. She didn't think her intruder would ring her doorbell. Riva peeked through the peephole in the door. When she didn't see anyone on the other side she crossed the room to the magazine rack. If whoever it was thought she was crazy enough to open her door without letting her see their face, they had lost their mind.

The bell rang again. Riva felt a frightening chill race through her as she headed back to her room, bumping into Lance. Her fears were replaced by the subtle shiver that coursed through her when she allowed her gaze to travel over his bare chest and stop at the waist of his brown pajamas. "I can't see who's outside," Riva said, catching herself staring at the black revolver Lance carried.

"I'll get the door." Lance brushed past her.

Again Riva caught herself staring, this time at his broad back, and she decided that it would take the entire night for Udell's wine to stop effecting her good sense.

"Who is it?" Riva heard Lance say.

Riva heard a man speak, but she couldn't make out who the voice belonged to. It didn't sound like Dylan; besides, Dylan didn't know where she lived. She would've known if it were her father. He would have called her first before coming over at that hour of the night, anyway. Riva mulled over her thoughts as she watched Lance look through the peephole and close his hand over the knob.

"Who?" Lance asked.

"Henry." This time the man's voice was loud enough for Riva and Lance to hear.

Riva stood patiently, watching Lance open the door and raise the pistol. "Can I help you?" Lance said, stepping out into the hallway and aiming the pistol at the gangly man, who Riva noticed raised his both hands over his head.

"I . . . I . . ." was all Riva heard the man say.

Lance's voice rose. "Vanessa, what the hell are you doing here?" Lance asked as he lowered the pistol. "Put your hands down, man."

Riva opened the door wider and faced Vanessa, waiting for her to tell Lance her reason for paying him a visit, if Vanessa could ever stop staring at him.

"Is this the way you greet all the people who visit her?" Vanessa asked Lance, pointing a finger in Riva's direction. Riva felt the hair on her neck prickle and rise.

"Apparently only you, since you didn't have sense enough to use a telephone," Riva answered.

"Are you saying that I'm crazy?" Vanessa snapped.

"Yes," Riva said, stepping farther out into the hall, facing the woman.

"Uh-uh," nobody calls me crazy!" Vanessa stepped toward Riva, dropping her purse.

"Get out of my face." Riva spread her arms out from her sides.

"Vanessa, tell us what you're here for and leave." Lance reached out and pulled Riva back toward him.

"Get your hands off me." Riva jerked out of Lance's grip, glancing at Henry. He looked as if he'd been tricked into making a visit he could have done without.

"Henry is my date," Vanessa said.

"So what if he is your date, does this look like a hotel to you?" Riva planted both hands on her hips. From behind her, she heard apartment doors opening. The last thing Riva needed was for the neighbors to hear and see more confusion coming from her apartment. However, Riva was not having Vanessa visiting her home to see Lance.

"What do you want, Vanessa?" Lance asked her again.

"I called home and Adam told me you were here, so I stopped by thinking that I could relieve you. Because you have a long day ahead of you tomorrow."

"Honey, you can't stay with me." Riva gave Vanessa a short chuckle, allowing her gaze to leave Vanessa's face and slide down to her shoes.

"I guess not. I don't believe your apartment was broken into. I think you concocted this lie so Lance would stay with you," Vanessa said.

"Vanessa, you're not worth my time or my energy, and I would appreciate it if you used the phone the next time you get the urge to stop by," Riva replied hotly, thinking this was the perfect moment to thin Vanessa's thick tresses.

"Vanessa, if I need anything from you, I'll give you a call," Lance said.

Riva felt Lance's hand on her wrist. This time she didn't jerk away from him; she calmly went inside with Lance right behind her, leaving Henry staring at Vanessa in disbelief.

Once they were inside the living room, Riva slammed the door.

"Riva—"

"Don't talk to me," Riva said, taking the magazine she had planned to read before she went to sleep. There was no need to try to control the anger inside her. Vanessa had wanted to see Lance, and the only reason she wanted to stay with Riva was to keep Lance from staying the night.

"Can we talk?" Lance asked. Riva.

"No, we can't talk again. Never!" Riva hurried down the hallway to her room, leaving Lance standing in the living room. *This is the last night Lance*

Cain is going to stay with me. She tried to tell herself she was happy she was going to be a single woman again. Riva got into her bed, not bothering to pull the sheet over her. She flipped the pages in the magazine and prayed that once she and Lance were divorced, she wouldn't set her sights on a man and then make a fool of herself just to get his attention.

Riva flipped back to the contents in the magazine, deciding to search for an interesting article to read. If she was angry, reading always helped her forget how angry she was. But this time Riva's method failed her, and she turned the pages like the madwoman she was, while half glancing at the beautiful, stylish clothes and jewels displayed in the magazine. Finally she found the article she was looking for, "Pulling Life Together after Divorce." Riva was getting comfortable and ready to read when her bedroom door opened. She looked over the top of the magazine, seeing Lance walk inside as if he were in his rightful place.

"Did you leave something in here?" Riva asked Lance, and turned the page again. Just as she had begun putting the memories of her fight with Vanessa behind her, Lance stood in her room, tempting her to forget her promises.

"Riva, we do need to discuss this divorce," Lance said, not bothering to stop and sit in the chair he usually sat in when he visited with her. He sat on the bed close to her.

"There's nothing to discuss," Riva said.

"I don't want a divorce," Lance stated flatly.

"Well, you're getting a divorce whether you want one or not," Riva said, flipping the pages in the magazine to keep her mind off Lance, who still had not bothered to put on the top to his pajamas.

"Riva, I told you about the money my father put away for me when I was a boy."

Riva continued to look at the article she was about to read, until she felt Lance pulling the magazine out of her hand and laying it on the nightstand.

"I remember," Riva said, not wanting to have anything to do with Lance and his money.

"We're still married, and I would like to share it with you," Lance offered.

"If you think I'm going to take your money because we're divorcing, don't worry, Lance—I don't want your money." She would not have taken the apartment if she didn't need a place to stay.

"Then why can't we stop the divorce?" Lance leaned closer to her, and Riva inhaled the fresh smell of soap and a hint of aftershave.

Riva pushed herself farther up in the bed into a more comfortable sitting position, giving Lance her full attention and studying his handsome features. Before they had been chased by the man who wanted Lance dead for having sent him to prison, she thought she and Lance would spend their lives together. She knew better now, but she still wasn't going to put up with Vanessa.

"Lance, I have forgiven you. But we're getting the divorce because you have a new life."

"What do you mean I have a new life?"

"Give me a break, okay?" Riva stopped speaking to calm herself because she was beginning to feel her anger returning. *One, two, three* . . . She silently began counting to ten.

"Babe—"

"Don't call me babe," Riva said, her concentration broken. *Four* . . . *five* . . . *six.*

"Don't tell me you're seeing someone, because

if you are, I won't promise you I'm not going to stand in your way." Riva felt Lance's weight shift as he straightened on the bed.

You won't stand in *my* way?" Riva lashed out at Lance, her anger rising and she forgot about counting to ten. "It's you who's living with Vanessa," Riva said, and she immediately wished she could have taken the words back.

"Let me explain my living arrangements to you again." Lance rose, pulling her off the bed with him, before she could continue to argue her point.

With strict composure and rigid determination, Riva stood, her breasts grazing Lance's chest. Riva relaxed a little, feeling his arms circling her waist.

"Tiffany, her son, and Vanessa are living with me because they are related to Samuel," Lance explained.

"Lance, that is the worst reason for living with anyone I've ever heard." Riva drew away from Lance.

"Let me finish, Riva," Lance said.

"Okay, finish, Lance." Riva was curious.

"Vanessa and her husband got a divorce, and he was awarded the house. Tiffany and her baby were living with Vanessa at the time, and neither one of them had anyplace to stay."

"If Vanessa and Tiffany knew they weren't going to have a place to stay, why were they looking for an apartment?" Riva asked, thinking that if Lance had wanted her apartment, she would've found herself a home.

"They found a home."

"With Samuel?" Riva asked. Lance's living arrangement was beginning to make sense to her.

"Yes, until they could get their own place. When I found myself with a problem, Samuel asked me if I wanted to live in his house too. Adam moved in after his divorce and shortly after I moved into Moses's house. He also told me, Vanessa, Tiffany, and Adam that he planned to sell the house."

Riva listened to Lance, and she believed him. But she didn't speak.

"Babe, Samuel named a price for the house that I can't refuse. I'm buying the house, and—"

"A house full of divorcées," Riva said, listening to Lance.

"Everyone living in that house has the same problem." Lance grinned. "Anyway, Adam is buying a town house. Tiffany is waiting for the closing on her apartment."

"And Vanessa?" Riva was curious.

"Vanessa is supposed to be looking for a place to stay." Lance held Riva at arm's length.

"And you said all of this to me why?" Riva asked, searching Lance's face.

"Vanessa and I aren't lovers."

Riva listened. She thought he was telling the truth, but Lance's truth still did not clear the fact that Vanessa was out to get him, and Riva would not share Lance. "I guess Vanessa has good reasons for not finding an apartment," Riva said.

"Riva, did you hear anything I said to you?"

"I don't know," Riva said thoughtfully.

"What is it that you don't know, Riva?" Lance seemed to have calmed down.

"The way Vanessa carried on tonight, I would think that you slept with her at least once," Riva said as Lance held up his hand to stop her.

"Riva—" Lance made an attempt to interrupt.

"And today, when I stopped by Moses Investigations, she made it sound as if the two of you were lovers," Riva remarked, determined to keep her thinking straight. She was always making one kind of decision or another at work. She had never had a problem making a decision about her personal life until she met Lance.

"Babe, you know me. I don't sleep around." Lance's voice was husky as he pulled her closer to him.

Riva rested against his chest, feeling his heart beat, and she believed Lance. It seemed to have taken them forever before they'd finally made love when they were dating, and as far as Riva was concerned, it was worth the wait. But still she needed time to think. Did she really want Lance back in her life knowing that one day he could be hurt? She wanted him to be the father of her children. But would their children have a father? It was tempting to cancel the divorce. But as her aunt Udell and her father and mother often said, some things were better left the way they were.

Riva lifted her head to speak. She was unsuccessful. Lance's lips settled against hers, and she celebrated his kiss.

"We don't have anything to think about," Lance said, lifting his head and breaking their passion for a moment.

Any response Riva had was again smothered by his lips.

"We'll be fine." He lifted his head long enough to reassure her, then kissed her again before she could protest.

Lance had lifted Riva and was laying her on the bed when the phone rang. Riva didn't protest when he reached back and laid the receiver on the nightstand before he turned out the lights.

Undeniable passion reared its beautiful head as he nuzzled her neck and played keynotes on her spine, satisfying her hunger and the many months she'd longed for his touch. She didn't protest or unravel herself from his embrace when she felt his fingers slip the straps of her gown from her shoulders, exposing two firm mounds. Riva heard a deep rumbling escape him as he stroked her smooth flesh. It was as if he sent a message to the core of her spirit, drawing red-hot, aching desire from a well inside her she didn't know existed.

Riva stroked Lance's broad shoulders, allowing her fingers to feather over his back, and she felt him shiver under her touch as she moved her hands over his body. With unbridled pleasure, Riva allowed her passion to flow.

"I love you," Riva heard Lance whisper once he released his kiss and rested his lips against her neck. Riva didn't resist as Lance raised her gown, slipping the silk up around her thighs. She tried to think, but her thoughts were jumbled as she quivered under his grazing movement, the sensations threatening to make her lose her sound judgment—and break her promise to herself about Lance.

The doorbell rang, drawing Riva to her senses and diminishing the crazed emotions raging through her. "Don't answer the door," she heard Lance's muffled voice say, as he buried his head in the crevice of her neck.

Riva squirmed, freeing herself from him. "I have to see who's there," she said, pulling out of Lance's embrace and glancing over at the clock. It was a few minutes past one o'clock in the morning. Riva glanced at the telephone receiver lying on the nightstand. She was sure someone tried to call her because something terrible had happened. The line had been busy, and now maybe her aunt was stopping by to tell her that her father was ill, or that Jasper's condition had changed for the worse.

Riva got up and watched Lance as he rolled over and lay facedown on the bed, clutching the edge of the mattress.

"Whoever it is had better have a good reason for being here," Lance grumbled.

Riva silently agreed with Lance as she stuck her feet in a pair of bedroom slippers, not bothering to put on her housecoat, and went to answer the door. She walked out of the room, blaming Udell's wine for her temporary loss of sanity, and thanking the Almighty for doorbells as she made an attempt to shake off the desire to make love with Lance. She went to answer the door, sorting out her feelings, and finally concluded that she'd lost a part of her mind.

"Yes?" She peeked through the hole in her door, seeing the man who had been with Vanessa earlier.

"Who is it, Riva?" she heard Lance behind her. Riva turned and noticed he was carrying his black revolver.

"I think Vanessa is back," Riva said, glancing down at the front of Lance's pajamas.

Lance looked through the glass hole and opened the door. "What do you want now, Vanessa?"

Riva couldn't help but hear the strain in Lance's voice. She stole another look at the slight bulge in the center of his pajama bottoms and stood in front of him, irritated at the unwanted salaciousness coiling through her as her hips grazed against Lance.

"I lost my credit card. When I was here earlier, I think my purse was open and I dropped it," Vanessa said. She seemed to be waiting for Lance to reply. When he didn't, she continued, "I thought I might have lost it here."

"And that requires getting us out of bed?" Riva stepped forward.

"Riva, helpless women like you make me sick." Vanessa shot Riva a chilly glance.

"And needy women like you get on my nerves." Riva matched her gaze, while she kept her voice low. It didn't make sense to wake the neighbors a second time.

"We didn't see a credit card, Vanessa. Good night," Lance said.

Riva felt Lance nudging her forward with his stomach, as if he wanted to go inside.

Riva looked at the woman who had disturbed her night twice. "Good night, Vanessa."

"If you find the credit card will you return it to me?" Vanessa asked, directing her question to Lance.

Riva studied Vanessa.

"What are you looking at?" Vanessa asked.

"You," Riva answered, not taking her eyes off the other woman. Riva was satisfied that Vanessa's intentions were to stop by her apartment just to disturb her and Lance. The thought of Vanessa trying to control her life coaxed Riva's anger to return. "If we find your credit card, we'll return it to you," Riva said, determined to control her fury.

"Yeah," Lance agreed, and Riva felt him push his stomach against her again, as if he wanted to go inside.

"Some people will do anything to get attention." Vanessa addressed her comment to her date, Henry, who was looking as nervous as he had the first time he'd visited the Cains.

"Are you talking to me, or are you talking about

me to your boyfriend?" Riva dug her slippers into the corridor's carpet, preventing Lance from pulling her any farther with his hard, flat stomach.

"What do you think?" Vanessa questioned Riva.

"I think you need to get a life," Riva stated, her voice rising more than she wanted. At that moment Riva's thoughts slipped back to her earlier consideration—how she did not want to become a desperate woman after her and Lance's divorce was final. Chasing men was not one of her best skills.

"I have everything I need," Vanessa said, her mouth twisting into a distasteful smirk.

"Except for the credit card you didn't lose in this hallway, so why don't you search the parking lot? You could've lost it there on your first trip to my place," Riva snapped. It was clear that Vanessa had no shame. If she lost her credit card, all she had to do was report the card lost. Instead she preferred stalking her and Lance in the wee hours of the morning. Riva's voice rose louder than she intended.

"Don't you yell at me," Vanessa said to Riva.

"Vanessa." Lance moved Riva inside.

"What?" Vanessa glared at Lance.

"You need to go," Lance said.

"Riva's yelling at me."

"I can yell as much as I want. You're disturbing me." Riva's voice bounced and echoed off the walls as she struggled against Lance, who had wrapped his arm around her and was beginning to lift and carry her inside.

"I don't think so," Vanessa remarked firmly. "But at least I don't have to fake a break-in to live with Lance. We live together."

"If you don't get away from the door, we are going to the hospital for an operation. To take my foot out of your—" Riva wiggled around in Lance's arms enough to look at Vanessa; then Lance nudged her inside and started closing the door.

"Mister, I don't want no trouble," Riva heard Vanessa's date, Henry, saying to Lance, and even though she couldn't see him, Riva assumed he was looking as frightened as he sounded. "I don't know what's going on, but I'm leaving." Henry started walking to the elevator.

Lance set Riva down and she slammed the door and headed toward her bedroom, her nightgown swishing around her ankles.

"Riva," Lance called out to her.

She heard Lance but she didn't look back. From this night on, Lance didn't exist in her mind or her soul. She had two months to get Lance out of her life forever, and she had no intention of changing her mind.

"Riva, talk to me." She heard Lance outside her bedroom.

Riva opened her bedroom door, looked at him, and slammed the door in his face so hard that the picture on the bedroom wall trembled.

Lance rested his arms against the wall and pressed his forehead against Riva's door. He stood in that position for several minutes before he wheeled himself around and slid down on the floor, sitting outside blocking Riva's bedroom entrance. Vanessa had gone too far, and if he had to, he would bodily throw her out of the house. "Damn!" Lance cursed, burying his head in his hands.

Finally Lance got up off the floor and went to his room. He had a meeting with Mason around noon and he needed his rest. But with Riva across the hall from him, he doubted sleep would come easily.

Eighteen

The next morning, Riva pulled a black sleeveless dress and waist-length matching jacket from the racks in her closet.

Riva showered, dressed, and combed her hair before she went to the kitchen to make herself a cup of chamomile-mango herb tea. She left her bedroom, observing that Lance's room door was open. The wrinkled light blue bedspread was the only indication that he'd slept on the bed last night. Riva went to the kitchen to make the tea that usually calmed her nerves, since she was still feeling slightly frazzled from last night's commotion.

Riva entered the living room on her way to her tiny kitchen, noticing that the suit she intended to take to the laundry and cleaners had disappeared. Her first thought was that the intruder had entered her home while she and Lance were asleep, and her familiar fear returned—until she saw a note on the coffee table from Lance, informing her that he'd taken the suit to her truck.

Riva folded the note in half and took it to the kitchen with her, dropping the paper in the wastebasket, then made the tea. She opened the blinds in the tiny connecting dining room, allowing the sun's yellow rays to slip through the cracks of the half-open vertical blinds.

Later Riva sat at the counter in her kitchen, sipping the warm herbal tea and reflecting on the early part of the morning. She hadn't slept well, and because of her desire, she'd almost given in to her need to be with Lance. If Vanessa hadn't interrupted her and Lance for the second time, her promise to keep Lance out of her bed would have been broken.

Promises or not, Riva decided, the appalling truth was that she wanted Lance in her life. Riva finished the tea and decided again to keep her promise, reminding herself to get her apartment keys from Lance. With that thought in mind, she went to get her purse and left for work.

A half hour later Riva arrived at work after driving through the stop-and-go traffic. She went to her office and put her purse away, then picked up a photo pack that was on her desk and opened it, finding pictures of her, Laura, and Theresa in the pack. Riva figured Laura must have left the pictures on her desk that morning. Riva laid the pictures aside and began checking an ad that was due soon, making sure things were running smoothly and that the ad would be completed on schedule. She hadn't even gotten through the first part of the folder before her mind began wandering back to her and Lance's pending divorce, and the turn her life had taken. Without warning a disaster had happened to her, and Lance was back in her life. She didn't know what to do. Riva closed the folder and stared out the window, thinking of the predicament she was in and trying to figure a way out.

"Are you all right, Riva?" Harvey Miller, the graphic arts technician, stood beside Riva as she stared blindly out the office window. "Riva?"

"I'm sorry; I didn't hear you," Riva said. Added

to her ruminations was the unabashed soaring sensation she allowed Lance to unleash inside of her. However, after her fight with Vanessa last night, any hopes she'd had of reconciling with Lance seemed impossible. "I hope you're here to tell me that the computer is fixed," Riva said to Harvey.

"Yes, and I have a draft of the sketch you wanted." Harvey held out a tan folder to her.

Riva took the folder from him and flipped it open. "Nice," she said, admiring the gold tube and the slogan that made up Isaiah Fuller's ad. "Thanks."

"Anytime." Harvey smiled, and hurried out.

Riva put the pictures in her purse, then seated herself on the edge of the desk and dialed Isaiah Fuller's number. "I think we'll be right on schedule with your project," Riva said to Fuller when he finally answered her call.

"Riva, thanks for helping me out," Isaiah said.

"You're welcome, but first you'll have to stop by and see if you like the layout."

"I'll stop by later this afternoon," Isaiah promised.

"If I'm not in the office, Laura can help you," Riva said, thinking how Fuller's advertisement may have been the root of all her recent evils. "Okay, Mr. Fuller, we'll talk soon." Riva was about to hang up when Fuller stopped her.

"How is Jasper?" Isaiah asked, sounding concerned.

"He's doing okay," Riva said. "I didn't call the hospital this morning, but yesterday the nurse said he was making progress." Isaiah's concern for Jasper reminded Riva to give Brenda money to buy a get-well card for Jasper and have everyone sign it.

"I'm glad Jasper is going to be okay, Riva. We'll talk soon," Fuller said.

"Yes, we will," Riva replied, and set the receiver down on the cradle, rubbing her hands together.

It was Isaiah Fuller's project that had started the trouble, Riva mused, reflecting on her argument with Jasper, who was still in the hospital recovering from his gunshot wound. If she'd picked a secluded place to meet with Jasper the first time, she probably wouldn't have been overheard arguing with him, and her life would be moving along smoothly.

Nonetheless, because of her big mouth, Riva concluded, her personal life was almost shattered into tiny pieces. Lance was living with her again to protect her until the cameras were installed in her apartment, and while he was there, he managed to awaken all her libidinous and wanton desires. Vanessa was showing up at her door, probably to make sure that she and Lance made as little bodily contact as possible, and an intruder had taken the liberty of walking inside her home and rearranging her personal belongings. The only good thing now was that Jasper would pull through, regardless of the nurse's information that the doctors were keeping an eye on his blood pressure.

"Riva." She swiveled her chair and noticed that Dylan was standing in her office entrance.

"Hi," Riva said, once again drawn out of her reflections on her life. She observed Dylan's brown eyes, which seemed to light up along with his wide, white smile. Come in," Riva offered, gesturing to the chair in front of the desk that she was seated behind.

"I don't want to sit," Dylan said, still smiling.

"What can I do for you?" Riva asked, admiring his smooth tan complexion and his dark suit that made him look as if he'd just stepped out of an expensive department store's showcase.

"Don't tell me you forgot," Dylan said, moving farther into the room.

"Oh." Riva chuckled lightly, covering her face with her hand. She'd forgotten that she'd promised Dylan she would have lunch with him. So much had happened since she'd made the promise to him last week. "You know, I forgot." Riva stood.

"I heard about Jasper," Dylan said. "How is he?"

"He's doing well." Riva moved to the side of the desk.

"And you?" Dylan asked Riva.

She shrugged her shoulders. "I'm doing okay."

"I'm glad to hear that. Girl, I thought I was going to have visit you in jail." Dylan flashed Riva another smile.

"I was thinking the same thing at one time." Riva forced a smile. She imagined everyone in town knew what happened to her.

"So are you ready to go to lunch?" Dylan moved past the chair and stood close to the desk.

Riva gave him a meek smile. "I . . . ." She didn't really feel like going to lunch with Dylan today. She hadn't slept well last night.

"I'm not taking no for an answer. So get your purse and let's go."

Against her better judgment, Riva decided to have lunch with Dylan. He was an excellent client, directing additional business to the company, and his conversations were mostly business and personal situations happening in his life. Riva just mostly listened to him, but today she was going to suggest that he meet her cousin Theresa. That way she wouldn't be tempted to talk about her problems, since she knew she couldn't tell him about the problem she'd discovered she had with Lance. At the same time, she could set Dylan up with a date, since he sometimes asked her to fix him up with one of the women from her club. "Give me a minute." Riva went to the closet, got her purse, and pulled off the matching black jacket to her dress, then made a beeline to the bathroom to check her hair and make sure her face wasn't shining.

About five minutes later Riva joined Dylan and found Adam standing next to him. His tall, muscular frame was clad in a dark blue suit, and he was giving her a knowing look. Riva wondered if Lance shared every detail of his life with his best friend.

"Adam, how do you like your position?" Riva teased him, knowing Adam's real reason for working for the advertising firm.

"It's not bad." Adam grinned. "Have you seen Laura?"

"No." Riva raised one eyebrow. It seemed that Adam Johnson and Laura were getting to know each other. Even though she hadn't spoken to Laura to find out the latest happenings in her life, Riva decided that her speculation was true.

"If you see her before I do, tell her I'm going to a meeting with Mason," Adam said, backing out of the room.

"If I happen to see her on my way to lunch, I'll tell her you're looking for her." Riva waited until Adam was out of the room before she straightened off her desk and put the files away. She locked her cabinets and desk drawer, then turned to Dylan. "I'm ready."

"Let's get out of here." Dylan grinned.

"Where are we going?" Riva asked Dylan, taking the photos off her desk and dropping them inside her purse. They left the building and crossed the lot to Dylan's car.

"An out-of-the-way restaurant where we can be alone and talk," Dylan said as he drove out into traffic, blasting the car horn at a pedestrian who was about to walk across the street in front of his car.

"I don't want to take a long lunch break." Riva turned to Dylan. "So let's not go too far out of town."

"It's not far," Dylan remarked with a hint of amusement twinkling in his eyes.

"Okay, you've been warned." Riva spoke lightly, leaning back and enjoying the ride and the music filling the car. Cool air circulated from the air vents, and Riva relaxed against the soft seats.

"When I saw on the news that you had some trouble with Jasper," Dylan said as he wheeled the car on the main highway, "I could not believe someone was stupid enough to shoot Jasper and try to frame you."

"Me either," Riva said, not wanting to discuss her troubles. "I'm too afraid of guns." She cast Dylan a sidelong glance. "But I must admit, Jasper and I have had some pretty heated arguments."

"That I believe," Dylan said, chuckling. "Jasper can be a hard man."

Riva smiled. Dylan knew Jasper well enough to make that conclusion, since Jasper, Dylan, and her father belonged to the same men's club.

"Yes, he can," Riva agreed with him. "But I have someone I want you to meet," she said, switching the subject.

"Riva, if this is a blind date you're setting me up with, she'd better be good."

"You're the one who's always asking me to introduce you to one of the women from the club."

"From the club, huh?" Dylan smiled, as if he

was pleased that he was finally going to meet a woman from Riva's private club.

"Yes, and I think you'll like Theresa Hart."

"Do you know her well?" Dylan asked Riva.

Riva laughed. She and Theresa were sandbox buddies; they'd even ridden tricycles together. "Yes. Would you like her phone number?"

"She's single, with no man in her life?" Dylan asked, looking straight ahead and slowing the car.

"Yes," Riva said as Dylan drove slowly past a restaurant, then turned into the parking lot.

"She's a good person?" Dylan asked, driving into a parking space.

"Of course she is. I think my cousin is a good person."

"All right. Can I have a description?"

"Dylan, I didn't know you were so particular," Riva said, opening her purse.

"Riva, don't start any stuff." Dylan grinned.

"I think I can show you better than I can tell you." Riva reached into her purse and took out a picture that she, Theresa, and Laura had had taken at the club one night by a photographer who wanted to date Theresa. She handed the picture to Dylan and watched him study Theresa's features. The photograph wasn't that big, but Riva was sure Dylan could make out Theresa's high cheekbones, beige complexion, and black shoulder-length hair.

"Hmm, nice." Dylan said, handing the picture back to Riva.

"Thank you," Riva said, as if Dylan had just complimented her on the beauty of her child.

Dylan laughed. "Do you think she'll mind if you give me her phone number?"

"I don't think she'll mind at all," Riva said, telling Dylan that she'd mentioned him to Theresa just last night. "I'll call her and check," Riva said, taking out her phone and calling Theresa at the courthouse where she worked. After about a minute of conversation with Theresa, Riva hung up. "You can give her a call."

"Okay, I will," Dylan said, hesitating.

"Dylan, don't tell me you're afraid of rejection." Riva smiled.

"I am." Dylan laughed as he got out of the car and started around to open the door for Riva.

Riva was out of the car before Dylan got around to open the door. "You guys are alike. Hard on the outside, and mush on the inside." Riva smiled at him as she closed the car door, pulling the door handle to make sure the door was locked.

"Are you male-bashing?" Dylan asked her as they headed to the restaurant.

"No, I'm just speaking the truth," Riva replied as they walked inside the restaurant and were guided to their table by the waiter standing near the entrance.

The dining room was crowded, filled mostly with businesspeople Riva and Dylan recognized, all of whom were seated around round tables covered with black cloths, small green plants in the center of each table. Soft music played in the background, filling the dining room with ambience.

As soon as Riva and Dylan were seated the waiter took their orders. The second the waiter left their table, Dylan started in on his problems, as was usual when Riva had lunch with him.

"Riva, I got in trouble," Dylan said, opening the menu the waiter had left in front of him.

"What is it now?" Riva asked, preparing herself to listen to Dylan's latest problem. Not that she minded. He'd listened to her problems when she'd first filed for divorce from Lance. Dylan thought the whole idea of her divorcing Lance was ridiculous. Dylan had met Lance twice at two of her father's parties. She had introduced Lance to Dylan, and Dylan had introduced his wife to Lance.

Dylan chuckled. "I'm serious. I tried to buy a house."

"Are congratulations in order?" Riva asked, scanning the lunch menu.

"I said *tried*. My ex-wide ran up our credit card before the divorce was final."

"Excuse me," the waiter interrupted, setting glasses of water on the table. "Would you like to order now?"

"Yes," Riva said, ordering a fruit salad. Then she waited for Dylan to give the waiter his order.

"Thanks," Riva said, and turned her attention back to Dylan's problem. "Does this mean that you're not buying a house?" Riva asked, recalling how she and Lance still had joint cards, which she'd forgotten about until Dylan had mentioned his ex-wide's behavior.

"I paid the bill, so I guess I'll have a house soon," Dylan said, surveying the room.

Riva's gaze followed Dylan's, and she noticed Lance seated at a nearby table with her father and Adam. She lifted her water glass and took a small sip, still paying attention to Lance, Adam, and her father, who all seemed to be in a serious discussion. Riva assumed their meeting concerned Jasper's case, and turned her attention back to Dylan.

"Fruit salad for you," the waiter announced, appearing at Riva and Dylan's table with a large tray. "And pasta for you." The waiter set the food in front of them. "Enjoy," he said, rushing to the table across from Riva and Dylan.

Riva spread her napkin and cut into the yellow melon on her plate. "What kind of house are you buying?" she asked, pushing the fork into the juicy slice she'd just cut.

"Something spacious," Dylan said, looking toward Lance's table.

Riva stole another glance at Lance and stuck the melon into her mouth. "Spacious sounds nice," she said, and chewed slowly.

"Yeah," Dylan remarked, twirling a string of pasta on his fork. "So did you divorce that guy yet?" Dylan nodded his head in Lance's direction.

This was a discussion that Riva hadn't planned to have. It was bad enough that Dylan chose a restaurant where Lance was eating his lunch and she was forced to look at him. Riva swallowed the sweet melon. "We have two months before the divorce is final." Riva looked toward the table Lance was sharing with her father and Adam, noticing that Lance had leaned back in his chair and was looking at her.

"You'll be a free woman." Dylan spoke the words as if her freedom were a good thing.

"Yes," Riva said, eating a small wedge of pineapple.

"You say 'yes' like you don't want the divorce to happen." Dylan twirled his fork around more pasta.

"I don't want to talk about it," Riva said, thinking it better to leave the news that Lance was living with her because an intruder had entered her home for another lunch and conversation, since Lance was trying to find the person who had committed the crime. She knew she wouldn't be able to tell Dylan that Lance was living at her apartment; Dylan would want to know what happened

to force her to allow Lance to live with her, and
he knew Lance was a private detective. It wasn't
that she didn't trust Dylan with the information—
they had been friends for years. Riva just decided
it was better not to talk about that particular problem.

"Well, breaking up is never sweet," Dylan said,
and started talking about Theresa.

Riva cut into another piece of fruit and ate
slowly, enjoying Dylan's interest in Theresa.

"Why didn't I meet Theresa at one of Mason's
parties?" Dylan asked, polishing off the pasta.

"Probably because Theresa wasn't there," Riva
said, remembering how on Saturday nights her
cousin wouldn't dream of going to one of Mason's
parties. Riva smiled, thinking of how Theresa
frowned on being at a party where everyone was
married except for her uncle Mason, her mother,
and Jasper.

"I guess you're right. Everyone at Mason's parties was married except for your father, Jasper, and
Udell."

"Aunt Udell is Theresa's mother."

"Get out of here." Dylan threw his head back
and laughed.

"Mm-hm," Riva murmured. "Let me give you
Theresa's phone number before I forget." Riva
reached inside her purse and took out a card with
Theresa's e-mail address and phone numbers, and
passed the card across to Dylan.

"Thart3@bellsouth.net." Dylan read Theresa's e-
mail address aloud and chuckled. "Thanks, I might
give her call."

"That would be nice," Riva said, not adding that
his having a conversation with Theresa, and possibly taking her out, would give Theresa something

else to talk about other than her and Lance's business.

"I think I should be getting back." Riva checked her watch, refraining from looking across the room at Lance again. She could feel his eyes on her. She placed her napkin beside her plate and stood up. "I'll be right back." Riva crossed the room to the ladies' room, stopping to speak to Mason, Lance, and Adam.

Lance smiled at her, and she noticed the smile didn't match the look in his eyes. Nonetheless, Riva returned Lance's smile and headed to the ladies' room.

She returned quickly, noticing that Dylan was standing at her father's table talking to him and Adam. Riva didn't see Lance, and she thought that he had probably left the restaurant. "I'll be outside," Riva said to Dylan, passing the table quickly, not wanting to get into the men's conversation. Although she knew their meeting was business, it was just that most men she knew had a habit of discussing some sports game or politics. Right after lunch those subjects didn't interest her.

Riva walked through the dining room and slowed, looking down, paying close attention to the small stack of steps she was about to walk down to go out into the lobby. When she looked up, Lance was standing in front of her.

"What are you doing with Dylan?" Lance asked.

"We had lunch; do you mind?" Riva moved around Lance, and he followed her toward the door.

"You told me last night that you weren't seeing anybody." Lance cornered Riva near the door.

"Lance, you know Dylan and I are friends."

"I also know that Dylan is divorced."

"So?" Riva said, still annoyed at Lance from the previous evening.

"I don't want you with him." Lance lowered his voice to a whisper when a few diners passed them.

"Excuse me?" Riva matched Lance's whisper. "We had lunch; we're not making preparations to get married."

"Stay away from Dylan, Riva."

"I will not dismiss my friends because you don't like them." Riva wanted to scream. "Can we have this discussion later?" Riva asked, noticing that Lance was changing his stance to a wide-leg position, and planting both hands on his hips, exposing a small portion of the black revolver strapped to his shoulder.

"If you're available," Lance stated, looking at her, making it almost impossible for Riva to unlock her eyes from his gaze.

"Lance, I think I need to get Riva back to work." Dylan walked up to them.

"We'll talk tonight," Lance said to Riva, and she noticed he didn't look at Dylan.

Dylan didn't talk much while he drove Riva back to work, and she was glad. All she could think about was Lance's reaction to her lunch with Dylan, acting as if he were jealous. Riva fumed. He had nerve, telling her who she could have lunch with when he was living in a house with Vanessa.

Riva attempted to suspend the thoughts sprinting through her mind. She turned her attention to signs along the road advertising stores, homes, and cars, and any other billboards that would distract her thoughts, but nothing was working, not even the soft music filtering out from Dylan's car speakers. The air-conditioning that she'd basked in while

they'd driven to the restaurant might as well have
been a heater, as all of her memories from last
night flowed back to her, and this time she had
visions of Vanessa wearing a wig—for necessary reasons.

Nineteen

"Riva, someone tried to frame you for trying to murder Jasper, then broke into your apartment." Paula Nelson, Riva's mother, shook her head. "Why didn't you call me?"

"I didn't want to disturb you while you were away," Riva responded. "I'm fine. The only thing we're trying to find out now is who entered my home without my permission," Riva said to her mother, who was crossing one long, slender leg over the other.

Paula was tall, with the same cashew-colored complexion as her daughter. Her tinted light brown shoulder-length hair was streaked with just enough golden highlights to set off the sparkle in her dark brown eyes.

"We?" Paula's smooth forehead creased into a frown.

"Lance is helping me," Riva answered, not wanting to discuss her pending divorce with her mother.

"I see," Paula said, rubbing her thumb over one manicured flesh-colored nail. "So where are you staying?" Paula inquired.

"I'm living in my apartment," Riva replied.

"Riva, why are you staying in an apartment where people are just walking in when they want to."

"Lance stayed with me last night," Riva said, still hoping that the conversation wouldn't turn to her pending divorce.

"Uh-huh," Paula said.

Riva noticed her mother's expression, and wondered why Paula hadn't broached the subject of why Riva wouldn't consider dropping the divorce proceedings. Riva thought that maybe her mother was concerned about her troubles, so she thought once again that it might be better if she didn't mention her divorce. "Lance is placing surveillance cameras in the apartment today," Riva added, still studying her mother.

"That's good. I'm glad Lance is staying with you," Paula replied, swinging her crossed leg.

"I would rather Lance *didn't* stay with me," Riva said, noticing the bland expression that crossed Paula's face, which was a sure sign that she was getting ready to fuss her out. Riva turned her attention to the canal at the edge of her mother's backyard and waited for Paula's response.

"Riva, I can't give you much advice on why you should stay married, because I'm a divorcée myself. But Lance is a fine man. I don't see that he did anything wrong." Paula stopped swinging her foot.

"Are you telling me that you're sorry about divorcing Daddy?" Riva asked.

"Honey, that's my point," Paula said, spreading her hands. "I wanted a business, and Mason decided that I shouldn't waste my time selling vacations to people. You should understand. I've told you many times the reason for my divorce."

Riva shifted in her seat, not liking the thoughts that were beginning to confront her.

"Riva, you're just like Mason. You're doing to Lance what Mason did to me."

Riva had always wanted to be like her mother. Her father was too demanding, forcing others to do exactly what he wanted, or else. Riva cast another glance at the canal, watching as the red, orange, and pink rays of the fading sunlight cast reflections of the early-evening sky against the water. She'd forced Lance away from her, and now she was angry because she thought he'd moved on with his life. "I don't think Lance and I are going to get back together," Riva finally said.

"Why is that?" Paula leaned forward as if not to miss a word of Riva's explanation.

"I think Lance may have found someone else to share his life with," Riva said, experiencing a tinge of frustration.

"What do you expect Lance to do? You don't want him." Paula reminded Riva.

Riva felt tears burning the edges of her eyes. She held her head down to keep her mother from noticing. "It's too late for us," Riva said, wishing that she'd never filed those divorce papers.

"It's not too late as long as you realize what you've done," Paula replied.

Riva considered Paula's advice. Lance had told her that he didn't share his nights with Vanessa, and she believed him. But when Vanessa had returned to Riva's apartment late last night, she had had serious doubts.

Again jealousy raised its ugly head and slithered through her like a rattlesnake as a picture of Vanessa's face reeled through her mind.

"Riva, if you think it's too late, well . . ." Paula's voice faded. Riva noticed that she was watching her as if looking for signs of hope that Riva was willing to change her mind about her marriage.

"I don't know," Riva said. She knew only one

thing: she didn't want to be like her father. It never occurred to her that she'd forced Lance to make a choice. He was still working in the field he loved. However, his position was no longer as dangerous as it had been when he was with the police force. "You have to understand," Riva said to Paula. "Lance was chased by an ex-prisoner, and we could've been killed."

"Riva, cars crash every day, and people are threatened by folks who never saw the inside of a prison." Paula paused. "And those worries you have about Lance moving on with his life?"

"Yes?" Riva said.

"If you don't pull yourself together, your worries are going to become a reality."

Riva rose to her feet on that note of advice. She didn't want to think about or discuss her loss. She didn't want to imagine Lance with someone else. The very thought made her stomach knot. And what was even worse, her mother was speaking the truth. "I'll see soon," Riva said, reaching down for her purse.

"Riva, I understand that you have your father's genes, and it's hard for you to be wrong about some things, but consider our discussion," Paula warned Riva.

"I'll do my best," Riva said, seriously planning to consider her mother's advice.

"Speaking of Mason, how is he doing?" Paula asked as she stood and began walking with Riva through sitting room of her town house.

"Daddy is okay. He enjoyed his vacation, and in about two months he's getting married," Riva said.

"I'm glad for him," Paula said.

"If he's happy, I'm happy for him too," Riva replied as she made her way through the dining room, tempted to take a red apple from the bowl, that served as a centerpiece on the flaxen dining room table.

"Riva, at least you don't think like Udell; she's dead-set against Mason getting married," Paula said, stepping off into the small kitchen opposite the dining room and turning on the light in the yellow kitchen.

"Aunt Udell thinks Daddy shouldn't get married." Riva smiled. "She thinks you and Daddy should be together."

"I know, but Mason and I are history," Paula said as she moved from the dining room to the entrance of Paula's town house, catching a view of the lovely sunken living room.

Riva stopped and rested her hand on the corner of the stair's varnished rail. "I used to wish . . ." Riva stopped herself from telling her mother that she used to wish her mother and father had worked out their differences and stayed married; then she remembered her mother's warning and advice. She *was* like her father—she was forcing Lance out of her life just as her father had essentially forced her mother to divorce him.

"I sent flowers to Jasper today," Paula said as Riva moved to the door.

"I still haven't gone by to see him," Riva said, making a mental note to pay Jasper a visit. The week had been hectic. "I'm waiting until the weekend to visit him." Riva had decided a weekend visit would give her more time to spend with Jasper.

"I'll probably stop by on my lunch break tomorrow," Paula said, "because tomorrow night I have a date."

"A date?" Riva repeated the word as if it were foreign. She was sure her mother dated; it was the rational thing to do. She had been a single woman for a long time.

"Yes, Riva, I have a date. One evening soon I'll have to introduce Charlie to you."

"I can hardly wait to meet him." Riva smiled as she walked to her car. Just as she turned the key in the ignition, Theresa called her. "Hello?" Riva answered, then listened to her cousin tell her that there was an emergency meeting at the club tonight. "I'll be there," Riva said. After listening to more details concerning the meeting, Riva hung up and considered her mother's advice. It seemed that her family was moving on with their lives, and she was the only one stuck in the past with regrets and uncertainties.

Twenty

Lance stopped at the supermarket to pick up a few personal items. His toothpaste and shaving cream were low. While in the supermarket he decided to buy food, since Riva didn't have any. She probably ate her dinners with Dylan. Lance recalled the jealousy that had clawed at his heart when he had seen Riva with Dylan today. He headed down the toiletries aisle and dropped a tube of toothpaste in the basket, then moved down to the shaving cream, choosing his favorite brand. He moved past the medicated creams until he reached the end of the aisle, then headed to the meat counter.

So far his business day had gone well. He'd met with Mason and explained his suspicions concerning Alicia Owens. However, his personal life wasn't going exactly as he wanted it to, especially when he had seen Riva today. She seemed to have been enjoying Dylan's company at lunch.

Lance had to admit that he was jealous. He rang the bell on the meat counter, and waited for the butcher to come out and serve him. While Lance waited to order two veal chops, his thoughts wandered back to Riva. The image of Dylan hovering over his wife grabbed at the center of his stomach.

Lance brushed the thought to the back of his

mind, and turned his attention back to his work. Mason was at the top of his list.

For some reason Lance had an inkling that if he dug long and deep enough he would find Alicia Owens at the core of all Riva's trouble. However, Lance couldn't point a finger at Alicia at the moment. It wasn't a crime for her to move in with Mason before the wedding, which was still a couple of months away. It was not a crime for one of her husbands to have died, as Lance had discovered. However, Lance had had a meeting scheduled with the husband Alicia had divorced. Maybe he could shine some light on Alicia for him.

Lance pushed his thoughts of Alicia Owens aside when the butcher arrived behind the meat counter to serve him.

"Yes, sir?" the butcher said to Lance.

"I need two veal chops," Lance said, not wanting to buy the plastic-covered meat in the tray below him.

"Will that be all?" the man asked.

"That's all." Lance replied.

While the butcher went to the back to slice veal chops for Lance and Riva's dinner, Lance took out his phone and called Riva. When he didn't get an answer, he left a message on the apartment phone, then called her cellular number. Still he didn't get an answer from her, so he left a message telling her that he would be home soon with dinner, and that he was cooking.

Lance stuck the phone back inside his suit jacket pocket, waited for the butcher to return, and allowed his thoughts to circle back to his wife's soon-to-be stepmother.

Lance's investigation into Alicia's past brought more questions to his mind. However, what he'd

found was not a crime. He'd learned that she still
had an apartment only a few blocks away from Mason's neighborhood. He understood from Mason
that Alicia had given up her apartment to move in
with him. Alicia wasn't being honest. Lance mulled
over his findings, which he'd discussed with Mason
today over lunch.

"Two veal chops." The butcher was back at the
counter, passing the white wrapped package to
Lance.

Lance took the package and dropped it into the
basket while moving down to another aisle, turning
off to pick up a box of five-minute rice. He
dropped the rice in the basket as he continued to
mull over Alicia, trying figure out if she was the
missing piece to the puzzle.

Out of curiosity, Lance had asked Mason to get
a copy of his own medical records. Lance learned
from Mason's report that the doctor had suggested
that Mason take a vacation because of stress and
exhaustion. However, Mason didn't take a blood
test, because he had wanted to get back to work.
Lance made Mason promise to return to the doctor, take a blood test, and give Lance the results
of the test. Mason had been back from his vacation
for almost a week, and he was beginning to feel
tired again. Lance suspected that Mason's exhaustion might have been linked to something other
than his work.

Lance headed to the vegetable department, picking out a head of lettuce, one large tomato, and
a bottle of salad dressing, then headed to the
checkout counter, stopping to pick up a bottle of
white wine.

While Lance waited in the checkout line, he
tried to piece together who could have heard Riva

and Jasper talking. It wasn't as if the café were a huge restaurant. If Alicia had been there, Riva would have seen her.

Lance paid for his purchases and left the supermarket, a little confused as he continued to calculate the issues that seemed to pop up in the case and repeat themselves one after another.

He was sure that he should have been well on his way with the case by now, even in such a short time. So far Adam hadn't come up with any specific information while he was working at Dae Advertising. But Adam had successfully bugged the offices and made himself available to the employees, stopping in to visit with the creative team and other staff, since he was Mason's assistant. Adam had told Lance today that he'd talked to few of the guys on the creative team and learned that Phillip Davis had given up on Riva's going out on a date with him.

Hmm. Lance dismissed the thought. It seemed that Riva was spending her time with Dylan. Lance was still toying with Adam's information as he turned off the street and drove through the gate to Riva's apartment.

Lance was staying with Riva again tonight. He also planned to check the surveillance equipment that had been installed in the apartment today.

He used his key and entered Riva's apartment, checking the areas where another detective agent working for Moses Investigations had told him they'd installed the miniature cameras.

Lance was satisfied, knowing that if someone entered the apartment, the person could at least be identified later and turned over to the police, once he or she was found. Still, the question remained: how did a break-in tie in with Jasper's attempted murder?

Though Lance considered the possibility that the break-in could have been irrelevant to Jasper's case, the idea continued to nag him. He carried the bags to the kitchen and set them on the counter, turning his attention to Riva's reactions last night and today as he put the wine in the refrigerator to chill. He didn't blame Riva for being angry. Vanessa had ruined their evening.

But every time he thought about Riva with Dylan, the whole thing made *him* angry.

Lance took everything out of the grocery bag except the toothpaste and shaving cream. On his way to his room he noticed that Riva's bedroom door was closed. Out of concern, he walked in to see if she was in her room. The scent of powder and Riva's perfume greeted him. The bathroom door was open just enough for him to hear the sound of water from the shower.

"Riva." Lance walked to the bathroom door and called out to her. When she didn't answer him, Lance pushed the door open enough to look inside. Her nightgown and housecoat lay on the vanity chair, and a pair of bedroom slippers sat near the laundry hamper. But Riva was not in the shower. Dark fear gripped Lance and seemed to creep at a snail's pace around his stomach and finally to his throat. Lance calmed himself and turned off the shower. He had only two explanations for this event: either the intruder had entered Riva's apartment again today, or Riva hadn't turned the shower off this morning when she left for work.

His second idea made no sense. Riva never forgot to turn the water off when she got out of the shower. Right then Lance decided that he had to get Riva out of the apartment. He left the room and checked the closet and other areas of the small apartment. He had to stay calm.

After he checked the apartment, he went to his room and called Riva, learning that she was on her way home, and the fact that she'd stopped on her way from work to visit her mother made Lance feel better. As calmly as he could, Lance told Riva to hurry home. Lance decided to make dinner before he took the surveillance equipment to the lab to view the tape. Tonight he would see the person who was entering the apartment.

Lance stripped, discarding his suit across the back of the chair. He put away his gun and went to the bathroom for a shower, turning the water to a medium temperature, wetting himself all over, and working the soap into a thick lather. He managed to keep his mind off his problems. But he wouldn't stop worrying about Riva until she was home.

The stunt Vanessa had pulled last night resurfaced in his mind. After Vanessa had returned for a second time, Lance hadn't been sure if Riva believed him anymore when he told her that Vanessa was just a housemate, the same as Tiffany, her son, and Adam. However, trying to talk to Riva had been impossible, unless he talked to her through her locked bedroom door after she slammed it in his face. Lance was left to sort through the pointless behavior Vanessa had displayed twice in one evening. Just as he was making headway with Riva, Vanessa wanted to help out with the case, and on her second trip she had supposedly returned to search for a lost credit card. After that scene, Lance's problems had escalated, and he should have known that any precious progress he'd made with Riva would be null and void.

Lance dismissed his annoying reflections, and as

he lathered herbal shampoo into his hair, he reminded himself again that he had a few questions for Riva that he hadn't had time to clear up today about Dylan. Any misunderstandings they had about each other were going to be clarified.

Lance rinsed the suds from his hair, stepped out of the shower, and dried off. He loved Riva despite all of their problems, and he wasn't giving up. It was as if fate had given them another chance at a life together. Lance wrapped the towel around himself, remembering the reasons he and Riva had separated and were waiting for their divorce to become final. It was his fault. He was supposed to take a desk job. But the minute the opportunity had been presented to work undercover, he had taken the job and told Riva later, after he was about to work on a dangerous assignment.

Thanks to Samuel Moses, Lance had gotten the chance to manage Moses Investigations while Samuel was in New Orleans taking care of family business and closing a deal on his retirement home.

Lance didn't particularly like sitting behind a desk, but he couldn't refuse Samuel's offer, especially if it meant Riva would stay married to him. He loved his work, and he had to find a way to make Riva understand. Even working with Samuel involved dangerous encounters. Lance mulled over that thought for a moment. He couldn't give up his work, and he couldn't give up Riva either. If Riva didn't want him, he would go so far undercover it would take months for him to return. By then, Riva should have moved on with her life.

Twenty-one

Lance's whistling of one of her favorite tunes greeted Riva as she walked inside her apartment, making her realize that he'd made himself at home in her apartment twice in one week. Riva scanned the apartment, searching for the cameras that were supposed to be placed there. When she didn't see any in the living room, Riva checked the kitchen, seeing the bags of groceries on the counter. She looked around the dining room area, and still she didn't see any foreign objects that resembled a camera, or any indication that surveillance equipment had been installed.

On her way out of the kitchen, Riva stopped and peeked into the grocery bags. Lance had bought the fixings for one of their favorite meals to prepare for dinner. Riva looked inside the refrigerator, noticing a bottle of white wine. The dinner Lance was planning to prepare for them tonight brought back memories of how things used to be with them.

Discarding the old memories, Riva went to her room. There was nothing like a quick shower and comfortable clothes after a day's work to rid her of the hassles she'd encountered. But this week was different. She'd found herself not only thinking about her troubles, but about how Lance had managed to get back into her life.

From the hallway she could see Lance's partially open door. The aroma of aftershave floated out, greeting her. She went to her room, closed the door, changed out of her black dress, and headed for the shower. Riva stepped inside the stall and noticed the dampness. Her shower was always dry by the end of the day. Riva worried that maybe someone had been inside her home today, then decided that maybe she had left the water dripping. She took a quick shower and pulled on a long, thin sleeveless black lounger.

Minutes later Riva was in the kitchen. "Hi," she said when she saw Lance already there, automatically admiring the T-shirt that stopped at the band of his well-fitting faded jeans.

"Hi," Lance said, sliding the broiler pan that held two thick veal chops inside the oven.

"I didn't think you were staying tonight," Riva said, ripping the plastic off the lettuce that Lance had taken from the bag and rinsing the lettuce.

"I intend to stay with you as long as I have to," Lance said, straightening up from putting the veal into the oven and looking at her.

"I don't think it's necessary for you to stay with me." Riva maintained her composure, thinking that maybe she should go to a hotel until her problems were solved. Who knew when the intruder would be captured and put in jail? Riva was sure she didn't want Lance around until the crimes were solved.

"You have a choice," Lance said, expressing what Riva believed was his final alternative.

"What do you mean, I have a choice?" Riva asked, taking a knife from the drawer and preparing to cut the lettuce into small chucks so she could put them into the shredder.

"You can stay at a hotel or you can stay with me." Lance reached for a pot hanging over the island kitchen counter.

"I think I'm capable of making my own decision."

"If you decide to live at a hotel, I'll take care of the bill." Lance seemed adamant in his decision, in his offer to help with her living expenses.

"No, you won't." Riva stabbed the knife into the lettuce and sliced the head in half.

"I would prefer if you lived with me, Riva," Lance said, taking a measuring cup from the cabinet over the stove and joining Riva at the sink, filling the cup with just the right amount of water for the rice. Riva studied Lance quickly, noticing that he was as stubborn as ever in his thinking. Riva continued to cut the lettuce into chunks as she scolded herself for allowing Lance inside her home in the first place. She should have gone to a hotel when her troubles began. Riva lifted the top off the shredder. "First of all," Riva said to Lance as she dropped a few chunks of lettuce inside the machine and pushed the start button, "you don't have enough room for me to live with you." She looked at him then, observing the sensual look in his eyes. "Don't look at me like that," she said, looking away. Sharing the same home with Vanessa came to mind as another objection, and Riva knew that even if she wanted to accept Lance's invitation, she would never be able to stay with him, under the circumstances. Riva kept her thoughts to herself; the less said about the bushy-haired woman who had visited last night, the better.

"My bed is big enough for both of us," Lance said, raising his voice over the sound of the shredder, and despite the noise, Riva noticed that Lance's voice matched the sensuality in his eyes.

"Stop kidding, Lance," Riva said, brushing away the warm feeling filling her. She took a salad bowl from the cabinet and emptied the lettuce into it.

"Do I look like I'm kidding?" Lance asked her.

Riva would have to look at Lance to answer his question, so instead of doing that, she took a large wooden spoon and fork from the drawer and laid the utensils on the counter. "No, I think you're serious," Riva replied, still avoiding eye contact with Lance.

"I don't want you to live alone until the person is captured, honey." Lance checked the veal and set a pot on the stove to cook the rice. "Anyway, living with me is not the worst living arrangement."

Living with you may be worse than you think. Riva took a tomato from the countertop, turned on the water, and began washing it.

"Did you find out anything interesting about Jasper's case?" Riva asked, making an attempt to change the subject of where she would live until the intruder was safely placed in a jail cell.

"I might have some information that might be helpful."

"Really?" Riva was curious.

"I'm not sure, so don't repeat me." Lance eased the fork into the second veal chop and eased it out. He closed the oven and checked the boiling water for the rice.

"I won't repeat." Riva was anxious to hear what Lance had found out.

"I think Alicia is the person we want," Lance said, checking the veal chops.

"Alicia?" Riva added the tomato to the bowl with the lettuce and tossed the mixture with the wooden spoon and fork. "That does not make sense, Lance," Riva replied, watching Lance rip open the bag and pour five-minute rice into the boiling water.

"I checked Alicia out. When she moved in with Mason, she didn't give up her apartment," Lance said, securing the lid over the rice.

"She did give up her apartment." Riva removed the wrapping from the preheated dinner rolls and set them aside.

"No, she didn't," Lance replied. "Alicia still has that apartment."

"Are you sure, Lance?" Riva asked. "I don't think Alicia would lie to Daddy. She loves him."

"I'm not sure of her love for Mason, either," Lance said.

"Oh, come on, honey, just because a person doesn't give up her home doesn't mean she's a criminal." Riva chuckled.

"Maybe not, but I'm beginning to think that Alicia is not as good as she wants you and the others in your family to think she is." Lance took the lid off the rice pot and peeked inside, then turned off the stove.

While Lance crossed over to the dining area, taking two plates from the china cabinet, Riva checked the dinner rolls, considering his information on Alicia. Riva couldn't imagine Alicia being at the center of a crime. She wasn't Riva's favorite person, but Alicia made her father happy, and that was all that mattered, as far as Riva was concerned.

"You'd better wash those plates, Lance; we don't know if the intruder touched them," Riva said.

While Lance washed the plates, Riva kept her thoughts about Lance's findings and about Alicia to herself. She took the veal from the oven and put the dinner rolls in, turning the temperature down.

Riva sighed to herself, taking out the yellow tablecloth and matching napkins, setting the table.

"Riva, I know it's hard to believe, but it's possible." Riva turned to Lance, noticing him placing two chops on their plates, then returned to the refrigerator for the wine, retrieving a corkscrew from a drawer.

Riva sat across from Lance at the table and waited while he to uncorked the wine. "Huh," Riva murmured, and got up, going to get bacon bits and salad dressing and removing the rolls from the oven. She returned, taking her seat at the table, squeezing dressing on her salad, and sprinkling bacon bits on top. Riva speared her fork into the salad and began eating, crunching down on bacon bits and shaking her head. "Did you tell Daddy any of this during your meeting?" Riva asked Lance.

"Don't worry about Mason, Riva; he'll be fine. But I'm telling you what I'm thinking because I want you to know that I'm worried and I don't want anything to happen to you."

"I'm not sure that Alicia is involved," Riva said. However, she couldn't be certain.

Lance cut into his veal, and changed the subject. "I'm also serious about you not going out with Dylan, and I don't care if you're only having lunch with him."

"We're not back to discussing Dylan again," Riva said. She'd had enough of Lance's attitude toward her lunch date with Dylan today. She stuck her fork into a bite-size chunk of tomato.

"I think it's best if you don't go out with anyone right now." Lance said.

"I think I'm entitled to a good friend. Anyway,

you know that Dylan and I have been friends for years." Riva cut into the veal and ate a bite.

"Don't get comfortable with him. You're still my wife," Lance replied in the same tone he'd used when he'd stopped her at the restaurant.

"Oh, and you don't date?' Riva asked, pouring herself a glass of wine.

"My dates are business," Lance said.

"And my dates are all pleasure?" Riva asked, her wineglass poised in midair as she gazed at Lance and waited for an answer. While Lance was warning her about Dylan, she had wondered if Vanessa thought *his* dates were business. Obviously not, Riva decided, judging by the way Vanessa followed Lance around town like a Neanderthal woman, hunting him with intentions of dragging him back to her cave. Riva felt herself getting angry again. "At least I don't live in the same house with my dates!" Her blood seemed to race through her, fueling her already hot temper.

"How many times do I have to tell you that just like Adam is a housemate, Vanessa and Tiffany are also my housemates?" Riva heard a catch in Lance's voice as he lowered his tone.

"If you say so," Riva said, going back to eating her dinner. She would not allow an argument concerning Vanessa and Dylan to interrupt her dinner. Another word from her would only add fuel to the already smoldering fire burning inside her. Riva sipped her wine and gave serious consideration to her own living arrangements. She didn't want to live in a hotel. She was not going to live with her father or her aunt Udell or her mother; those alternatives were out of the question. "I think I'll move into a hotel." Riva pushed away from the table and finished her wine.

"I also think you need to take time off from work," Lance said, eating his salad.

"Lance, I have bills to pay, and Daddy doesn't give away free paychecks." Riva set her glass down.

"I'll help you out," Lance said.

"No." Riva didn't want Lance taking care of her. She had been an independent woman when she'd met and married Lance, and she had no intention of changing her status.

"Ah, come on, Riva; stop being so damn stubborn."

"Lance, don't you think it will be better—or at least safer—if I'm at work? No one is going to harm me at work." Riva waited for Lance's response. Instead he cut into the last of his veal and chewed slowly. "Well?" Riva said when he'd finished eating.

"I have a few concerns about your going to work," Lance finally answered her.

"If you're concerned about Alicia stopping by to visit me and the creative team, you have no need to worry; she's too busy planning her wedding."

"Babe, I can't tell you everything I suspect. But I think there's more to all of this than meets the eye."

Riva tilted her head to one side and gazed at Lance. "Are you serious?"

"Yeah." Lance drank some wine and continued to eat his dinner.

Riva and Lance grew quiet. Riva ate, sipped more wine, and gave Lance's suspicions serious consideration.

"So you think there's someone at work who's out to get me? Can you link all of your findings to me and Jasper?" Riva felt her fears begin to rise. Had a murderer been hired at Dae Advertising and no one knew? "Lance?"

"I'm checking the surveillance equipment to-night." Lance pushed away from the table, taking his and Riva's plates, the small salad bowls, and the wineglasses off the table as he headed into the kitchen.

"Wait." Riva got up, took a tray from underneath a cabinet in the kitchen and, putting the rolls, salad dressing, and bacon bits on it, cleared the table. "Where are the cameras?"

"There's one." Lance pointed to the clock in the kitchen.

"I don't see a camera," Riva said, straining to get a better look at her clock, when Lance removed a button-size camera from the edge of the clock.

Riva hurried to the living room with Lance as he removed a miniature camera from the television set, then headed to the bedroom.

Riva was satisfied that if someone had entered her apartment today, she would know. She went to the kitchen to wash the dishes, and Lance followed to help her.

"I'm going to the lab," Lance said, handing Riva the last of the dishes to dry and put away. He wiped his hands on a dry towel. "Have you made up your mind where you're going to live?"

Riva knew that she didn't want to live in a hotel, but she didn't want to live with Lance either. "I'm still thinking," Riva said, taking the dishes and glasses to the china cabinet. She put the china away and turned to find Lance blocking the narrow entrance to the kitchen.

"Make up your mind, because you're not staying here while I'm out," Lance said. "My place or the hotel?"

"Will you give me a chance to decide?" Riva moved around Lance.

"You can't stay with Mason; I don't trust Alicia. So it'll have to be my house, the hotel, Laura's, your mother's, or Udell's." Lance grinned.

None of Lance's choices were inviting, but the options grew progressively worse, not to mention the fact that Laura was probably cuddled up with Adam. Riva didn't want to put a damper on her girlfriend's life.

"I'll stay at your place," Riva decided, going to her room to pack.

Lance smiled. "Okay."

Riva took her largest piece of luggage and an overnight case from closet and started packing. When she finished, she took off the black lounger and pulled on a pair of jeans and a shirt, dressing for what would probably turn out to be a fun evening at the club tonight. Fun was what she needed, Riva mused. A game of pool after the meeting would take her mind off her problems for a while.

"Are you ready?" Riva heard Lance ask as she stood in the closet, putting on a pair of navy heels.

"Almost," Riva said. Turning out the closet light and pulling her luggage behind her, she walked out. "I'm stopping at the club for a meeting," Riva said, walking out of her room.

"I'll stop by the club later," Lance said. "We'll go home together."

Riva knew she was in danger, if Lance was suspecting Alicia and the people at Dae Advertising. She felt the muscles in her neck tense, like a rubber band pulling, and she wished she were going to the spa instead of attending one of Theresa's meetings to argue about nothing important.

Riva hoped that by the time she left the club she

would be relaxed and ready to join Lance and his roommates at his home. Riva pondered over that idea for a moment, thinking that staying at a hotel until her troubles were over was beginning to sound better than sharing Lance's house.

I'll take this." Lance reached for Riva's luggage and gave her his gym bag. He hoisted his garment bag over his shoulder and pulled Riva's luggage out into the hallway.

Riva set her overnight case and Lance's gym bag on the floor in the corridor so she could lock the front door, then walked with Lance to the elevator.

"You know, you're making the right choice by living with me," Lance said as they stepped onto the elevator.

"I'll let you know later." Riva smiled up him.

"I think living with me will be safer, Riva," Lance said, still smiling.

"You sound sure of yourself." Riva pushed the ground-floor button. The door closed and the elevator began to move as Riva noticed Lance's smile fade.

"When I came home this evening, your shower was on." Lance seemed to relax against Riva's suitcase.

"Why didn't you tell me?" Riva asked. She never left home without turning off the water and lights, and she remembered thinking it was strange that her shower had been damp after a long day. "I was thinking that I might have forgotten because I was rushing this morning. . . ." Riva's voice trailed off. "You think someone was in the apartment today?"

"I think so," Lance said. "I didn't tell you because I didn't want you to start doubting your memory."

"What?" Riva asked as the elevator door opened

and she walked off ahead of Lance and turned to
wait for him.

"I think this person wants you to think that
you're losing your mind."

"My mind?" Riva walked beside Lance, unable
to control the fear coiling through her. "But why?"
Riva wanted to know. She couldn't think of a reason. "I didn't do anything bad to anyone."

"You don't have to have done anything bad to
anyone, Riva. That's why you're staying with me,
and you're not going to work." Lance seemed adamant in his decision as they crossed the parking
lot to their trucks.

"You think Alicia is walking into my house . . .
don't you?" Riva waited while Lance propped her
luggage against her truck and reached for her key
to unlock the door.

"Be careful tonight," Lance said, not answering
Riva's question. He laid his garment bag on the
hood of the truck, then placed Riva's suitcase in
the double cab behind the driver's seat.

"Uh!" Lance grunted playfully. "Girl, what did
you pack?"

Riva laughed. Lance always teased her when they
went on vacations that she packed more than she
needed. But Riva wasn't sure when she would return to her apartment, and she needed everything
in the suitcase. Riva smiled at Lance. "I packed the
usual stuff. Suits, slacks, blouses, jeans, tennis shoes,
heels, bedroom slippers, nightgowns, and two
housecoats." Riva smiled up at him. "And my favorite jewelry."

"Get in," Lance said, laughing and closing the
truck's door.

"I'll wait for you at the club." Riva wound the

window down and turned the key in the engine, starting the motor.

"Is Theresa still running the Speak Easy?" Lance asked, and Riva couldn't help but laugh. When Theresa had suggested a club where women could spend time having fun after work, Lance had named the women's club the Speak Easy.

"It's not an illegal club," Riva said, still laughing, and turning on the truck's headlights.

"Whatever." Lance chuckled. "I'll follow you to the club; after that, be careful."

"I'll be fine," Riva promised Lance. She was sure her intruder wasn't at the club.

"I'm serious, babe; this person is crazy, and I don't like your being out at night alone."

Riva agreed that the intruder must be insane. However, she didn't think whoever was entering her apartment was following her around town.

Riva pushed the gearshift into reverse. "I think I should call Daddy and let him know I'll be staying at your place tonight," Riva said.

"I don't think calling Mason is a good idea," Lance remarked. "But if you do call him, call his cellular phone. It's like I told you earlier; I don't want anyone listening in on the call."

Lance was back to pointing a finger at Alicia again. "Lance, I know you have the nose to sniff out criminals and suspects, but I don't think Alicia is doing anything but planning for her wedding."

"Maybe, but I still don't trust her," Lance said, leaning his head inside the window and giving Riva a quick kiss on her cheek.

"I'll see you later." Lance backed away from the truck.

Riva nodded, still feeling the touch of Lance's soft kiss against her cheek, and she wanted more. She

dismissed the annoying thought. Being interrupted
by Vanessa last night was a blessing in disguise. Tonight she didn't know if she would be lucky enough
to escape their unwanted passion—which might be
forced to end because of her and Lance's divorce.
She had to be firm. Lance wanted his career, and
Riva realized that Lance would never change profes-
sions. She'd been selfish, and, unwillingly, now she
was prepared to give him up.

Riva slipped a CD into the disc player, and listened to the love song filling the cab before she
drove out of the parking lot and through the apartment security gate. She glanced into her rearview
mirror, noticing Lance tailing her as she drove out
into the street, heading to the club.

Several blocks later, Riva pulled into the club's
parking lot, parking close to the front of the building. "I'll see you later," Riva said to Lance, getting
out and going inside. She glanced over her shoulder and saw him leaving for the lab to view the
surveillance tapes.

Riva was just about to join the other club members when her telephone rang, cutting into the
conversation and laughter from the members that
filtered into the parking lot. Riva reached inside
her purse. "Hello?"

"Riva, could you stop by for a minute?" Paula
sounded cheerful.

"Sure, Mother," Riva said, turning around and
going back to her truck. "Are you all right?"

"I'm fine. I want you to meet Charlie," Paula
said.

Riva could almost hear the smile in her mother's
voice. "I'm on my way." She glanced at her watch.
Her mother had told her that she was going out
tonight. Riva wondered if she had changed her

mind, or if she and Charlie had had their dinner already. But meeting Charlie was worth missing a few minutes of the club's meeting.

"Thanks, Riva," her mother said, as Riva hurried to the truck to drive to her mother's town house.

Riva pulled out into the street and, out of habit, glanced into her rearview mirror, noticing that a white car was following too close behind her. Riva flipped the signal and changed lanes, speeding, then glanced at her mirror again, noticing that the white car was following her. Dark, cold fear gripped Riva as she pressed the accelerator, only to notice that the white automobile matched her speed, forcing her to miss the turnoff to the street leading to her mother's house.

Riva slowed, and the driver in the white car matched her speed once again. She looked swiftly into the rearview mirror, trying to make out who was driving the car. Riva wasn't sure if the person was a woman or a man, especially when the driver of the car turned on its high-beam lights. Lance was suspicious of Alicia. However, Riva wasn't satisfied that driver was Alicia. She knew Alicia's red car.

Riva sped up, and the white car sped up as well. Fear coiled at the center of her stomach and moved in a slow pace, crawling up to her chest. *I have not done anything to anybody that I know of, so why is this person following me?* Riva's eyes brimmed with tears. *Why didn't I listen to Lance?* Riva asked herself, no longer interested in meeting Charlie. But finding a police station was at the top of Riva's list, as Lance's warning to be careful ripped across her mind. Riva prayed as she forced herself to pay attention to the street instead of to the person driving behind her.

Riva made an attempt to calm her fears and not panic as she drove into a different neighborhood with the white car still behind her. The speed limit was thirty-five miles an hour, and a posted sign read, DON'T EVEN THINK ABOUT SPEEDING. Riva had seen the sign many times and obeyed the law, but this time she speeded up, wishing that a police officer would stop her. She drove past homes and apartment buildings strung with tiny white lights, and a stone fountain spurting a rainbow mixture of yellow, green, blue, and red liquid. The headlights behind her drew her attention to the glare, almost blinding her.

Riva neared the neighborhood police station, fear and panic slashing at her as she drove the next three blocks. Riva's only thought was to drive as fast as she could to the police station. She pressed the gas pedal. Three blocks later she sped into the station's parking lot, missing the side of a police cruiser by inches. Riva zigzagged the steering wheel, pressing the brakes and skidding to a stop almost smashing into an electric pole.

Her heart hammered in her chest as she leaned back, resting her head against the seat, trying to determine whom had she made angry in the last week. She sorted through her thoughts, collecting any memories of fights she might have had with clients or employees, including the one she'd had with Jasper. Nothing came to mind, except that maybe someone Lance had helped land in prison was out and targeting her to get revenge on Lance.

A tap on Riva's truck window startled her, drawing her out of her considerations.

"Are you all right?" Bill Lee stood next to her car.

Riva rolled down the truck's window. "I . . .

yes . . . no." She swallowed hard, trying to compose herself. "Someone was following me," Riva finally said, glad to see an officer.

"Can you describe the car?" Bill asked Riva.

"The car was white. I couldn't make out who
was driving." Riva said, unable to steady her trembling voice, or to control the icy fear twisting her
heart.

Riva noticed Bill leaning his head inside the
truck, peering at her. "You don't look too good.
Would you like to come inside for a glass of water,
Riva?"

"No, give me a minute. I'll be okay," Riva replied
as she tried to calm her trembling voice.

"I don't have much to go on, but I'll look
around," Bill said. "Are you sure you don't—"

"No." Riva cut Bill off. "I'm going to my
mother's; she called me."

"I'm off duty. I can make sure you get to your
mother's house."

Riva nodded. "All right," she told Bill as he
walked away from her truck and got into his black
sedan.

Still slightly trembling and upset, Riva headed
over to Paula's town house, noticing in her rearview mirror that Bill was behind her.

Several minutes later Riva was parking in front
of a row of beige town houses with brown roofs,
fronted by small strips of thick green grass and surrounded by emerald hedges. Riva cut the engine
and waved to Bill as she hurried up the walk to
her mother's town house, letting him know that
she was thankful for his assistance.

Riva rang the bell and shifted from one foot to
the other as she waited for what seemed like all of
three minutes before her mother opened the door.

"Riva, what's wrong?" Paula asked as Riva hurried inside.

Riva wasn't sure if she should give Paula all the details of the trouble she was having or not. She didn't bother to go to the living room to sit; she walked in and sat on the first step of the staircase.

"Someone was following me," Riva said, unable to keep the information from her mother. The rest of the story about the break-in at her apartment, and how Lance was at the lab trying to see if anyone had been inside her home, spilled out.

"Why didn't you tell me?" Paula asked Riva. "You know you can stay with me."

"I'm staying with Lance," Riva said. She'd already made up her mind that she wouldn't move in with her mother.

"Now, Riva, you know I'm not going to be able work in peace while I'm away, knowing that you might be in serious trouble. And knowing you're in trouble, I don't feel like going to dinner anymore," Paula said.

"I'll call you every day," Riva said, beginning to feel calmer. "Go out and enjoy yourself."

"I'll be expecting your phone calls. Come on; let's sit in the living room," Paula said, gesturing for Riva to come with her. "I hate to mention this, but do you think it's someone out to get revenge on Lance?" Paula asked once she and Riva were seated.

The thought had crossed Riva's mind. Riva drew in a deep breath and exhaled slowly. "I don't think so." She was determined to stay strong. Riva pressed her manicured hand to her chest as if doing so would quell the fear circling her heart.

"Udell was about to tell me something that happened at your place when she called me this evening, but she got a phone call, and told me that she would call me later." Paula sank down onto a chair across from Riva. "Now, Riva, I saw you today, and you didn't say a word about this. What's going on, and why are people breaking into your apartment?"

"I don't know," Riva said. If she knew who was causing trouble in her life, the person would be in jail.

"Does this have anything to do with Jasper?" Paula reached for the portable phone on the table she was sitting next to.

"No. I mean, I don't know," Riva replied. "Who're you calling?"

"I'm calling Mason." Paula began dialing his number.

"No—don't do that!" Riva sprang up from the sofa.

"Really?" Paula stopped dialing Mason's number. "Why don't you want me to call your father?"

"I'll tell Daddy." Riva sat back down on the sofa.

"Riva, I do not like what's going on with you." Paula gave Riva a disturbed look. Riva noticed a line crease her mother's forehead as she replaced the receiver.

"Mother, I'm sure I'll be fine." Riva replied. Riva studied her mother, who had now clasped her palms in a praying position.

"I guess I am overreacting," Paula finally said.

"Mother . . ." Riva made an attempt to change the subject. "I stopped by to meet Charlie."

"Huh?" Paula's mind seemed to be distant.

"Where's is Charlie?" Riva asked Paula.

"Oh." Paula sounded as if she'd forgotten Riva's reason for visiting her. Paula smiled at Riva. "He should be here soon."

Riva got up off the sofa.

Paula walked Riva to the door. "He went to the store. We were out of water," Paula said.

"We?" Riva asked. It seemed that both her parents were actually enjoying their lives.

"Yes, Riva." Paula looked at her and raised an arched brow. "We like spring water."

"Look." Riva spread her hands. "You know, I'm glad you're happy."

Paula lowered her raised brow and took a couple of steps toward the front door, when the doorbell rang.

"That's Charlie," Paula said, looking through the peephole. She opened the door.

"Ladies," Charlie said. Charlie was tall with thick steel-gray hair, olive skin, and a neat mustache. His tan suit and expensive shoes made Riva wonder if Charlie Crooks earned a good living.

"Charlie, this is my daughter Riva Dae Cain," Paula began the introduction. "And Riva, this is Charlie Crooks."

Charlie shifted the bag with the spring water to his left hand. "It's good to meet you."

"It's nice to meet you too." Riva returned Charlie's firm handshake, then gave her mother an approving smile. "I have to go, and I'll call," Riva said. "Enjoy your evening."

"Thanks, Riva," Charlie said.

"Good night." Riva hurried to her truck.

Riva reached the club just in time to listen to a local singer showing off his talent to the club members. The club was dimly lit by a circle of multicolored lights, which cast a glow over the singers and band. They were all dressed in black shirts and trousers, rocking to the music they made on their instruments while the lead singer serenaded the crowd with a song from the late eighties.

Riva watched the singer and band members incite the clamoring crowd to a swaying of hands and a popping of fingers, before she went to find Laura and Theresa. She was tired, and her evening had been ruined when she was chased on her way to her mother's.

She pushed her way through the crowd of casually dressed women and a few men who had accompanied their wives or girlfriends to the meeting. In another room in the back of the club, where the card games were held and games of pool were played, Riva found Laura and Theresa. "Hi," Riva said to her friends.

"Riva, you're late and you missed the meeting," Theresa said.

"I know." Riva didn't give a reason or an explanation to Theresa or to Laura for why she was late. "What was the meeting about?"

"Key Lock's travel funds are short, and Mommy asked if we could have a fund-raising party. She wants to continue taking the kids on trips," Theresa explained.

"I thought it was a good idea," Laura remarked, seeming pleased.

Riva didn't mind the idea at all. When she had attended the Key Lock after-school program with Laura and Theresa, Udell had made sure the children with the best school grades were rewarded. The weekend trips were fun. "How do you plan to raise the money?" Riva asked, anxious to get started.

"The guys in the band agreed to play one night a week for free. So we agreed to give a dance party every Friday night, and invite the public for a fee. Plus, we all made pledges," Laura said. "I think we should be able to raise enough money to send the kids at Key Lock on a nice trip."

"How many students are going on the trip?" Riva asked.

"Five teens will be spending one week in Orlando," Theresa said, giving her all the details that Udell had planned for the trip.

"And, of course, Aunt Udell will need chaperones," Riva added thoughtfully.

"I'll add your name to the chaperone list," Laura agreed, heading toward a table for a pad and pen.

"I'll have to let you know later whether I'm going or not," Riva said, not wanting to make any out-of-town plans before she checked with Lance. She'd been chased tonight, her apartment had been vandalized, and Lance seemed sure that the person responsible for her misery knew her.

"Let's get a game of cards going," Theresa said to Riva, Laura, and another woman who had joined them.

"I'm shooting pool tonight." Laura giggled and headed over to a table.

"I'm not staying," Riva said, knowing that as soon as Lance finished at the lab, she was going home with him. But Riva didn't tell Theresa her plans.

"You're going to miss the fun," Theresa said.

"Theresa, I'm sorry, but I can't stay." Riva walked over to where Laura was chalking a pool cue, preparing to play a game.

Riva watched the game until Laura won, then checked her watch, wondering what was keeping Lance.

"I told him not to play me," Laura said with a laugh after she'd won the game.

Riva smiled.

"You don't look like you're in a partying mood," Laura said to Riva.

"I'm not." Riva went over and sat on a stool against the wall, scanning the room. "Is that who I think it is?" Riva asked Laura.

"Who?" Laura asked, looking in the direction Riva was looking.

"I thought I saw Phillip Davis," Riva said, straining to see whether he was still amid the crowd across the room.

"Phillip tried to get inside earlier tonight, and someone made him leave because we were in a meeting," Laura said.

"He's back," Riva said, wondering how Phillip had managed to get inside the second time.

"Theresa probably let him in. I saw him talking to her after he was asked to leave," Laura said, laughing.

"I wonder how he found the club?" Riva said. There were no signs indicating that the building they rented for fun was a club.

"I don't know," Laura said. "But you know how Phillip is. He probably overheard someone at work talking about it."

"Oh, yes, he's a nosy man. I hope Theresa asked him to make a donation. Make him spend some money—that'll cure his curiosity." Riva winked at Laura.

Riva's telephone rang. "Excuse me," she said to Laura, and headed to the ladies' room, since it was the quietest room in the building.

"Riva." Lance sounded worried. "I talked to Bill Lee a few minutes ago, and he told me that you were followed and chased."

Riva hadn't expected her chase to stay a secret, especially since she'd driven to the police station.

"I was being followed," Riva started.

"Why did you leave the club?" Lance asked her, his voice rising with every word.

Riva stayed calm. "Mother called me and asked me to come over."

"I can't stop by for you tonight. But if you go outside now, Adam will be waiting for you. He'll follow you home."

"What happened with the surveillance tapes?" Riva asked. She was anxious to know what was going on in her apartment while she was working.

"I'll tell you later," Lance said, giving her the key code that allowed her to enter his gated community, before hanging up.

Riva pushed the off button and dropped the phone into her purse.

Riva had thought she was smart, driving to a police station because she was being chased. She could run, but she couldn't hide.

The driver of the white car sat across the street watching Riva's truck parked in the club's parking lot. The driver hadn't expected to find her truck parked outside a building where people were mingling in the parking lot. The driver observed Riva walking out of the building toward her truck. After watching Riva acknowledge someone sitting in a truck in the parking lot, then seeing the driver of the truck follow Riva in a direction that didn't lead to her apartment, the driver of the white car decided to follow a few car lengths behind to see where the trip would end.

Fifteen minutes later Riva turned off on the exit for the street that took her to Lance's house, and speeded up, noticing that Adam was still tailing her. As Riva drove closer to Lance's neighborhood, she began to pay close attention to the street signs. Minutes later she reached the gate to Lance's development and stopped, punching in the code. The gate rolled backward, allowing Riva entrance to the development. Riva drove through, observing that Adam followed, using the excess time left on the gate. As the gate closed behind Adam, Riva glanced into her side mirror, thinking that she saw the white car that had followed her earlier in the evening. She dismissed the ridiculous thought. Her evening had been like a nightmare. She slowed, driving down the well-lit street, reading addresses on houses sitting only yards away from the street behind tall green palms with colorful flowers in all shades resting against green manicure lawns.

Riva neared the address Lance had given her and stopped in front of the house. The building rose two stories over a rich lawn, palm trees and multi-colored flowers decorating the each side of the walk. Lights shining from every window in the house seemed to send out a warm, golden greeting to her. But Riva didn't get out of her truck until Adam stopped behind her and got out.

"Adam," Riva said as she climbed out of her truck, once she saw him walking toward her.

"Lance told me you had a bumpy ride this evening." Adam grinned, leaning Riva's truck seat forward and reaching inside for her luggage.

"I was so scared," Riva said, waiting for Adam to pull the suitcase out from behind the seat. "My luggage is not lightweight." Riva chuckled.

"If I pull a muscle, I'll send you the doc, bill." Adam grinned as he lifted the suitcase out of Riva's truck.

"I will pay the doctor bill." Riva laughed. Her fears were gone, and it seemed as if she was going to have a good night after all. Riva mulled over that idea while walking beside Adam.

"Lance will have to give you a key." Adam unlocked the door and waited for Riva to enter before he headed through the foyer and up the stairs with Riva's suitcase.

Riva stood in the foyer, noticing an intercom set into the wall. She moved farther inside the house and stood next to a small study, observing the cherry desk and matching bookcases. Riva couldn't help but marvel at the home Samuel Moses had allowed Lance and his housemates to share. The cream walls looked as if they were newly painted. The dining room set was across from the living room, which resembled an indoor nursery, with tall green plants and medium-sized trees rising from silver plant holders. As Riva moved through the light gray and chrome living room and to the bottom of the staircase, she heard soft music coming from the back of the house.

"Riva," Adam called from the landing, cutting into her thoughts and admiration. "Lance's bedroom is the last room in the back on the right."

"I'll be up later," Riva said. She walked around the stairs to an opening leading to the large kitchen and adjoining sitting room, noticing the wide screen television and stereo against the wall in the sitting room. A glass door led out to the patio. Riva didn't bother to look outside. Instead she headed up to Lance's bedroom, climbing the steps and walking onto the landing. Riva walked along the hall, noticing a painting on the wall of the ocean with raging waves beating against rocks under tangerine and crimson clouds. A huge mirror on another wall hung over a table, with a small ceramic bullfighter centerpiece. Three other doors were closed, Riva observed, then looked out over the railing down into the living room and dining area. Seen from above, the rooms resembled a furniture store display.

She headed in the direction of Lance's room, passing a large, wide mirror trimmed in gold, hanging above a narrow glass table. Riva walked into Lance's bedroom; the king-size bed seemed to invite her to cuddle on the thick gray-and-black comforter. Once Riva was inside the room, she sat on the edge of the bed and kicked off her shoes, noticing another intercom and a small speaker on the wall near the door. Riva wondered if the intercom was part of a security system as she took her shoes to the closet that was large enough to fit a double bed.

Lance's shirts, suits, and trousers hung neatly on racks, his shoes stacked in plastic boxes on the shelves.

Riva considered how neat the closet and Lance's bedroom were, deciding the housemates had to have a cleaning person. Riva was certain Lance had not been transformed into a neat freak.

Riva opened her suitcase, taking out her clothes and hanging them on the empty racks on the opposite side of the closet. Riva finished stacking the few pairs of shoes she'd packed, and stuck her feet in her bedroom slippers before she went downstairs.

She stopped in the dining room, admiring the huge china cabinet filled with expensive china, and the green silk plant serving as a table centerpiece that was almost as large as her entire dining room table.

Riva walked through the kitchen and into the adjoining sitting room. From where she stood now, she could see someone sitting in a patio chair outside facing the canal. Riva opened the refrigerator and pulled out a bottle of water.

"Well, well, what do we have here?"

The sound of Vanessa's voice drew Riva around to face the woman who would probably kill to have the husband Riva was about to divorce.

"Go to hell," Riva shot back, calmly twisting the cap off the water bottle.

"You couldn't keep him at your house, so you followed him home."

"Like you followed Lance to my apartment?" Riva took a sip from the bottled springwater and planted one manicured hand firmly on her hip.

"I work with Lance; what's your excuse?" Vanessa's voice rose.

"We're still married." Riva set the water on the counter.

"You get on my nerves. Pretending to be helpless just to get Lance's attention," Vanessa snapped.

"At least I don't have to follow him around town to get his attention!" Vanessa's uninvited visit flashed across Riva's mind.

"Everything was going fine until you came up with some weak scheme." Vanessa stretched her hands wide. "Everything was perfect but you."

"Vanessa, shut up!" Riva drank another sip of water. Vanessa's ranting was giving her a headache.

"You don't tell me to shut up." Vanessa moved toward Riva.

"Hey, hey!" Adam walked in. "What's up with you, Vanessa?"

"She comes in here all high and mighty, like she owns this place." Vanessa pointed to Riva.

"If you think I'm going to stand here and let you insult me, you'd better think again, sister." Riva slid onto a stool. She could use her energy for more important things than arguing with Vanessa.

Vanessa clucked her tongue. "Adam, you and Lance make me sick."

"Vanessa, I'm sorry if you have ill feelings toward me; I can't speak for Lance. But I suggest that you feel better, because we have a few things to go over tonight on the Wade case," Adam said to Vanessa as he left the room.

Riva listened to Adam as he was leaving the room, and decided that maybe living with Lance wasn't a bad idea. At least she would find out the details of the case firsthand. It had never occurred to her that the detectives called meetings at home.

"Whatever." Vanessa walked out onto the patio and returned with a glass. She set the glass in the sink with such force, Riva was surprised the glass didn't break. "Every one of you makes me sick," Vanessa said.

"Vanessa, what are you ranting and raving about?" Riva heard another female voice and turned to see Tiffany entering the kitchen, the young woman who had greeted her at Samuel Moses's detective agency. Tiffany was carrying a chubby baby boy on her petite hip, and a blue bag over her shoulder.

"Tiffany, don't start with me, because you get on my nerves too," Vanessa said, making eye contact with Tiffany.

"I'm going to get on more than your nerves if you wake up my baby, again," Tiffany said to Vanessa. "But I'm not really upset with you, because I wanted Erin to wake up anyway." Tiffany kissed the baby on his cheek. "His grandmother is on her way to pick him up." Tiffany kissed Erin's cheek again. "He'll be gone the whole week."

"I wasn't talking that loud." Vanessa walked to the sofa and sat down.

"Yes, you were; I could hear you upstairs. You sounded like you'd lost your mind." Tiffany turned and noticed Riva. "Hi, Riva."

"Hello," Riva said to Tiffany between sips of water. Maybe she should have gone to a hotel, Riva mused. Resentment and dissatisfaction mingled in her, making Riva more determined than ever to get through the time she would spend with Lance.

The doorbell rang. "Erin, I think that's for you," Tiffany said, going to answer the door, the baby smiling and waving as they left the room.

Despite the dispute Riva had had with Vanessa, she couldn't help but smile and return the baby's wave as Tiffany carried him to his grandmother.

A few minutes later, Tiffany was back. "I think I'll have what you're drinking, Riva." She took a bottle of water from the refrigerator and sat on a stool on the other side of the counter.

"How's everybody?" Lance walked in and slid onto a stool beside Riva, setting his attaché case on the countertop.

"I guess we'll get through the night," Riva said to Lance, wishing that he weren't sitting so close to her. However, tonight she wasn't going to allow her emotions to get the best of her.

"Riva, you and I . . ." Lance voice trailed off. "We've got to talk girl. You could've gotten yourself hurt tonight." Lance popped the lid on the black leather case.

"Mother called and I went to see what she wanted. I didn't know I would be chased," Riva defended herself.

"I understand. But you've got to be careful," Lance said, turning his attention to his coworkers. "I have good news and I have bad news," he said, as Adam walked back in and joined the group.

Riva's heart lurched, and she wondered what news Lance had found as she watched him take a file from the briefcase.

"Who's on the tape?" Adam asked Lance, pulling back a stool and sitting next to Tiffany.

"Well, the good news is not that good." Lance grinned. "There was someone in your apartment." Lance looked at Riva.

"Who?" Riva asked Lance.

"That's the problem; we didn't get a chance to see the person's face because it was concealed."

"Was the person a woman or a man?"

"I don't know," Lance explained.

"That's not good," Riva said, wondering aloud if she would eventually get to know who was walking in and out of her apartment.

"Maybe the person is someone you know, Riva," Tiffany said.

"That's what I was thinking," Lance said, and Riva noticed him looking at her.

"What?" Riva asked.

"Nothing." Lance fold his arms across his chest. "We'll know soon enough."

"I don't know what he or she was looking for. No jewelry was taken," Riva said, hoping that the person would be found so she could go home.

"Maybe Cedric and Emma found something. They'll be here soon." Lance to Riva, sounding sure of himself.

"Should Riva be in the meeting about this?" Vanessa directed her question to Lance.

"Vanessa, this is about Riva," Adam said.

"But Lance said you wanted to talk to us about the Jasper Wade case."

"Vanessa, please!" Tiffany said, and Riva concluded that Vanessa was just a disgruntled woman, and probably couldn't get along with anyone.

"I don't think Riva should be in this meeting." Vanessa voiced her opinion again.

"All in favor of Riva staying for the meeting, raise your hand," Adam said, raising his hand. Riva watched as all the others held their hands high except for Vanessa. "All in favor of Riva leaving the meeting . . . ?"

Riva noticed that no one raised a hand. However, Vanessa didn't seem contented until she got Riva's attention and gave her an evil look.

Riva couldn't help but smile as the others chuckled softly, their laughter mingling with the ringing doorbell.

"Vanessa, you're outvoted," Tiffany said, pushing herself around on the stool.

"Hmm." Vanessa murmured on her way to the front door, returning with two people Riva didn't know.

"You guys finished?" Lance asked as the two circled the counter, and Riva realized these must be the two other detectives who worked for Moses Investigations, though she'd never met them.

The man—Cedric, Riva remembered Lance saying—was average height with a light complexion, and looked as if he was serious about his work. The woman—Emma—was tall, brown skinned, with black shoulder-length hair and a friendly smile.

"Riva, this is Emma, and this Cedric," Lance introduced the detectives.

"Hi," Riva said.

"This is my wife, Riva," Lance said to Emma and Cedric.

"It's nice to meet you." Emma held out her hand to Riva.

"Yes, Riva, welcome aboard." Cedric reached for Riva's hand.

"I'm not joining the team," Riva said, correcting the detective.

Emma smiled and handed Lance a bag and a file labeled ALICIA OWENS.

"I found the dress and hat in the garbage behind Alicia's apartment building," Emma said.

Riva looked at the long light blue dress and black wide-brim hat.

"Were there any gloves?" Lance asked Emma.

"No. I didn't find any gloves," Emma said, leaning against the counter.

"I'm thinking that gloves were used, because no fingerprints were found in Riva's apartment."

Riva sat speechless, listening to the detectives, and trying to figure out why Alicia had broken into and ransacked her apartment. "Why aren't you sending the police to arrest Alicia?" Riva asked Lance.

"Because we're not sure if Alicia is doing this," Lance said to Riva.

"But you told me earlier that you thought Alicia was—"

"I suspect Alicia is linked to you and to Jasper's case, but we have to prove it," Lance assured Riva.

"Are there any shoes?" Vanessa asked Lance.

"No." Lance passed the dress to Tiffany.

Riva wondered what was in Alicia's file, but she sat quietly and listened as the group discussed their views and opinions.

Finally Lance opened the file, pulling out a picture of Alicia. "We need to get someone inside of Mason's house." Lance looked at Riva.

Riva looked at Alicia's photo and wondered why Lance was looking at her. He'd already mentioned that he thought Alicia was involved, so she wasn't surprised that he had found information that would prove Alicia guilty.

"I'll see you guys in the morning," Riva said, getting up off the stool.

"Wait."

"I'm not a private detective," Riva said. "I'm going to bed."

"Wait," Vanessa said. "Riva, why don't you visit Alicia . . ."

"For what reason, Vanessa?" Riva asked. If anyone else in the group would have made the suggestion she might have taken them seriously, but would have refused.

"She's your father's fiancée. Who knows what you might find out talking to her?" Vanessa said.

"I don't think Alicia will share her secrets with me, Vanessa, especially if you're saying she knows who's breaking in my apartment."

"Ah, Riva, she'll never suspect you," Vanessa said.

"No, Vanessa," Lance said, before Riva could tell to keep her suggestion to herself. "That's not a good idea."

"There he goes again, protecting Miss Riva," Vanessa said.

"Like I said, I'm going to bed." Riva walked out of the room. It seemed to Riva that Vanessa never missed an opportunity to pick a fight with her, and tonight she didn't feel like getting into an argument with her. If Alicia was as dangerous as Lance seemed to think she was, she didn't want to be alone with Alicia anyway.

Upstairs in Lance's bedroom, Riva took her red nightgown and matching housecoat from the closet. Riva stepped out of her bedroom shoes and pulled off her jeans and top. She went to the bathroom for a quick shower, to wash off any lingering scent she'd picked up at the club earlier, along with the warm stickiness from the humid weather.

She turned on the water and stepped into the shower stall under the hot, spraying water, and allowed her thoughts to wander. She was more unable to make up her mind whether she should finalize the divorce now than ever. Lance hadn't been a bad husband. He'd walked away, giving her everything. He'd even offered her part of the trust fund his father had left him. This year Lance was allowed to cash in the fund, which was a small fortune now. However, Riva had refused when Lance had offered her part of the money. It was her idea to divorce him for no other reason than the fact that he loved his work.

Riva stepped out of the shower. After drying off and dabbing herself with her favorite perfume, she crawled into bed and began to doze. Through half-closed eyes, she noticed the nightstand drawer on her side of the bed was open just enough to make her want to close it. She pushed the drawer closed, and then, out of pure nosiness, Riva opened the drawer, checking the contents. A pad of paper, a pencil, a pen, and a small red leather binder with phone numbers lay in the drawer, along with a black box sealed with cellophane and labeled, SAMPLES. NOT FOR SALE. Riva edged her thumbnail along the side of the cellophane, removing the transparent paper, and lifted the top, seeing several packs of latex armor inside the box. Riva sat up, wide awake, and held the box in her hand, all sorts of suspicious questions running through her mind.

She hadn't expected Lance to live the life of a hermit. Riva thought about Lance's lovemaking techniques and a fresh wave of jealousy grabbed at her heart. She had no business worrying about whom he was sleeping with; it wasn't her business anymore. Riva looked down at the box she was holding, wishing the bitter and evil thoughts racing through her would dissipate. Riva was so involved in her thoughts, she didn't know Lance was in the room until he sat on the bed and pulled off his shoes.

"I thought you would've been asleep by now." Lance grinned at her as one shoe hit the carpet with a dull thud.

"I thought I would've been asleep too," Riva answered as another shoe hit the floor.

"I'm glad you're awake." Lance pulled his shirt over his head and turned to look at her. Riva noticed Lance's mouth tip into a philanderer's grin.

"You can wipe that wolf smile off your face," Riva said, still holding the box of protective armor.

"Oh, yeah?" He stood up and unsnapped his pants, pushing them down over his narrow hips, giving Riva a full view of his firm butt and muscular thighs, as he used to when they were together.

"Yeah," Riva said, wishing that Lance wouldn't give her a full display of his body. Unlike him, she'd been sex-free for months, and seeing him almost naked was not doing her libido any good.

"I think I'll keep the smile." Lance grinned, pitching his clothes onto a nearby chair across the room and parading his rugged physique to the bathroom, leaving Riva with the urge to seduce him and enjoy a night of hot, sizzling passion.

The bathroom door closed and Riva looked down at the box in her hand. She eased her fingers into the black box and pulled out a thin pack, tracing her fingers over the smooth covering.

Ten minutes later Riva was still contemplating how wonderful it would feel to recapture just a few minutes of lovemaking with Lance, for old time's sake, if for no other reason.

"We can use some of those if you want to."

Riva looked up and saw Lance towering over the bed, wearing nothing but the suit he was born with, and displaying every inch of his masculinity. She set the box down on the stand beside the bed and held out the pack she was holding to Lance. Without warning she rose up, working her way across the king-size bed to him. Drawing Lance down to her, she could hear a tormented growl slip from him, and she wanted him even more as she caressed his chest one stroke at a time. Riva made up her mind: tonight belonged to her.

With slow, intimate strokes, Riva caressed his hips and listened to another growl escape Lance, sounding as if the snarl had come from deep within before sliding from his throat and across his lips. Riva kissed him.

"Wait, babe," she heard Lance say.

"Uh-uh," Riva murmured while stroking him, realizing that she had hardly ever been the aggressor, and when she did take the liberty of approaching Lance first, he usually took control. But not tonight, Riva mused, giving Lance a sexy, wicked smile as she continued to stroke.

"If you don't stop I'm going to . . ." Lance lamented between inhales, drawing in his breath and allowing his sigh to filter out between his teeth as he gathered her in his arms, his mouth hard against hers.

Riva murmured softly as Lance rose up and tore open the pack.

"I don't need this, you know," Lance said to her, gesturing at the pack she'd given him earlier.

"Just in case," Riva heard herself say, and her voice sounded as if she were speaking from a faraway place. She didn't want to break the spell.

Riva reached out to Lance and stroked his chest. Little gasps of air escaped her as Lance lifted her red gown, moving the silk over her hips, and lowered his dark head, forging a magic trail to places that hadn't been caressed in months.

Like a slow, low-burning fire, Riva felt the flames rise, working their way through her, and she pulled him closer as he peeled the scarlet silk straps off her shoulders, caressing her until she thought her soul would explode as he touched and kissed every inch of her. Riva surrendered to the strong, rippling heat that seemed to bring every ounce of her blood to a bubbling boil. Somewhere from a distance, she heard coos mingled with growls that seemed to be echoing in the distance.

"Riva . . . babe." She heard Lance call her, but she didn't answer because she couldn't speak, as they basked in a glow of hot passion, lost in a world of their own, then repeated the process.

The next morning, Riva rolled over and noticed that Lance was not beside her. It was Friday, but she had no intentions of getting out of bed. Following Lance's advice, she called her father, telling him that Lance wanted her to stay out of the office for a while. However, she was prepared to work from home. Mason didn't seem surprised that Riva was not returning to work until Lance solved the case. Riva said good-bye to her father and slid further underneath the covers.

So far her week had been more than hectic. Riva silently counted off the disasters that had ripped through her life like a hurricane.

Jasper had been shot, and she'd been accused of committing the dirty deed. On top of that, she now had a trespasser wandering around in her home, and she'd been chased by a white car. The telephone beside her bed rang. Riva peeked from underneath the covers and decided to wait and see if anyone other than herself was in the house to answer the call.

"Riva, you have a call from Lance." Riva recognized Tiffany's voice floating out of the bedroom intercom.

Riva reached over to the opposite of the bed and lifted the receiver. "Hello?"

"Hi," Lance said, his voice stirring memories of last night. "What're you doing today?"

"I planned to visit Jasper later."

"How much later?" Lance asked.

Riva looked at the clock. It was already ten. "I'm visiting him after lunch."

"Meet me at Bayside for lunch?" Lance asked.

"Okay," Riva agreed. Her plan to stay in bed for another hour, as she sometimes did on her day off, was out of the question. But she wasn't sure if Lance just wanted to have lunch or if he'd learned something about the case and wanted her to know. "I'll see you at twelve-thirty?"

"Twelve-thirty is good," Lance replied.

Riva replaced the receiver, got out of bed, and

drifted to the bathroom. Once she was there, she changed her mind about taking a shower and decided to soak in the tub, which was almost as big as the hot tub at the spa. She turned the nozzles, adjusting the water temperature, and headed to the closet, choosing a long, slender, coral-colored dress with thin straps, and a matching pair of heels. Riva took a bottle of cherry bubble bath from her case before crossing the bedroom to the bathroom again.

While she soaked in hot, sudsy water, Riva wondered what she was going to do about her pending divorce. She pushed the recurring thought out of her mind, and basked in the memories of her night with Lance.

Minutes and minutes later, Riva pulled herself out of the tub, promising herself that if she and Lance did get a divorce, she was going to buy herself a house with the exact same tub.

It wasn't long before she was dressed. Riva went to the linen closet, taking fresh sheets and pillowcases, making the bed, then went downstairs for a cup of coffee.

"Hi," Tiffany greeted Riva as she entered the kitchen.

"Good morning." Riva crossed to the cabinets, taking a cup and filling it with coffee, then joined Tiffany at the counter, sitting on the stool she'd sat on last night.

"I guess you got what you came for last night." Riva looked up and observed Vanessa walking in.

"Good morning, Vanessa." Riva took a sip from the coffee and wondered why Vanessa was griping this morning.

"Vanessa, would you like a cup of coffee?" Tiffany got up to get a cup. From the look Tiffany gave Vanessa, it seemed to Riva that Tiffany wanted the woman to be quiet, or at least change the subject.

"I had coffee with Lance and Adam this morning," Vanessa said to Tiffany, and pulled out a stool to sit across from Riva.

"You were up early." Riva took another sip of her coffee. The least she could do was be civil to Vanessa, even if she and Vanessa didn't like each other.

"I'm surprised I woke up early myself, since I didn't sleep much last night," Vanessa said, and picked up the *Herald*.

"Insomnia?" Riva asked, watching Vanessa turn the pages in the newspaper, as she lifted her cup for another sip of coffee.

"No, you and Lance," Vanessa said.

Me and Lance? The question slid across her mind. "No sweat!" Riva held her coffee midair.

"Yes, you and Lance." Vanessa laid the paper down on the counter. "You see, Riva, the walls in this house are thin."

"I didn't hear anything," Tiffany said.

"Tiffany, I'm not surprised. You would've slept through Hurricane Andrew if you weren't awake when the winds started blowing."

"I'm sorry," Riva said.

"Now that you know I didn't sleep last night. Be quiet the next time." Vanessa picked up the paper and peered over the top. "Or go home."

"Don't start with me this morning, Vanessa." Riva got off her stool.

"I'm just telling you what I think you should do," Vanessa said.

"Let me give you something else to think about," Riva started around the counter.

"Ladies, please!" Tiffany spoke up. "I don't understand the anger."

"Tiffany, for your information, Riva is mad because she thinks I want Lance."

"I wonder what gave her that idea," Tiffany said, and got off the stool. "I'm going out."

"Me too," Riva got up, going upstairs to get her purse.

"Good. I'll have the house to myself," Riva heard Vanessa grumbling in the kitchen.

By the time Riva came downstairs on her way to meet Lance, the house was quiet, except for the sound of music playing low in the sitting area.

Twenty-two

Lance crossed his arms over his chest and reclined against the cherry counter, facing the shopping center's parking lot as he mulled over the information he'd read on Alicia's report last night. Lance continued thinking about Alicia while he studied the cars in the parking lot outside Moses Investigations for no particular reason. Sometimes Lance found it interesting to people-watch while thinking. Lance continued his train of thought until a white car drove up. A brown-skinned man of average height and medium build got out, and Lance watched him cross the parking lot and walk up to the dark-tinted window of Lance's building, peering between the large letters that read MOSES INVESTIGATIONS. Then he walked farther down, and as he moved slowly past the window, Lance watched his gait. Slow and sneaky, Lance mused, watching the man's movement.

Riva had thought a white car chased her last night. Lance mulled over the report Bill Lee had given him when he'd called Lance to let him know that Riva had almost knocked down a telephone pole at the station. With that thought in mind, Lance decided to take a look at the car's license plate. He headed out back, hoping that he didn't miss the guy if he got into his car and drove away before Lance could get to his truck. Lance hurried down the back of the buildings and walked through the alley that led to the parking lot. He went to his truck, noticing that the car was still parked. He walked to the back of the white car and memorized the license plate. Then he moved to an electrical pole a car length from his truck. He took out a small pad from his jacket pocket and wrote the car's license plate number on the paper, then called Riva.

"Yes?" Riva answered her phone.

"Babe."

"Yes, Lance."

"I'm going to be late. Can you wait for me?"

Riva agreed to wait for him, which gave him time to tail the white car. Lance dialed Adam's telephone number and waited for him to answer. When Adam picked up, Lance read off the license plate number of the white car and asked Adam to check the owner.

A few minutes later the man returned to his car. Lance gave him time to get almost to the edge of the street before he climbed into his truck and followed two car lengths behind.

Lance followed him to a row of apartment buildings not far from Mason's community. He slowed and turned off, knowing there was a shorter way to get to these apartments, hoping that by the time he got to the street from his shortcut, the driver would be parking the car.

Lance pulled up to the curb and waited on the other side of the street, thanking whomever had come up with the idea to tint windows.

Finally the white car drove up and parked at the curb. Lance watched the man get out and walk to the apartment building—the same building that

Alicia was supposed to have moved from when she'd moved in with Mason. Lance gave him a few minutes to get inside before he went to see how easy it would be for him to get inside the building.

In order for him to gain entrance to the apartment building Lance needed a key. He walked back to his truck. Even if he got inside the building, he wouldn't know which apartment the man lived in, and besides, he didn't know who the man was since Adam hadn't called him with the car's license plate number. That meant that the car didn't necessarily have to belong to the man driving.

Maybe he was wrong about everything concerning the Jasper Wade case. Added to that, he didn't have the slightest idea who broke into Riva's apartment. Maybe he was too close to the case since he knew all the people who had been hurt.

Worst of all he couldn't prove that Alicia was spiking Mason's drinks. He had to call Mason and let him know that he was giving up the case. He punched the redial button on the cellular, calling Dae Advertising, and waited for Mason to answer his call. His answering service picked up. Lance called Mason's cellular, and got his voice mail. It wasn't like Mason to cut off contact from the world. Lance took a chance and called his home, again Lance got his voice mail.

Lance hung up and called Adam.

"What's happening, Lance?" Adam asked.

"Nothing. Did you run the license number?"

"Yeah, the car is registered to Phillip Davis," Adam said.

"I followed that guy to an apartment building, but I need a key to get inside, or I, at least, need to know someone living there. But even if I got in I wouldn't have known where to go."

"So what're we going to do?" Adam asked.

"There' nothing we can do, because we don't have proof," Lance said. "I'm going to lunch with Riva."

"Do you mind if I join you?"

"No," Lance said. "We might come up with another idea besides dropping the case."

Twenty minutes later, Lance parked in front of the small café, where Riva and Jasper's trouble began. He dropped a few coins in the meter, and crossed the street to the café.

Lance chose a table near the back so he could talk to Riva and Adam without too much interruption.

"Hi." Riva walked to the table and spoke to Lance, then sat across from him. "You look upset.:

"I think Phillip chased you last night," Lance said.

"How do you know?" Riva asked.

"I'm not sure. But I followed a white car to that apartment building that Alicia lived in before she moved in with Mason."

"Oh, yeah."

"Adam ran a check on the license plate, and the car belongs to Phillip Davis."

"That's Phillip," Riva said.

"Maybe he's not the same Phillip that works for Mason," Lance said, a trace of frustration hanging on the edge of his voice. What good was it to follow instincts if he couldn't do anything about it?

Lance looked past Riva, and she turned to see what he was looking at. She saw Adam walking toward them.

"Hi," Riva spoke to Adam as he pulled out a

chair and sat down. He gave her a quick nod. Riva thought Adam looked upset too. "I wish I could go to the police and tell them that Phillip chased me last night."

"Just because the car is white, Riva, does not mean Phillip chased you," Adam said, motioning to their table.

"This is frustrating," Riva said. She stopped talking when the waiter came over and took their lunch orders.

With all the disappointment, Riva had lost her appetite. "I'll have a lemon soda," she said.

"Will that be all?" the waiter asked.

"Yes," she said, and toyed with the menu while Lance and Adam ordered sandwiches.

"I will return soon," the waiter said, and Riva watched him leave and stop at a soda fountain at the back of the room.

Lance stretched his arms behind his head and locked his fingers together. "Now, I really do believe that Alicia knows Phillip, and he's living in her apartment."

The waiter brought Riva's drink and Lance and Adam's lunch and she listened to them discuss the case they couldn't help the police solve because they had no proof.

"Did you call Daddy?" Riva asked.

"Yes, but I didn't get an answer," Lance said.

Lance slipped his arm around Riva's waist and walked her across the street to her truck. Lance couldn't help but notice the disturbed look on her face as they crossed the street.

"I'll see you later," Riva said, opening her truck door.

Lance pulled Riva into his arms and kissed her lips lightly. He tightened his embrace, gathering her closer to him, planting tiny, feathery kisses on her lips. Reluctantly Lance released Riva and slowly backed away. He knew that Riva hadn't changed her mind about divorcing him, no matter what happened between them last night, but he could not help himself. Lance turned and jogged across the street to his truck.

Once inside his truck and behind the wheel, Lance turned the key in the ignition, started the truck, then called Vanessa. "Where are you?"

"I'm trying to enjoy my day," Vanessa said.

"Riva is going to the hospital to visit Jasper." Lance named the hospital. "Go now, wait for her, and don't let her out of your sight."

"Is there anything happening that I need to know about?" Vanessa asked.

"No, except we're thinking about getting off this case," Lance said.

"Then why do I have to guard Riva?"

"Vanessa, don't fight with me," Lance said.

Lance pushed the off button on his phone and pulled out into the street, still tasting the flavor of Riva's kiss and promising himself that he was not going to touch, kiss, or hold Riva again until they'd made a decision whether they were getting a divorce or not. Lance knew that keeping his promise was not going to be easy with Riva sharing his home and bedroom, but trying times were necessary to establish the truth.

Twenty-three

On her way to the hospital to visit Jasper, Riva concluded that she and Lance were rekindling old flames. Last night had been a perfect example, and before she allowed herself to reignite her passion, she was going to keep her cravings under control. She was honest with herself. She and Lance shared the same house and bed, and making a decision to behave herself was questionable. But she would try. When she had an urge to reach out and touch Lance, Riva promised she would restrain herself. If he reached for her, she would move away from him. She had to set rules, because she wasn't certain whether she and Lance were going to continue their marriage. Riva's rules were simple enough; all she had to do was follow through.

Riva pulled up in the hospital's parking lot, parked, and got out. She'd heard from Udell that Jasper was doing much better and had been moved to a room. Udell had given her the room number. Riva walked into the hospital, inhaling the clean air and enjoying the serenity of the lobby, as people spoke in hushed voices and laughed in whispers, as if lively merriment would disturb recovering patients on the upper floors of the medical establishment.

Riva passed the desk clerk and took the elevator

to Jasper's floor. Riva greeted nurses, dressed in white and others in light blue uniforms as she passed the nurses' station and went to Jasper's room. "Hi," Riva greeted Jasper, noticing his face breaking into a broad smile. It appeared that Jasper had lost a few pounds. "How are you feeling?" Riva pulled the chair close to Jasper's bed and sat.

"I feel okay." Jasper smiled. "I won't be lifting weights any time soon." he laughed.

"Jasper, have you ever lifted weights?" Riva giggled.

"No, but I have strict orders from the doctor. I have to go the gym at least three times a week once I'm out of here and feeling better."

"Do you know when you're going home?" Riva asked.

"I understand from the doctor that I should be well enough to go home next week."

"That sounds promising," Riva said.

"Yes. I'm thankful to be alive." Jasper pushed himself up to a sitting position, then flinched as if he was in pain.

"I'll call a nurse to help you." Riva moved toward the bed to ring the buzzer.

"I can manage," Jasper said.

"Great." Riva sat and patted his hand. "I'm glad to see you and know that you're doing well, Jasper," Riva said, truly glad to see Jasper, and know that he was alive and well.

"Mason stopped by today. He told me you're taking a few days off work." Jasper gave Riva a weak smile. "You can't work without me," he teased her.

"We have had many fights, Jasper, but you know I wouldn't physically hurt you."

"I know. But when I received the call, I went to you." Jasper paused, and smiled at Riva.

"Jasper, after all these years you still don't know the sound of my voice?"

"Riva, to tell you the truth, I was so aggravated and tired, I hardly knew the sound of my own voice." He chuckled. " But I knew how upset you were about the ad, and I thought the person who wanted to meet with me was you."

"That was a dirty trick," Riva said. "If I hadn't been able to prove I was at the spa, I would be in jail right now."

"Yes, it was a dirty trick." A frown creased Jasper's forehead. "If the bullet had been any closer . . ." His voice faded.

Jasper didn't have to say more. He could have been killed, Riva concluded.

"Do you need anything, or would you like for me to check on your apartment?" Riva offered.

"Thanks, but Udell is taking care of my apartment." Jasper looked down at the pajama top he was wearing. "Udell stopped by my house and brought pajamas over for me."

"Oh, well." Riva chuckled.

Jasper's smile widened, and he changed the subject. "Anyway, the night I stopped by to meet with you again, I'd planned to tell you to work the ad the way you liked."

Riva chuckled softly. "Well, I met with Mr. Fuller, and he understands the changes in the ad."

"When Mason and I spoke this morning, I told him it was fine with me if he wanted to give Fuller a break. But Mason said he wasn't going to help Fuller out anymore." Jasper closed his eyes.

"I don't want you worrying about work." Riva patted his hand and stood. Jasper seemed to be tiring, and she didn't want to keep him from his rest. "I'm going, but I'll try to stop by again before you go home," Riva said, patting Jasper's hand.

"Thanks, Riva," Jasper opened his eyes just a slit and closed them again.

"You're welcome, Jasper."

"Mason told me that he saw the doctor before he visited with me today, Riva," Jasper said as Riva was about to leave his room.

"He did?" Riva stopped near the door, and turned to Jasper.

"Yes. He doesn't look good, Riva. You need to check on him. Mason looked exhausted."

Riva moved back to Jasper's bedside and leaned over to him. "Stop worrying about Daddy. I'll check on him," Riva said softly, feeling Jasper's concern. "Have a nice nap," she said, and tiptoed out of the room.

If it wasn't one thing it was another. Riva understood the aftermath of a vacation. She usually needed another week to recover after one week of fun. Learning from Jasper that her father wasn't looking good and seemed exhausted was unsettling. Riva was worried that he might be ill, especially when he'd looked well the day she saw him after he'd cut his vacation short to return because of her problem. Now Riva agreed with Lance; Alicia was probably trying to kill her father. Maybe she was spiking his drinks with poison. She probably also shot Jasper or had Phillip shoot him.

Riva took the elevator to the lobby and walked out of the building. Thanks to Phillip, she had a curfew. The last time Riva had had orders to be inside the house before dark, she'd been a girl.

Riva was walking to her truck when she saw Vanessa standing next to a hunter green car. "Hello, Vanessa," Riva said as she unlocked her truck door.

"You visited so long, I thought I had to go in and get you." Vanessa unlocked the door to her car.

"Vanessa, I'm fine," Riva said, looking at her watch. She was determined not to allow Vanessa to push her buttons. "I have to stop and see my father before I go home."

"No, you're not," Vanessa said, opening the car door. "We're going home."

"I think I misunderstood you," Riva said, circling the front of her truck and planting one hand on her hip and bending one ankle against the other.

"Oh, no, you understood what I said." Vanessa moved toward Riva just as the security guard rode past.

"Vanessa, I'm going to visit my father, you're welcome to follow me." Riva went to her truck, got in, and headed to Mason's house. She didn't bother to check to see if the hunter green car was behind her.

The sun was only just beginning to slip behind a ribbon of pink and lavender clouds, and Vanessa was in a tizzy because she wanted to go home.

It seemed to take forever for Mason to open the door after Riva rang the doorbell. She waited patiently, glancing back at Vanessa, who was sitting in her car pouting.

Finally the door opened and a tired Mason greeted Riva. "Riva. Hi," Mason said, and stepped out on the small porch, his keys dangling between his fingers.

"How are you feeling?" Riva inquired, concerned for her father's health.

"I'm okay," Mason said, pulling the door behind him and inserting the key in the lock.

"I just came from visiting Jasper, and he told me

you saw the doctor today." Riva moved closer to Mason, getting a look at the dark circles under his eyes. "Jasper is right; you look exhausted."

"I'll be all right," Mason said, moving away from Riva to the edge of the porch.

Riva walked off the porch and stood in front of Mason. If her father died, she didn't know what she would do.

Mason gave Riva a weak smile. "I have to go out. Can we talk later?"

"Where is Alicia?" Riva asked.

"Alicia took a friend to the airport," Mason said, walking to the front of the garage, where his car was parked; then he stopped. "Why don't you wait until I get back? I won't be gone long."

"I can't. I'll talk to you tomorrow," Riva said, hoping that she wouldn't have to visit her father in the hospital instead of visiting him at his home. "Daddy, the doctor didn't tell you what's wrong with you?"

"No. But I took a test. As soon as I know, I'll tell you," Mason said, moving to his car.

Riva didn't know what to do or say. She couldn't tell her father that she thought Alicia or Phillip was trying to kill him.

"All right. Tomorrow." Mason got into his black Mercedes.

Riva was already headed toward her truck when Vanessa honked her horn.

"Be patient," Riva yelled out to Vanessa, then got into the truck, started the engine, and drove off down the street, driving at least fifty miles an hour.

The phone rang and Riva slowed as she dug around in her purse, then pulled out her telephone. "Yes?" Riva answered.

"Riva." Theresa said.

"Yes, Theresa." From the sound of Theresa's voice, Riva knew her cousin was upset.

"Dylan called me last night and we went out."

Riva smiled. "That's nice. Did you enjoy yourself?"

"Riva, Dylan is boring," Theresa complained. "I'm not going out with him again."

Riva chuckled. "What do you want me to do?"

"Nothing. I wanted to tell you how boring he is. When I went jogging this morning and I didn't see your truck, I knew you didn't stay at home last night," Theresa said to Riva.

"No, I didn't stay at home last night," Riva replied.

"So where did you stay, in a hotel?" Theresa asked Riva.

"No, I'm staying with Lance," Riva replied.

"Give me Lance's address, I'm visiting you tonight," Theresa said. "We need to talk." Theresa was still talking when Riva punched in the code at the gate, giving her access to Lance's community.

"Theresa, do you want to talk about Dylan?" Riva drove through the gate, knowing how much Dylan wanted to meet someone.

"Not really, I'm just saying that he's boring. All he talked about was his ex-wife, his divorce, and how he was buying a house, and he asked me a thousand personal questions."

Riva laughed. "I tried. I'm sorry your date with Dylan didn't work out."

"I'll be over there in a little while," Theresa said, and hung up.

Riva pulled up to the edge of the driveway, leaving room for Lance and Adam to park in the garage or the driveway, and got out. She noticed

Vanessa had parked on the opposite side of the street and was crossing over to the house. Her forehead was wrinkled into a frown, and she looked as if she never smiled.

"Vanessa, are you always angry?" Riva asked Vanessa before she realized that she was asking. "Don't you ever go out and have fun?"

"What's it to you if I never go out and have fun?" Vanessa stopped in front of Riva. "I work all the time, and maybe if I didn't have to baby-sit you, I could go out tonight."

"What, you don't like your job?" Riva asked curiously.

"I like my job, Riva. Unfortunately my job doesn't give me the opportunity to go out and meet Mr. Right."

Riva knew she and Vanessa would never be friends, and Riva's reasons were valid. Not only did Vanessa have her claws out to grab Lance, but she was rude and just plain mean. However, Riva decided that as long as she and Vanessa were sharing the same house, she would be nice to her. "Would you like to meet a nice man?"

"I don't think there are any nice men left. Thanks to you, the chance I thought I could have with Lance is gone."

Riva didn't speak. Vanessa had just verified what she'd suspected. However, Riva wasn't going to allow Vanessa's desires to stop her from being civilized.

"Vanessa, would you like to meet a friend of mine?" Riva asked as she and Vanessa walked toward the house.

"Does he have a disease?" Vanessa asked as she continued toward the front door.

"No, and never mind," Riva said. It was clear

that Vanessa didn't like her and thought she was trying to palm off a diseased man on her.

"All right, who would you like for me to meet?" Vanessa stopped.

"His name is Dylan Edwards, and he's looking for a friend," Riva said.

"Really? And this little introduction to Dylan wouldn't be because you're afraid I'm going to take your man?"

Riva stopped and took a deep breath before she exhaled slowly. "You are a miserable woman." Riva started walking to the house, then stopped again. "Vanessa, even though Lance and I aren't divorced yet, if I think you're even thinking about flirting with him, I'll snatch your hair out!"

"Okay . . . okay." Vanessa smiled. "Is Dylan good-looking?"

"He's handsome," Riva said, thinking that Vanessa couldn't be too concerned about looks. The date she had been with a few nights ago would never win the Mr. Handsome of the Year contest.

"When can I meet him?" Vanessa asked as she unlocked the door.

"I'll have to talk to Dylan first," Riva said.

"Riva, if this is some evil little scheme you're playing—"

"Vanessa, be serious. Why would I do a thing like that?"

"Ha!" Vanessa threw her head back and strolled through the door.

Riva didn't bother to go into the kitchen; she went to the bedroom and pulled off her dress, changing into an old pair of black shorts, since those were the only ones that her intruder hadn't thrown on the floor. Riva pulled on a tank top and headed for the stairs.

From the top of the staircase, she heard Theresa at the front door: "We're here to see Riva."

"She's upstairs," Riva heard Vanessa say to Theresa.

"Riva!" Theresa was as loud and talkative as ever, Riva concluded, and went downstairs, wondering who Theresa had brought with her.

"Laura." Riva ran down the last two steps. "What's up, girlfriend?"

"I figured the only way I was going to see you was to ride with Theresa." Laura chuckled, shifting three boxes of pizza into Riva's arms as they headed to the sitting area and kitchen.

"Thanks for the food." Riva carried the pizzas to the kitchen.

"Oh, Lord, Tiffany, the whole clan is here." Riva heard Vanessa speaking to Tiffany and realized that no matter how civil she was to Vanessa, the woman would still hate her.

"That must be Vanessa," Laura whispered to Riva. "Theresa told me about her."

"Uh-huh, that's Vanessa," Riva said.

"Child, please." Laura giggled. "Miss Thing got issues."

"Vanessa has a few issues, and one is that she doesn't want me living here," Riva said.

"Anyway," Theresa said, "where is the music, the wine, and the men?"

"Tiffany and Vanessa, this is my girlfriend Laura and my cousin Theresa."

"Hi," Tiffany said. "I'm Tiffany." Tiffany looked at Vanessa. "This is Vanessa. What kind of music do you like?"

"Anything good," Theresa said.

"Oh, yeah," Tiffany said, opening the entertainment cabinet and taking out a tray filled with discs.

"Play whatever you like," Tiffany said to Theresa, then took a bottle of wine from a cabinet and stuck it in the freezer to get cold.

Riva, Theresa, Laura, Vanessa, and Tiffany ate pizza, talked, laughed, and drank wine. "I'm introducing Vanessa to Dylan," Riva said to Theresa.

"Knock yourself out." Theresa grinned. "She can have him."

"So this man is one of Theresa's leftovers?" Vanessa asked, overhearing Riva and Theresa's conversation.

"Girl, please," Riva said, turning to find Vanessa standing behind her.

"Listen, Vanessa," Theresa said. "I had every intention of dating Dylan. But let me tell you right now"—Theresa broke the crust off the edge of the slice of pizza she was holding, nibbled on the cheese—"Dylan is not a bad-looking man, he's got a business and plenty of money, he dresses like a model, and he's boring as hell."

"Theresa, stop before I choke on this pizza." Laura laughed.

"Well, I'm just letting Vanessa know what's she in for." Theresa smiled. "Don't get me wrong," Theresa added. "Dylan and I went out once, and that was all it took for me to know that he was not the one. I don't care how much money he has."

"You don't care how much money who has?" Lance walked in, challenging Theresa as he moved to the other end of the curved kitchen counter, snatching a paper towel off the roll and taking a slice of pizza from the open box.

Theresa smiled. "This conversation is for women. Stay out of it, Lance." She went back to eating her pizza.

Lance chuckled. "All right, Theresa."

For the first time since her troubles began, Riva felt good. It was just nice to sit among her friends and family and housemates, enjoying pizza, wine, music, and laughter.

"Hello," Adam walked in and said.

"Hi," everyone said in unison.

"Hmm." Theresa groaned, eyeing Adam as he went to a closet at the back of the sitting room and pulled out a stool.

"Excuse me, Theresa, will you step over here for a minute?" Laura beckoned to Riva's cousin.

"You're gonna get it now, T." Riva smiled.

"What do you want, Laura?" Theresa asked.

"Don't even think about flirting with Adam." Laura smiled sweetly. "And I'm not teasing."

Lance's gentle chuckle at Laura's remark filtered through the room as he moved behind the counter and sat onto the stool behind Riva, forcing her to scoot forward.

"Girl, please, Adam is hot." Theresa giggled, moving back to her stool.

Riva finished eating and leaned back against Lance's chest. It felt good being close to him, inhaling his subtle masculine cologne that had begun wearing off by the end of the workday. She sank closer to him, feeling the beat of his heart against her back, and reminded herself of her rules.

Riva's favorite slow song began to play. She slid off the stool and grabbed Lance's hand, pulling him off the stool. "May I have this dance?" Riva asked Lance as if they were attending a formal affair, chuckling lightly.

"I thought you would never ask." Lance slipped his arms around Riva as they headed to the sitting room.

Riva felt as if she would melt against Lance, remembering all the times that they had had together before she'd dismissed him from her life. Lance leaned down and nuzzled the side of her neck.

"This is not fair," Riva heard Vanessa shout out over the music. "Riva, why don't you call Dylan?"

Riva looked up at Lance. "Do you mind if Dylan comes over?"

"Yeah, I mind," Lance said.

"I told Vanessa about Dylan, and she wants to meet him," Riva said.

"Why does she have to meet him here?" Lance asked.

"Don't tell me you're still upset because I went to lunch with Dylan." Riva stopped dancing and looked at him.

"Riva, Dylan likes you."

"We're friends."

"Baby, you may be just a friend to Dylan, but he has different ideas," Lance replied.

"Come on, Lance. Vanessa really wants to meet him."

Lance looked back at Vanessa and then at Riva. "All right. Just this one time, and after tonight he can't come back and visit you."

"Is there a problem?" Vanessa asked Riva and Lance.

"No, Vanessa," Riva said. "Theresa, call Dylan."

"If Theresa calls Dylan, he might think she's calling for herself," Vanessa said.

"Oh, no, he won't. Me and homeboy have a good understanding," Theresa said, picking up the receiver and dialing 411. "I forgot his phone number."

"Tell him to bring a friend," Tiffany called out

to Theresa from across the room as she sorted through more songs to play.

"Tell Dylan to bring two friends," Riva said to Theresa. "Don't you need a dance partner?"

"You got that right." Theresa held up her hand as if she wanted complete quiet as she spoke to Dylan. Riva didn't pay much attention to the call Theresa was making; she was enjoying being cradled in Lance's arms and wishing the song would never end.

The evening turned into a full-blown party when Dylan and his buddies, Randy and Clint, arrived.

Lance directed Riva to the pantry. She took out potato chips, pretzels, and nuts, filling the bowls Vanessa took from the cabinet, while Adam went to get the Jack Daniel's and the Johnnie Walker Red from the liquor cabinet in the dining room. Lance excused himself, disappearing with his truck keys, and returned later with what looked like a third of the deli department from the supermarket, along with a steak for everyone.

After dinner and more dancing, Riva noticed that Vanessa and Dylan seemed to be getting along well. Tiffany and Clint were dancing, and Theresa was showing Randy the latest dance steps that she had probably learned from one of the teens in the Key Lock program.

Riva sat next to Lance on the sofa, sipping wine and trying not to think sexy thoughts about him. She'd set rules for herself, and made promises that she would not seduce Lance. So far, in the short time she'd shared Lance's bedroom, she hadn't broken her promise since the last time they'd made love. Riva was proud that she was behaving herself.

"I'll talk to you tomorrow," Riva said. After she got off the sofa, she walked past Theresa on her way upstairs. Riva got Theresa's attention. "Good night."

"I'll talk to you tomorrow," Theresa said, smiling.

"Okay," Riva said, noticing that Theresa seemed happier than Riva had seen her in a long time. Riva headed out of the room and into the living room to take the stairs, seeing Laura and Adam speaking in whispers. Everyone seemed to be going on with their lives, and in spite of herself, Riva was happy the women were enjoying themselves.

"Riva." Riva heard Lance behind her.

She waited at the foot of the stairs for Lance to pick up his jacket off the chair where he'd dropped it when he came home, before they went upstairs to the bedroom.

At the threshold of the bedroom door, a vision of hooking her arms around Lance's neck and kissing him, long, soft and sweet, backing inside the room, forcing him to follow her, played across her mind like a motion picture, but she dismissed the thought. Once inside, Riva tugged at the edge of her shirt, pulling the red tank top over her head and tossing it to the chair, while Lance turned off the intercom and discarded his shirt and pants. Neither one spoke to the other. Lance sat on the bed, one leg propped on the bed and the other on the floor, a position Riva was certain would separate her from her promise. So, to keep herself out of trouble, she went to the closet for her gown and housecoat and headed to the bathroom.

Minutes later, after a quick shower, Riva walked to the bedroom with plans to behave herself. She squeezed lotion into her palm and began massaging it on her body.

"Let me do that," Lance offered, squeezing the

sweet-smelling lotion in his palm and sliding the strap of her nightgown off her shoulders.

Riva closed her eyes, enjoying his soft touch.

"No." Riva turned to take the lotion from Lance, stopping him from touching her. She couldn't help but notice the heated desire smoldering in his eyes. "I think I can—" Riva started, but was interrupted as Lance gathered her in his arms, his hands stroking her hips, igniting a fiery passion that she knew would force her to break all her rules. Riva didn't care anymore. She tingled and shivered with excitement, not wanting to stop. She felt feverish as Lance's mouth covered hers again. Riva's thoughts began to spin, her common sense warning her to stop, but she would not listen as Lance lifted her in his arms and gently laid her on the bed, exploring and sampling every inch of her body, until Riva felt as if she were spinning on an axis, reeling in space and time. Riva accepted Lance's caresses, allowing scorching flames to flow until they were satisfied.

Lance turned off the light and lay awake, staring at the ceiling while Riva slept. He'd promised himself that he wouldn't touch Riva again until they'd discussed their pending divorce. Lance looked at Riva. She was so sweet and he had broken the promise he'd made to himself.

The phone rang, drawing Lance out of his regrets. "Yeah," Lance answered, wondering who could be calling him at this time of the night.

"Did you talk to your father-in-law?" Bill Lee asked.

"Not yet," Lance said, intending to call Mason the next day to get permission to put a camera in his house. That was the only way they would know if Alicia was lacing his drinks with phenol. "I'll talk to him tomorrow."

"Mason might let you look around his house and see what you can find," Bill said.

"I don't see why he wouldn't," Lance said.

"Who's that, Lance?" Riva asked, sounding as if she was half asleep.

"Bill," Lance said.

"Huh?" Bill said.

"I was talking to Riva," Lance said.

The next day Lance was given permission to put cameras in Mason's house. However, nothing was going as planned because Mason was on his way to the hospital after he'd learned that traces of carbolic acid had been found in his blood.

Even though Mason sounded tired, he seemed as anxious as Lance to find out what was going on inside his home and gave Lance permission to search his house.

When he finished talking to Mason, Lance called Riva asking her to meet him for lunch.

Riva agreed to have lunch with him, and Lance hung up. He leaned back in his chair again, planting his long legs on the top of his desk. He suspected Alicia was at the core of the crimes. Finding out if there was poison in Mason's home that matched the poison in his system was important.

Lance quieted his mind. He had to stand still and collect his thoughts. If Alicia was involved, he would get her.

A knock on the door drew Lance out of his pondering. "The door is open," Lance said.

"Lance." Grace Cain crossed over to Lance and sat in the chair in front of his desk.

A smile lit Lance's face, matching his mother's grin. "What're you doing here?" Lance pushed away from the desk, swinging his legs off the top.

"I haven't seen you in a while."

His mother's cheerful smile was exactly what he needed. "I've been busy." Lance straightened in his chair.

"Now tell me that you're all right." Grace crossed one leg over the other and rested her purse in her lap.

Lance glanced up at her and then down at the desk. She knew him and from the expression on her face, she was certain things were not as great as he wanted her to think. "I'm fine," Lance answered his mother.

"How is Riva?" his mother asked, as she always had before he and Riva had separated.

"Riva is doing well." Lance started from the best place he knew to begin. He watched his mother lean back in her chair, legs still crossed and purse perched on her lap. "In a couple of months, we'll have our divorce."

Grace Cain clutched her purse with one manicured hand and stroked the smooth black leather with the tip of her finger. "It would be nice if you and Riva could work out your differences."

"It *would* be nice." Lance kept his gaze lowered, not wanting his mother to see his pain. "Riva and I will do what's best."

"I do worry about you, Lance. I think you work too much, and you don't get enough free time." Grace leaned toward the desk, clearly concerned for her son's happiness.

"You're right; I plan to take a vacation as soon as I solve the case I'm working on."

"I can hardly wait for you to finish." Grace rose

from the chair. "I can't visit with you long. I was buying myself a tennis racket and stopped by on my way from the store."

Lance chuckled, getting up and walking around the desk. After his father died, in addition to her job, his mother kept herself busy. She'd learned to play tennis when Lance was in his late teens, and once a month on a Saturday nights she and her girlfriends went on a dinner cruise. Lance was sure his mother enjoyed the casino more than any other activity on the cruise ship.

"Samuel called last night." Grace moved toward the door.

"He did?" Lance was glad to hear the news. He also knew that Samuel wanted a definite answer from him on whether he was buying his house or not. "How is he?"

"Samuel is doing fine. He'll be here next week." Grace opened the door.

A grin crossed Lance's face. A year ago he'd noticed that Samuel and his mother's relationship seemed to have changed. Before Samuel left to take care of family business back home in New Orleans, he and his mother had begun going to dinner and to other events every week. His mother assured Lance that she and Samuel were just friends and enjoyed many of the same things.

Lance never pried for information concerning her relationship with his mentor. But he was sure his mother liked Samuel more than she was admitting. Lance smiled to himself. Every time she talked about Samuel, Lance noticed the light in her eyes.

"I'll see you soon," Lance said to his mother, walking her to her car. "Be careful."

"I'm always careful. I want you to stay safe," Grace said as she got into her car.

. "I'll you talk to you later," Lance said, and went to his truck. He and Riva had a lunch date.

"Lance, I do believe that Alicia is crazy enough to poison Daddy. You should've seen his eyes." Riva picked up a French fry and bit off the end. "Daddy said he thinks there's something wrong inside the house," Riva said while she chewed.

Lance bit into the chicken breast sandwich and ate, looking as if his mind was far away. "That's why I had a search warrant ordered," he said.

"Alicia probably won't be home. I would like to be there when the officers search the house," Riva said.

"She probably is crazy," Lance said. "Riva, I need your key to Mason's house."

"Do you think you'll find the poison?"

"I hope so," Lance said.

"Suppose she carries the poison in her purse, and while she visits Daddy at work, she drops the poison in the water he keeps in his office?" Riva speculated.

"No, Adam and I checked the surveillance cameras in the offices, and there is no indication that Mason's water is being spiked." Lance took a long drink from his cola. "Mason has to be getting the drug from home. The drug is either in his food or his drink."

"It's not in his food, because Alicia doesn't cook," Riva replied.

"Okay," Lance said, taking another bite of the sandwich.

Twenty-four

Lance unlocked the front door to Mason's house, walked in and stood in the foyer. He glanced around, noticing the living room door was open, and Alicia's wedding gown was draped casually over the back of the sofa.

Lance walked into the study to Mason's liquor cabinet. The cabinet was clear except for the multicolored Chinese vase sitting on top. He pulled opened the double doors, displaying a half-full bottle of rum, and several unopened bottles of Scotch.

Lance set the bottles on the floor, searching for a container filled with clear liquid. He set the liquor bottles back on the shelf and closed the cabinet doors.

Riva had said that Alicia couldn't cook, but it wouldn't hurt to look in the kitchen, Lance thought, leaving the study and going to the kitchen to search the cabinets, noticing the camera that had been installed earlier that day.

He found nothing that looked like poison underneath the kitchen sink or in the drawers. After checking the rest of the house and finding nothing to prove that Mason had been poisoned in his home, Lance was beginning to think that Riva was right. Maybe Alicia carried the poison in her purse.

He walked back to the study and stood staring

at the mahogany liquor cabinet before he walked over to Mason's desk. He looked in all the drawers, even the pencil holder on top of the desk and still found nothing.

Lance went back to the cabinet and picked up the vase, careful not to drop it.

He looked inside, seeing a bag. He slowly turned the vase upside down, moving the blue velvet bag to the mouth of the vase and then pulled the bag out.

He set the vase on top of the cabinet and began removing the contents from the bag. He fished around and felt a small bottle. Lance carried the bag to the kitchen and ripped a paper towel from the roll—just in case he'd found the poison that was in Mason's blood, he wanted the fingerprints of the person that handled the bottle of liquid.

He pulled out a small clear bottle of liquid and called Bill. If he could get the liquid tested positive for phenol he would be making progress, all he had to do was get the bottle back to Mason's before Alicia came home from work. Still, if she was seen on camera even handling the bottle, there was still no proof that she laced Mason's rum. He would like to see her lacing the liquor.

Riva returned to work. She could hardly concentrate for wondering what the test results would show in the liquid that had been found in the liquor cabinet. Finally she settled down, only to have her mind and her thoughts travel to her and Lance. They were still sharing the same bed. However, they both kept their distance while they slept. Riva could hardly stand the arrangement. It was hard lying next to him at night while they both kept a cool distance from each other. However, after their last night of lovemaking, Riva had decided that she would keep her distance.

Twenty-five

The next day Lance awaited the results of the test on the liquid he had found in Mason's liquor cabinet. Lance sat on the stool behind the receptionist's desk. Every fiber in his body told him that the substance the police had found was the poison that had landed Mason in the hospital.

The phone rang. "Moses," Lance answered the call. "What's up?" Lance asked Bill Lee. He listened to the officer without speaking. Finally Bill hung up. "Yes!" Lance said, raising his fist.

The drug that had been retrieved from Mason's liquor cabinet matched the drug in Mason's body, however, he still could only speculate that Alicia put the poison in Mason's drink.

Lance stared out into the parking lot from where he was sitting and allowed his mind to skip to Riva. It was torture being next to her at night and not being able to hold her. However, it seemed that Riva wasn't interested in making their marriage work. Although she'd shown interest in his work, Riva's main interest seemed to be related to her father. If Mason hadn't been involved, he doubted he and Riva would be as close as they were.

However, Lance allowed himself to do a little wishful thinking, hoping that Riva would change her mind about how dangerous his work was. He banished his wishful thinking. Lance doubted Riva would ever think his work was safe. She'd never forgotten the chase and crash, and how they both could have been killed the day the ex-con had decided to take out his revenge on Lance.

The time was upon him now, and Lance knew it wouldn't be long before he and Riva would go their separate ways.

"Lance, I found an apartment, I hope you're happy." Vanessa walked up to the desk, drawing Lance out of his thoughts.

"You're right. I'm glad." Lance chuckled. "When are you moving?"

"I'll be out by the end of the week," Vanessa replied.

"That soon?" Lance was surprised.

"Would you like for me stay longer?" Lance noticed Vanessa was smiling—and for the second time since the night of the party, when Vanessa had first met Dylan. Lance realized Vanessa was happy.

"I'm glad for you," Lance said.

"Thanks. I'm leaving early so I can go home and pack."

Lance smiled and nodded. "Vanessa, we got the test results from the drug that was found at Mason's."

"Oh, yeah?" Vanessa's smile faded.

"The poison matched the poison in Mason's blood," Lance said.

"Did you tell Riva?" Vanessa asked as she headed out the door, leaving to go home and pack to move into her apartment.

"I told her."

He lifted the handset to call Riva again. It wasn't much, but finding the poison—even he could prove Alicia hid it in the vase—was worth a cele-

bration. "Riva, we have to celebrate," he said when
she answered.

"What're we celebrating?" Riva asked. "Did we
win the lottery?"

Lance chuckled. "No, but finding the poison
might be a reason to celebrate."

Riva's laughter floated out to him.

"I thought maybe we could go to the movies."

"The movies?" Riva laughed again, as if he'd
told her a joke.

"I didn't think you wanted to go out on a serious
date." Lance chuckled.

"Are you talking about dinner, wine, and dancing?" Riva asked.

"Yes, but you wouldn't be interested. Right?"
Riva's slow breathing reached out to him while he
waited for an answer to his question.

"Why don't you make dinner reservations," Riva
finally said. "I'm leaving work early so I can visit
with Daddy. I'll be home soon."

"All right," Lance said slowly. He could hardly
believe that Riva had accepted his invitation to have
dinner with him, regardless of the occasion. "I'll
make reservations at our favorite—the restaurant
we like." Lance stopped himself from saying they
would have dinner at their favorite restaurant.

"Sounds good," Riva said. "Lance, thanks for
helping Daddy."

Lance hung up. He would enjoy one last night
with her and hold the memory next to his heart
forever.

Riva dressed in a long, slender black linen halter
dress, black heels, and her best jewelry. She applied
her makeup and kept her mind free from thinking

about Lance. She knew their celebration was because of Lance's work to help find the people responsible for trying to hurt her and the people she loved. Nevertheless, Riva wished that she and Lance could stay married.

She dabbed her favorite perfume on her pulse points and went downstairs to wait for Lance. Lance refused to stay in the bedroom with her while she dressed. A pang settled in her stomach, and she knew that whether she went through with the divorce or not, Lance obviously didn't want her to be his wife anymore.

Soft music mingled with quiet conversations filled the restaurant, and it was like old times as Riva and Lance enjoyed a romantic dinner and evening under cozy dim lights together. Riva couldn't help but notice how handsome Lance looked, dressed in a dark suit, looking as if he should have been on a runway modeling for a men's magazine.

Riva ate her dinner and sipped wine while Lance discussed Jasper's case.

Finally, Riva changed the subject. "Lance, do you think we can stay married?" Riva asked him, not because they were sharing an evening together, but because she'd given her mother's advice serious consideration. She *was* like her father, and coming to terms with that fact was not easy. She had no right to force Lance out of a career he loved.

"Are you sure you want to stay married to me?" Lance asked Riva.

"I was thinking that maybe we could make our marriage work," Riva said, beginning to wonder if Lance was happy the way things were.

"Why don't we think about what we're going to

do for a few days, and by then maybe we'll have an answer."

"We?" Riva looked at Lance over the rim of her wineglass. She was probably right; Lance had moved forward and she'd lost the only man she wanted to spend her life with.

"Riva, I love you, and you know that. But I have been on an emotional roller coaster. I'm not going to put myself through that pain again. If you want me, you'll have to accept what I do for a living."

Riva noticed that Lance had been cool toward her lately. Or had Lance found someone else to fill his life? "I'm being honest," Riva said.

"I want you be certain that you want to stay married to me." Lance finished his wine and pushed away from the table. "If you feel the same way at the end of the week, we'll talk," Lance said.

Riva lowered her gaze, hiding the tears that gathered in her eyes. She understood Lance, and she couldn't blame him. She didn't resist when he pulled her up from the table and led her to the dance floor in the back of the restaurant. She settled in his arms and savored their close contact, knowing it would probably be her last with him.

Twenty-six

The weekend finally arrived. Riva rolled out of bed Saturday morning, knowing that she had to give Lance an answer to his question concerning their divorce. She also knew it was up to her to solve the problem, and she decided that honesty was the best way as she made her way to the shower. She'd had another sleepless night, knowing Lance was sleeping beside her, though they refused to touch each other.

Riva finished her shower and dressed in a pair of jeans and a T-shirt, dabbed on her favorite perfume, and went downstairs.

The house was quiet and held a special serenity. Large boxes were stacked in the living room, and Riva wondered who was moving, Tiffany or Vanessa—or were both women moving out? Riva walked past the brown cardboard boxes. As she started into the kitchen to pour herself a cup of coffee, she noticed that Vanessa was on the patio.

The doorbell rang and Vanessa hurried inside.

"Riva, I'm moving," Vanessa said, opening the front door. A man wearing a white shirt with the name of a moving company walked in. Riva greeted him, noticing a white truck with name of the moving company written on the side of the truck's door.

"That's good," Riva said.

"I hope to see you again," Vanessa said, as the man rolled a box out to the truck on a dolly.

"I hope to see you again too, Vanessa," Riva said, going to the kitchen, doubting that she would ever see Vanessa after today.

Riva went to the kitchen and poured herself a cup of coffee as waves of sadness washed over her. The weeks she had lived with Lance hadn't been bad. She'd watched him work with his housemates, and noticed how he made hard work look like fun. Riva dropped a cube of sugar in the coffee and reached for a stirrer on the counter. She stirred slowly as her mind wandered to the life she was choosing for herself.

While Riva drank her coffee, she called the hospital to speak to her father to let him know that she would be by in a few minutes to visit him.

"He was released about an hour ago," the nurse said to Riva.

"An hour ago?" Riva asked the nurse. She'd visited her father just yesterday, and he hadn't said that he was expecting to be released the next day.

"Yes, the doctor left orders to release Mr. Dae last night." Riva listened to the nurse, glad that her father was well enough to go home. "I'll see him at home," Riva said, and hung up.

Riva got off the stool, poured out the rest of her coffee, and washed the cup. When she finished she called her father. She didn't get an answer, so she ran upstairs for her purse and truck keys, noticing that Vanessa and her boxes were gone.

She grabbed her purse and keys and hurried down the stairs, bumping into Lance.

"Hey, girl, where're you going in such a rush?"

Riva felt his hands clasp her waist, keeping her from falling.

"Daddy has been released from the hospital. I'm going by to see how he's feeling."

Lance chuckled, and Riva allowed him to guide her into the kitchen.

"Wait, I'll give you'll a ride," Lance said, heading toward the garage door.

Riva followed Lance, thinking how nice it was for him to drive her in his truck instead of her fighting the weekend traffic this morning. Riva stepped into the shadowed garage which was lit by a few bands of sunshine crawling through an upper window in the wall. Riva gasped, letting out a low whistle. "When did you buy the car?" she asked, admiring the black two-seater sports car.

"I ordered it last week," Lance said, unlocking the door for Riva and waiting for her to get inside. "And I picked it up this morning."

Riva sat and as she waited for Lance to get in, she knew her life with Lance was over. When she'd met him, he had owned a sports car, but he sold it to help with the down payment on their apartment. She'd begged him not to sell his car, because Mason had offered them the down payment on the apartment. Lance was a proud man, and refused to take money from her father. It seemed now that he was ready to be single again, and another wave of sadness swept over Riva as they backed out of the garage and silently headed to Mason's house.

Fifteen minutes later, Lance pulled up in Mason's driveway. Riva got out and ran to the door, ringing the bell.

Mason opened the door and Riva grabbed him, giving him a hug. "Thank God you're okay," she said, releasing her father.

"I'm glad to be feeling better," Mason said.

"All we have to do now is prove that she poisoned you," Lance said, as they sat to discuss the near-death horrors and the physical and mental pain they'd all experienced. "Alicia is gone."

"Does Mother know that you're okay?" Riva asked Mason, then remembered that her mother was out of the country.

"No, Udell told me that Paula was on a business trip." Mason straightened in his easy chair and stretched out his legs.

Lance's chuckle filled the room. "Mason, not all women are bad."

"I guess you're right." Mason smiled. "But I never thought Alicia would poison me.".

"With any luck, we won't see Alicia again," Riva said.

Riva and Lance talked to Mason for a while longer.

"I'll see you, Daddy," Riva said, getting up, with Lance standing up beside her.

Mason stood. "I'll be back to work Monday."

"Are you sure you're feeling up to working?" Riva asked Mason.

"Yes, Riva. "I'm sure." Mason grinned; then his smile faded. "Jasper will be out a while longer, and I'm going to have to find someone to take his place."

"Temporarily," Riva added, as she and Lance walked out to the car.

"Yes," Mason said.

"Oh, Daddy," Riva called out to him while Lance unlocked the car door. "Alicia had planned a birthday party for you. Are you interested?" Riva asked, telling Mason which evening Alicia had planned to have the party.

Mason laughed. "I think I could use a good party."

Riva got into the car and closed the door. She could use a party too.

Riva and Lance drove home, discussing the case and wondering when the police were going to find Jasper's shooter. There was no telling where he was hiding, since he'd disappeared. Riva and Lance discussed Phillip until they reached home, and Lance drove the shiny black sports car into the garage, leaving the garage door open.

Riva went inside, still not ready to discuss the divorce. However, she knew Lance wasn't waiting any longer to know her plans. It was Saturday, and time to broach the subject of whether or not they were divorcing. Riva watched Lance slide a tape out of the entertainment center and insert it in the player near the kitchen entrance on the wall. He pushed the button, and Riva knew every room in the house was filled with the sweet melody of the love song vibrating the walls.

Riva walked to the pool table in the sitting room and lifted a pool cue off the rack on the wall. "Let's play," Riva challenged Lance, stalling for time.

"I don't know why you want to play me. You can't win." Lance let out a short laugh.

"I've won a few times with you, so who's to say I won't win this time?" Riva asked, wishing that she didn't have to listen to the lyrics to the song: "If you think you're lonely now, wait until tonight." The words seemed to take on a new meaning for Riva. The shattered pieces of her life were still disconnected, like a puzzle with too many lost pieces. Riva felt as if her life was never going to fit together again. She chalked the tip of her cue, and watched Lance take a cue off the wall.

"You can shoot first." Riva stood away from the table, watching Lance chalk the tip of his pool cue.

"Are you sure you want me to take the first shot?" Lance seemed to study her, and Riva knew he had no idea what the rules were going to be. But first, before they played, Riva decided to talk to Lance about their pending divorce. The quicker she told him her feelings, the better she would feel.

"I think we should talk about the divorce first," Riva said, and watched Lance. He seemed to be studying her expression.

"All right." Lance sat on the edge of the table. Riva sat next to him. "I really love you."

"Okay," Lance said.

"I must admit that I allowed my fears to cloud my judgment."

"All right," Lance said to her.

"Recently, I realized that . . ." Riva stopped and watched Lance. It was hard for her to admit the truth, but she had to tell him, and she was ashamed of herself. "I realized that I was trying to control you. I guess I was trying to stop you from doing the work you loved."

"Okay," Lance said, and she watched a smile play around his mouth.

"I'm sorry," Riva said. "So I understand if you don't want to reconcile our marriage. I—"

"You're forgiven." Lance interrupted her, then laid his cue on the table and clasped both hands on the edge of the pool table.

"I still love you . . . I don't want a divorce. But I understand that you are afraid of my work, and you worry." Riva watched him lift himself off the edge of the pool table and move toward her.

"I'm not going to tell you that I won't worry about you while you're working, but I don't want a divorce," Riva said.

"Come here." Lance reached for her.

Riva went to him.

"I love you, and the more I tried to get you out of my system, the more I wanted us to stay married." Lance lowered his head, brushing his lips against hers, arousing tingling sensations in her. "I thought I was going to lose my mind." His feathery kiss deepened as he parted her lips with his, and Riva sank against him.

"Hello," Riva heard Tiffany speak as she entered the room, and she and Lance pulled out each other's embrace. "I'm sorry I interrupted," Tiffany apologized.

"Hi." Riva smiled at her, not embarrassed that Tiffany had walked in on her and Lance. She noticed that Lance didn't speak; instead he let out an irritated sigh.

"I just wanted to say good-bye," Tiffany said. "And to thank Lance for letting Erin and me stay until we could move into our condo."

"You're welcome, Tiffany," Lance said, and sat back on the edge of the pool table.

"Riva, I hope to see you again," Tiffany said, turning to leave.

"You will see Riva again." Lance glanced at Riva and she felt her heart warm.

"I'm glad." Tiffany smiled. "I'll see you guys later. I have to pick up Erin."

"Take care, Tiffany." Riva watched her leave, and again the house was quiet, except for the music piping from the speakers on the wall.

"Are you ready to play?" Riva asked Lance, and picked up her cue. She had other plans in store for Lance now that she knew they weren't getting a divorce.

"Yeah, let's play." Lance grinned and grabbed his pool cue.

"If I win you'll have to do everything I want you to do." Riva grinned mischievously.

"I hope the rule applies to you as well. Because I've got things I've been wanting you to do to me for days." Lance's grin matched Riva's. He racked the balls and split them, scattering the array of colors across the table.

As Lance aimed and shot one ball after another into the pockets, Riva hoped she could live up to her own promise to win the game.

The phone rang and Lance missed a shot.

"I'll get it," Riva said, going to answer the call, listening to Lance let out a disgruntled moan. She knew the ringing telephone had broken his concentration as he rose from his bending position over the pool table after he missed the shot he aimed for.

"The caller hung up," Riva said, taking her place at the pool table. Now was her chance to show Lance her improved pool skills. She wasn't an expert, but she was better than the last time she'd shot pool with Lance.

Riva called the ball she intended to pocket, aimed, and hit it, scattering the balls across the table, pocketing the one she'd chosen. By the time they'd finished the game, Riva had won. She hung up her pool cue and rested one hand on her hip, then crooked her forefinger and beckoned to Lance. "Come here."

Lance chuckled. "What are you going to do to me?" He moved to her.

"You'll know soon enough," Riva said, standing

behind him and pushing him out of the sitting room to the stairs.

"Does this have something to do with your rules?"

"Yes." Riva leaned around, giving Lance a mischievous grin.

"Don't play with me, Riva." Lance chuckled again.

"Who's playing?" She pushed him into the bedroom at the top of the stairs and closed the door. "Do you remember when we were first married and you asked me why I didn't want to be the aggressor?" Riva touched his waist and snatched his shirt out of his pants, and began lifting the shirt up over Lance's head.

"Yes." Lance took off his shirt and hurled it across the room.

"I didn't understand then that your idea might have been fun." Riva unsnapped the silver catch on his pants and drew the zipper down, pushing the pants over his narrow hips.

"I think you were aggressive a few weeks ago," Lance said to her.

While he discarded his trousers, Riva stripped down to her black teddy and went to her bag in the closet, taking out a spray bottle filled with red liquid. She returned as Lance pitched the trousers across the bedroom.

"I hope that's not what I think it is." Lance grinned.

"I don't want you to speak. So say nothing," Riva said, understanding Lance's protest against her spicy love concoction. When they'd been working out their problems, before he'd moved out of the apartment, Lance had tried to entice her by intro-

ducing the strawberry elixir to her one evening.
She'd refused to have any part of his playfulness.

"Babe, I can't handle that stuff." Lance chuckled.

"Then you'll just have to control yourself . . .
won't you?" She squeezed the nozzle, spritzing scarlet liquid against Lance's wide chest. As she sprayed
him, Lance moved back until he was resting against
the edge of the dresser.

"You're not playing fair, Riva," Lance murmured
as she blew on his chest, then slowly licked the
sweet flavor.

"Come on, Riva." Lance groaned.

Riva sprayed his thighs and masculine center before setting the bottle down.

"Who's playing?" She stroked his chest.

Lance reached out for her, and Riva backed away
from him.

"You're not touching me until I tell you to
touch." Riva smiled up at him, noticing that
Lance's head was back and his eyes were closed.
Riva was sure she was getting the best of him. She
kissed him again, and listened his breath catch in
his throat.

"Babe, if I knew you weren't going to play
fair . . ." Lance stopped speaking as Riva feathered
her hand against his masculine center, making his
body grow firm against her palm.

"Stop." Lance reached for her and Riva tried to
step back, only to be dragged to him and crushed
against his chest. "You want to play, don't you?"
Lance asked her.

Before Riva could respond Lance covered her
lips, smothering her with warm and hungry kisses,
making her sink against him, forgetting the rules.

"Mmmm," Riva murmured when Lance came up

304   *Marcella Sanders*

for air. Rising on her toes, she planted a warm kiss on his lips. He wheeled around and traded places with her against the dresser. Just as he was lowering his head, the doorbell rang.

They ignored the bell. It rang again, and this time the chimes seemed louder, cutting into the music that piped its way through the speakers in the house and into their bedroom.

"This had better be important," Lance said, releasing his grip on Riva and turning to hold on to the edge of the dresser, taking a few deep breaths. He put on his pants and went to open the door.

Riva put on her housecoat, and stood at the top of the stairs, watching as Lance descended with long strides, taking two steps at a time, muttering curses she hoped he hadn't used while Tiffany's baby was living in the house. Riva moved down to the middle of the stairs.

"A man can't relax without someone stopping by to talk, sell something, or get in the way!" Lance opened the door. "Sam." From the stairs Riva heard Lance greeting Samuel Moses.

She could see the tall, light-skinned man who was responsible for Lance's career.

"Come in." Riva heard Lance invite Samuel Moses inside.

"It look like you were in the middle of something," Riva overheard Samuel say as he and Lance moved into the living room.

"Riva and I were busy," Lance said, looking toward the stairs.

"How are you?" Samuel said, catching sight of Riva.

"I'm good," Riva said, and headed back up to the second floor, leaving Lance and Samuel to their discussion.

By then the playful, romantic mood she'd been in had tapered off, so Riva got dressed. *There will be other times,* she mused as she pulled on her clothes and headed back downstairs. It had been a while since she'd seen Samuel.

"Did Samuel leave?" Riva asked, walking into the kitchen and noticing that Lance was pouring himself a tall glass of orange juice.

"Yes. We're meeting with him later." Lance set the orange juice inside the refrigerator and closed the door.

"What's going on?" Riva asked, anxious to know exactly why Samuel's visit was so short.

"Let's get to the meeting with Samuel. We're buying a house."

"We are?" Riva asked.

"Yes, we are." Lance said. "We going to discuss the deal he's offering us on this house," Lance said as they climbed the stairs. Riva smiled. She and Lance were finally a team again.

Phillip knew he couldn't enter the gated community without a card or some identification, or notifying the guard and saying who he planned to visit. He pushed the buzzer, alerting the bus driver to stop. Phillip stepped off of the bus and scurried through the vacant lot next to the canal. If he could move through the lot and behind the neighboring houses until he reached Lance's street, he would be inside the gated neighborhood and free to carry out his plan. Phillip gripped the springwater bottles he'd filled with gasoline, and patted his pocket, making sure he hadn't forgotten the matches.

If he had done his research earlier, he might have learned what Riva's husband did for a living,

Phillip mused, stopping at the edge of the canal when a couple walked past with fishing poles.

Who did Riva think she was anyway? He mulled over how he'd learned that Riva was married to a private detective. He had Laura to thank for that. She'd been in the hall talking to Adam. Evil feelings crept through Phillip as he fumed over the fact that he and Alicia had been played for fools. The plan had been to kill Jasper and blame the murder on Riva. Everyone at Dae Advertising knew she and Jasper didn't get along. The reasons for their fights weren't hard to figure out: Riva wanted her way and Jasper wouldn't agree with her.

Phillip scampered up behind a row of two-story houses and walked until he reached the sidewalk, rehashing his and Alicia's ruined plan as he neared Lance's home. If he had known that Riva was going to the spa, he would have never disguised himself as a woman and shot Jasper. When his plan backfired, Alicia had suggested that he drive Riva crazy. Even if she didn't end up in a mental institution, she would be deemed incompetent, too unstable to run the company after Mason was dead. He and Alicia planned to sell Dae Advertising after they were married. Phillip walked out from behind the houses and out onto the street, heading toward Lance's house.

Finding out where Lance lived hadn't been easy, but thanks to one of the several disguises he owned he'd been successful. Phillip had chosen a thick mustache, light brown contacts, two gold teeth, and phony identification. He was proud that he'd been able to sneak in and out of the state without anyone becoming suspicious. It was just his luck that he'd overheard one of the women at Dae Advertising asking Laura if Riva was sick. Laura told her that Riva hadn't been feeling well. When the woman asked Laura for Riva's address, Phillip almost walked away, until he heard Laura give an address and the name of the subdivision that he knew wasn't Riva's address. When Laura told the woman that Riva was living there with her husband, Phillip was shocked. Alicia had told him that Riva was getting a divorce.

On his way out of the building, Phillip had stopped at the receptionist's desk. It was no secret that the receptionist loved to gossip. So he told her that he had heard that Riva wasn't feeling well. He wanted to send her some flowers, but he wasn't sure how Riva's husband would react to his sending flowers.

The receptionist told him that Riva's husband probably wouldn't mind, since she'd heard that they were in the process of getting a divorce. The receptionist must have noticed his surprised expression, because she'd filled him in on all the details. The receptionist had heard that Riva was divorcing her husband because he was a private detective and had almost gotten them both killed. The night he'd shot Jasper, Phillip had stayed in an area behind a clump of trees afterward. He couldn't hear much, but he heard that a detective from Moses Investigations was in the area. Phillip remembered that the last Friday he was in town, he drove to the shopping center and noticed MOSES INVESTIGATIONS written on the window. He'd wondered if this was the detective office, and had tried to look inside. He couldn't see anyone because the window was tinted almost black.

Phillip was grateful for the receptionist's information. His questions were answered, and he was angry. Riva had probably moved in with her husband for protection. Phillip moved down the street and finally found Lance's address.

It wasn't long before he was walking up to the house, seeing Riva's truck parked out front and another truck parked behind hers. This would be the last time Riva and her husband would drive anything, because he was going to kill them both.

"Yeah," Phillip mumbled, walking to the open garage door. "This will be the last case you'll solve."

This time his plan would work, Phillip mused, walking past a small black car. He walked out of the garage and into the laundry room.

It was just like people living in the suburbs, Phillip thought; they liked leaving the doors open. He tiptoed inside, passing the washing machine and dryer, and inched past the study, peeking around the corner. He could hear a man's voice moving closer to him. Phillip stood still, looking for a place to hide. When he didn't hear the man talking, Phillip relaxed.

Phillip moved swiftly as a cat through the study, working his way to the kitchen. He had to find a place to hide until nighttime, when Riva and her husband would be in bed, or at least upstairs, before he set their house on fire.

Phillip noticed keys on the kitchen counter and reached for them.

"Drop the keys," Phillip heard a man's voice say behind him. Phillip froze, unable to turn around. He composed himself, and immediately began deciding whether he should drop the keys or throw the gas. The matches in his pocket would strike on just about anything, since the matches were easy to strike.

"No, I'm not dropping the keys," Phillip said; then he heard steel click behind him.

"Turn around slowly." Phillip heard the man, and decided that it was in his best interests to obey. He turned around, wondering how he was going to use his gas.

"Detective Lance Cain?" Phillip smirked, his face distorted with hatred as he looked down at the barrel.

"So shut the hell up," Lance said.

"You don't tell me to . . ." Phillip started unscrewing the cap on the gas bottle.

"Easy," Lance said, moving toward Phillip. "Set both bottles on the counter."

Phillip didn't like taking orders, but looking into the barrel of the gun was like looking into a crystal ball and foreseeing his own death.

Phillip set the bottles on the counter. "Why don't you put the gun, down man. I'm leaving."

"You're not going anywhere." Lance moved closer to Phillip.

"Lance." Riva came into the kitchen. "Oh, my God!" Riva screamed and ran to get the phone, drawing Lance's attention away from Phillip.

Phillip hit Lance across the face with his fist, sending him into a full spin.

Lance faced Phillip and knocked him into the counter. Phillip staggered, then picked up one of the bottles.

"If you make that phone call, Riva, I'll light him up."

"Lance, please . . ." Riva cried.

"Be quiet, Riva," Lance said, aiming the gun at Phillip's head. "Call the police, Riva," Lance said, not taking his eyes off Phillip.

"Man, you think I'm joking?" Phillip said.

Lance's voice was calm. "Throw the gas, Phillip, and I will blow your head off."

Phillip set the gas on the counter. Lance was probably crazy enough to shoot him. If he could get his hands on his matches . . . Phillip saw Riva making the call to the police, and he grabbed Lance's arm, trying to force the weapon from his hand. Lance pulled away from Phillip and stuck the pistol into the waistband of his jeans.

Lance and Phillip struggled. Lance slammed Phillip against the counter before they wrestled their way to the sitting area, where Lance knocked Phillip across the cocktail table, sending him sprawling out on the sofa. Philip got up and rushed toward Lance, and slammed him against the kitchen table. Lance straddled Phillip, reaching for his gun.

"No, Lance, don't kill him here!" Riva screamed.

Lance ignored Riva. "How did you find out where I lived, scum?" Lance asked, clenching his teeth.

Phillip didn't answer him, and Lance touched the trigger on his now-drawn gun.

"Ah . . . the receptionist," Phillip said. "Brenda. Man, let me go. Riva, tell him to let me go."

"You listen to me: you don't speak unless I ask you to speak. Do you understand me?" Lance twisted the collar of Phillip's shirt in his hand and yanked, making it hard for Phillip to breathe.

"Shut up, Phillip," Riva said, listening to Phillip struggling for breath.

A loud knock on the door sent Riva running to open it. "He's in here," Riva said to the two officers, directing them to the kitchen, where she noticed that Lance had eased off Phillip.

Phillip scurried toward the gas, grabbing it and

running out toward the garage with the officers behind him.

By the time the officers had made it to the garage entrance, Phillip had splashed gas in the laundry room, the garage, and on his clothes. "I will light this house up!" Philip yelled, ignoring the officers' warnings to drop the gas and the matches.

Instead of surrendering, Phillip struck a match against the driveway. His clothes and hands blazed as yellow and orange and red flames engulfed him. Phillip let out a shrieking howl and started running, while Lance and one of the officers chased him.

"Drop and roll!" Riva heard one of the cops instructing Phillip. It was clear that if he heard, he didn't stop. The flames seemed to leap as the wind helped the fire burn Phillip's body more. Riva began to chase after Phillip along with the officers and Lance.

"Stop that fool before he burns himself up," Riva heard a neighbor yelling from across the street.

Riva noticed one of the officers making a call. Shortly afterward, a rescue unit arrived, the fire truck followed, and Riva watched. Maybe she should have felt sorry for Phillip's pain, but she didn't. Phillip and Alicia had wanted her, her father, and Jasper to die.

Riva stood on the sidewalk with the neighbors, and watched as Lance trotted back to her. "Will Phillip be all right?"

"I don't know. He's badly burned," Lance said, gathering Riva to him. "We'll meet with Samuel later. We need go down and give a report," Lance said, holding on to Riva.

Finally, after Phillip was carried to the ambulance,

Lance locked the garage door, and Riva got her purse. They rode to the station to give their statements and make a report. When they finished and were headed back to Lance's car, Riva slipped her arm around his waist.

"Lance, what all did you find out about Phillip?"

"Are you sure you want to know?" Lance asked Riva.

"Yes," Riva said.

"Riva, Phillip and Alicia were lovers," Lance said.

"Get out of here!" Riva couldn't believe Alicia and Phillip had been lovers. Riva shook her head. "Maybe now we can be safe."

"Maybe," Lance said. "Let's go home, Riva."

Twenty-seven

An array of colorful lanterns lit Mason's back-yard. Gray smoke wiggled up from red-hot coals, and the smell of barbecue sauce scented the late-evening air. Music from the sixties played, as men and women swayed to songs from yesteryear.

"Aunt Udell, don't call me tomorrow complaining about your aching back," Riva called out across the yard to where Udell had just finished swinging her hips, following the instructions on the song of how to do the Swim.

"Riva, child, this is how I get my exercise." Udell moved back to the chair on the patio and sat beside Jasper, not bothering to dance to another song.

Riva giggled, noticing that her mother was busy gearing up to bump hips with her father, while Laura and Adam stood holding each other.

"Come on, Riva." Theresa and Clint got up from the table, where they had been sharing a glass of Udell's homemade wine with Riva and Lance. "Let's join this dance line." Theresa nudged Clint.

"I think Theresa may be on to something." Lance chuckled, pulling Riva up from the table. "If my mother and Samuel can bump and grind, baby, we need to join the dance line."

Riva laughed as she and Lance joined Tiffany,

Randy, Vanessa, Dylan, her parents, and several employees from Dae Advertising. Everyone clapped and cheered as one couple after another imitated dances they'd seen on television dance shows.

Finally the deejay slowed the music and Lance gathered Riva close. Riva savored the moment, glad that she and Lance had reconciled. She rose up and kissed his lips lightly as they moved to the slow beat of the music.

Finally the food was served. Everyone seated themselves at the long picnic table close to the patio, and helped themselves to barbecued chicken, potato salad, cole slaw, baked beans, hot dogs, and several other dishes.

Riva watched her parents, seated next to each other, her mother being very attentive to her father. Riva knew her parents would never remarry, but she was sure they would remain friends.

"You didn't invite Charlie to the party?" Riva asked her mother.

"Charlie?" Mason asked Riva, while he looked at Paula.

"Charlie couldn't be here tonight," Paula said.

"Who's Charlie?" he asked again.

"He's Mother's boyfriend," Riva said.

"Boyfriend," Mason said, giving Paula a look that Riva had never seen before.

"Mason, please—I didn't say one word to you when you were engaged to that woman," Paula said.

"I was asking," Mason said. "I didn't know."

The few friends and dates Paula had over the years since her and Mason's divorce hadn't been a secret. She just never discussed her personal life with him, and now he was acting surprised because she had a lover. "Now you know."

"Are you going to marry him?"

"I might."

"Paula . . ."

"I'll see you guys later," Riva said, leaving her parents.

It appeared to Riva that the birthday was a way of bringing people together. Riva mused over that idea while watching Grace Cain and Samuel Moses, and all the friends that Theresa, Vanessa, Laura, and Tiffany finally seemed to have met. She felt happy, but most of all, Riva was satisfied that she and Lance were together.

Feeling content with her and Lance's choice to reconcile, Riva watched the happy couples. Had it not been for the disaster in her life that was caused by Phillip and Alicia, Riva wondered whether she and Lance would have reconciled their marriage.

Riva mulled over that idea as everyone headed inside so Mason could open his gifts. As Riva sat next to Lance, she watched Udell and Jasper, and Riva was certain that her aunt could have been correct when she said everything happened for the best.

By midnight, Mason was opening his last gift. Riva noticed that the gift was from Alicia when Aunt Udell noticed the name on the tag. "I told Mason about that woman," Udell said, gesturing to Alicia's gift. "But he didn't listen to me because he's hardheaded."

The room filled with chuckles as Udell continued to tell Mason his main fault was not taking her advice.

"Udell, don't start." Mason stopped unwrapping Alicia's gift, and turned his attention to his sister. "You never listen to me," Mason said, grinning.

"Mason, you never gave me any advice," Udell said, propping her hand on her hip.

"You don't remember how I warned you about that good-for-nothing truck driver you started going out with a couple of years after Fred died?" Mason chuckled, and Riva and the others joined him in his laughter.

"All right, Mason, there are too many people in this house for you to start telling family secrets."

"Hey, Jasper, didn't I tell Udell not to start with me?" Mason asked Jasper between chuckles.

"I'm not getting into that conversation." Jasper smiled at Udell.

"I'm going home," Udell said, looking around as if she'd lost something. "Theresa . . . Riva . . . did one of you see my wine urn?"

"No, Aunt Udell." Riva got up, and Lance stood beside her. Riva noticed that Theresa didn't bother to answer Udell. It was common for Udell to bring her homemade wine to parties and later misplace the urn she'd carried it in.

"I found it," Udell said, and turned to Jasper. "Are you ready?"

Riva smiled. It seemed that the Cains', Daes', and Harts' lives were back to normal, Riva mused. Alicia was in jail, Phillip was dead, and her father and Jasper were in good health.

Riva caught Lance's wrist. "Happy birthday, Daddy," she said, watching how attentive her mother was to her father.

"Do you think they'll get back together?" Lance asked, cutting into Riva's thoughts.

"No," Riva said, remembering her mother's telling her that she and Mason were history.

Nevertheless, Riva knew everything was fine. Jasper hadn't returned to work; he was on an extended paid vacation, and had plans to accompany Udell to Orlando to assist with the group of teens who had been chosen for the Key Lock trip. In the meantime Jasper was helping Riva, Theresa, Laura, and the other club members raise money for the after-school program.

Riva and Lance walked out to their car, and under the full moonlight, she circled her arms around Lance and allowed him to gather her into his arms. Riva savored being close to him, and promised herself that she would never again try to force Lance to change his career.

"It's good being back together, Riva." Lance squeezed her to him.

"I don't know about you, Mr. Cain, but I intend to make this marriage a long love affair." Riva tipped her face up and pulled Lance to her, giving him a kiss.

COMING IN JANUARY 2002
FROM ARABESQUE ROMANCES

__LOVE ON THE RUN
by Angela Winters   1-58314-216-9   \$6.99US/\$9.99CAN
Gabrielle "Bree" Hart was making the most of her new life, far away from
her overbearing family, when she learned that they had hired Graham Lane
to bring her home. But when she found out he was investigating a dangerous
mystery, Bree was determined to help him solve it—and discover whether
they could create a lasting love. . . .

__HEART OF THE MATTER
by Raynetta Manees   1-58314-262-2   \$6.99US/\$9.99CAN
Newly elected Mayor Affrica Bryant has ambitious plans for improving her
city. Chief of Police Alex Bartholomew wonders if she is the right person for
the job . . . Until she shows him that beneath her lovely exterior lies determination. Affrica and Alex must put their trust in each other, if they—and
their blossoming love—are to survive.

__THE ART OF DESIRE
by Selena Montgomery   1-58314-264-9   \$5.99US/\$7.99CAN
Agent Phillip Thurman is trying to rebuild a normal life. His first assignment
is to pick up Alex Walton, the maid of honor for his best friend's wedding,
at the airport. His second is to deal with his instant attraction to her. His third
is to keep Alex out of danger as his past—and her need to know about it—
threaten to destroy their future.

__LOVE IN BLOOM
by Francine Craft, Linda Hudson-Smith, and Janice Sims
                        1-58314-319-X   \$5.99US/\$7.99CAN
Three beloved Arabesque authors bring romance alive in these captivating
tales of first love, second chances, and promises fulfilled. . . . Make this a
Valentine's Day to treasure forever with a very special celebration of love.

Call toll free **1-888-345-BOOK** to order by phone or use this coupon
to order by mail. ALL BOOKS AVAILABLE JANUARY 1, 2002.
Name_____
Address_____
City_____ State_____ Zip_____
Please send me the books that I have checked above.
I am enclosing   \$_____
Plus postage and handling*   \$_____
Sales tax (in NY, TN, and DC)   \$_____
Total amount enclosed   \$_____
*Add \$2.50 for the first book and \$.50 for each additional book.
Send check or money order (no cash or CODs) to: **Arabesque Romances,
Dept. C.O., 850 Third Avenue 16th Floor, New York, NY 10022**
Prices and numbers subject to change without notice. Valid only in the U.S.
All orders subject to availability. **NO ADVANCE ORDERS.**
Visit our website at **www.arabesquebooks.com**.